AWOL
FROM
ELYSIUM PRESS

Cemetery Riots

CEMETERY RIOTS

A collection of dark cautionary tales
edited by T. C. Bennett *and*
Tracy L. Carbone
published by
AWOL FROM ELYSIUM PRESS

CEMETERY RIOTS
First published June 2016 by
Awol From Elysium Press

"Abused" first appeared in Gauntlet Magazine issue 16, 1998
"All Our Hearts Are Ghosts" first appeared in
Gutshot, PS Publishing, 2011
"Father and Son" first appeared as a limited edition chapbook,
Camelot Books and Gifts, 1999
"The Windows" first appeared in Dark Eclipse issue 7, 2012

Cover design by Beetiful Book Covers
beetifulbookcovers.com
Book layout and design by Robert Barr/Shadowridge Press
shadowridgepress.com

ISBN: 978-0692751107

awolfromelysiumpress.com

ACKNOWLEDGEMENTS

I want to enthusiastically thank co-editor and contributor, Tracy L. Carbone for a fantastic job on this anthology, because without her it would not be what it is.

With the same fiery enthusiasm, I want to thank this anthology's contributors: William F. Nolan, James Dorr, Tracy L. Carbone, Kelly Kurtzhals, Hal Bodner, John Palisano, Eric J. Guignard, Ray Garton, Chet Williamson, Michael Sebastian, Richard Christian Matheson, Michael D. Nye, Taylor Grant, Jack Ketchum, Kathryn E. McGee, Lisa Morton, Karen Dent, Roxanne E. Dent, John Everson, Peter Atkins and Dennis Etchison.

And lastly, with gratitude and friendship, Eric Miller, *The Saturday Group*, Robert Barr of *Shadowridge Press,* and Malcolm and Christine at *Mystery & Imagination BookShop.*

I dedicate this anthology to all the writers in the world and to all the cemeteries who will have us.

Also, to my daughter Mackenzie, son-in-law Ryan, my mother Vivian, my departed fathers David & George, my brothers Vance, his wife Christy and their family, Dwayne and his fiance Sarah and family, and Steve AKA Chico and his family.

And lastly, to she-who-will-not-be-named. We both know who you are.

—T. C. B.

STORIES

CEMETERY RIOTS

*Imagine yourself in a cemetery. Void of all light at
the base of a tree. But it's no ordinary tree.
This tree abounds with the dead.
Now envision that each tree limb is a story with its
own vision, its own length of words,
and its own insanity.
With that said, beware of the widow makers and
the strange foreboding dwelling beneath.
Remember, nothing's heavenly in
Cemetery Riots.*

Ray Garton

THE WAITING DEAD

The cemetery where Bethany had decided to end her life was small and somehow looked even smaller in the moonlight. It was backed up against a craggy hillside—thus the name Hillside Cemetery—and bordered on three sides by cypress trees that jutted like fangs from the lower jaw of an enormous mouth yawning up at the night sky. She had visited the cemetery many times before, but never at night. Her grandmother was buried there, the woman who had raised her and the person she missed most in the world.

Bethany zigzagged through the cemetery by moonlight, a flower in her hand and a large blue bag slung over her shoulder. She went around the creepy statue of two giant hands joined in prayer, toward the weeping willow in the far corner, until she reached Grandma's grave. She bent down to place the Tahiti daffodil on the flat marker. Grandma's favorite flower was the daffodil, and her favorite daffodil was the Tahiti, a sunny yellow with reddish-orange ruffles in the center. Then, with a little difficulty due to her girth, she sat down Indian-style on the grass, facing the marker.

"Hi, Grandma," she said. She always talked to Grandma when she visited her grave, but usually in whispers. Now, alone in the cemetery at night, she felt comfortable speaking out loud. "I miss you."

She felt the familiar lump in her throat—it had been there more often than not in recent months—and tipped her head back to look up at the night sky. Thin, patchy clouds crept slowly across the black velvet backdrop, obscuring most of the stars, but the full moon shone clearly and bathed the cemetery in a soft, bluish glow. It was a cool spring night, cool enough for Bethany to wear a heavy sweater.

Lowering her eyes to the grave again, she said, "I don't think I can do it anymore, Grandma. Not without you here. I'm only twenty-one, which means I've got, what, another sixty years to go? I . . . I just don't think I can do it."

She heard a soft noise overhead and looked up just in time to glimpse an owl swooping down out of the darkness and gliding over her head toward the hillside. Taking the strap from her shoulder, she put the bag on the grass beside her.

"I'm still fat, you know. I've lost a few pounds, but only because I was throwing up when I ate. But I couldn't keep that up. I'm not sure how bulimics do it. You know how much I hate to throw up. Remember that time when I was a kid and I had the flu and I threw up all over you? You laughed and laughed, but I felt so guilty. These days . . . it's weird, but I feel guilty all the time, and . . . I don't know why. I think maybe it's for . . . existing. That's the thing, see. Existing. I . . . I'm just no good at it."

She plunged her left hand into the bag and removed a package of Oreos.

"See? I'm not even trying now." She took a can from the bag and said, "It's a diet soda, but that's kind of silly, isn't it? I mean, with the Oreos? But I don't see any point in, you know . . . *not* eating whatever I want. It doesn't make any difference. I thought about the last thing I wanted to eat and because Dairy Queen was closed, I stopped at the AM/PM and got these. Next best thing."

The Oreo package crackled as she tore open the end, and the sound seemed louder in the night. She took in a deep breath and sighed before plucking a cookie from its tray and biting off half of it. She chewed for a while before speaking again.

"Remember when I got skinny? In high school? Practically starved myself to do it. But even then, I wasn't *that* skinny. Still kind of, you know, big and broad. And it didn't matter at school. They still called me Big-Butt Bethany, even though my butt was proportional then. I still didn't get invited to parties or dances. It just didn't matter."

She finished the cookie, thinking about what she had looked like back then. It was the only time she had been truly pleased while look-ing in the mirror, not because she was so beautiful but because of what she had accomplished. She had lost eighty-five pounds, which had seemed like an enormous amount of weight. But she still stood five feet, nine inches, and still had that large build. The fact that she truly was big-boned did not make it any easier to say those words out loud because it sounded like such a whiny excuse. The difference was that she could *see* her bones — not directly, of course, but it was the most defined they had ever been, and, as it turned out, ever would be. The rest of the time, they were consumed by all that freckled fat.

A couple of swallows from the bottle of Diet Dr. Pepper washed down the cookie before she removed another from the package.

"I have a gun in my bag, Grandma," she said. "I stole it from Richie's bedroom."

Richie was her cousin, who lived just a couple of blocks from her apartment building, and she knew he kept a loaded .38 in his nightstand drawer. She also knew where he hid his spare key in case he locked himself out of the little house where he lived with a roommate. Richie worked nights in the Costco distribution center and his roommate was out of town with his girlfriend for a few days, so she had helped herself to the gun. She had gone to the shooting range with Richie once and he had shown her how to use it.

After biting into her second cookie, she chewed for a moment, then said, "You never liked guns, I know, but this is just for me. Nobody else will get hurt, I promise." She looked around the cemetery at the flat lawn, the praying hands, the statue of an angel at the foot of the hillside overlooking all the graves, the willow in the corner, the surrounding cypress trees. "There's nobody else here but us, Grandma." Plopping the rest of the cookie into her mouth, she chewed. "And I know you're not here. Not really. If you were, you'd do everything to stop me. If you were, I wouldn't be doing this. But it always makes me feel good to talk to you. Because I miss you so much. You were the only person who really listened to me. Laughed at my jokes. Hugged me when I cried." Her head dropped forward as she felt the sting of tears in her eyes. "I guess I've always cried a lot, huh?" Then she chased the cookie with another swig of soda and began to sob.

Somewhere up the hillside, the owl made its sad call three times, then fell silent. A siren wailed in the far distance as she continued to cry, her upper body bent forward and jerking with sobs.

"I-i-is there something I can do?"

Bethany sat up with a shriek and scrambled to her feet, nearly falling over as she spun around to see the young man standing behind her.

"What? What do you want? Who are you?" The words tumbled out of her mouth one on top of the other as she dipped her knees and snatched up her bag with her right hand, then hugged it to her with both arms. Suddenly breathing heavily, she wanted to turn and run out of the cemetery but knew he could outrun her without trying because he was so slender and fit and suddenly she felt so stupid for coming to the cemetery in the middle of the night, and then she remembered the gun. Holding the bag with her left hand, she stabbed her right into it and felt for the cold metal.

"Don't be afraid, I don't want to hurt you," he said, raising his hands palms-out and spreading his fingers. "I *can't* hurt you, believe me, not even if I wanted to. But I saw you crying and I wanted to see if I could help. I-I-I probably can't, but I wanted to at least ask. I'm sorry I scared you. Really."

There was nothing menacing about him, not his body language or his voice, which was gentle and pleasant. Instead of the gun, she removed her flashlight from the bag, aimed it at him and thumbed the button. He did not flinch or cover or even *narrow* his eyes when the light hit his face and that somehow frightened Bethany more than the possibility that he might want to hurt her. It felt like her turn to talk. Her voice quavered as she said, "Whuh-what are you doing here? In the middle of the night?"

His narrow face opened up in a bright smile. "I live here."

Beginning to feel nauseated, she said, "You're homeless."

His hair was short and sandy brown, his eyes dark. Somewhere in his twenties. Raising his eyebrows, he slowly turned his head from side to side and said, "No. No, I'm not homeless. This is my home."

"I . . . I don't understand. But I should go, anyway." She began to back away.

"You don't have to run off because of me, really. I'll leave you alone if you want. I was just concerned. A lot of people who come here cry, but never alone in the middle of the night. So I thought I'd, you know, well . . . to be honest, I was here for a while. Listening." He closed his eyes a moment, embarrassed. "*Eavesdropping*, I know, I'm sorry, it's rude, but I couldn't help it because, like I said, nobody comes here at night. Except horny teens to get drunk and have sex. A bunch of them came on Halloween night a few years ago. Turned into an orgy. It was embarrassing. But . . . not too embarrassing to keep me from watching." He chuckled nervously. "Being dead . . . it kind of turns you into a voyeur."

The light she still held on his face trembled. "Being . . . you're . . ."

"You said you were going to kill yourself. I don't think you should. Even though I don't know you. My name is Gary, by the way, I'm Gary Bell, and I don't think you should kill yourself. It's a mistake. I should know, believe me. I killed myself. An O.D. of painkillers. Really strong painkillers."

"You did? Was it painful?"

"It was a hell of a lot worse than I expected. I figured I'd just go to sleep, you know? But I had some other stuff in me, too, like cocaine, and it didn't work out that way. First, I threw up. A *lot*. I was so sick, I wanted to die. And then I did. But it took a while."

"I tried to do that once."

"With painkillers?"

"And tranquilizers. I wanted to make sure it worked."

He nodded.

"But it didn't. I have this extremely sensitive gag reflex, see, and trying to swallow pills usually makes me gag and I just spit them back up again. Which is disgusting. I'm sorry."

"I understand. You chewed them up, didn't you?"

She nodded. "Two at a time. They tasted so bad, they made me gag, so I took them slowly and at a couple spoonfuls of apple sauce in between. I took them too slowly and I got sick before I could finish. I puked a lot, too. But Grandma didn't let me die. She found me, called an ambulance, and they made me keep puking. They kept me in the hospital overnight and I had to see a therapist."

"You're smirking."

"Yeah, you know what Grandma said to me? She said, 'If you ever do that again, I'll kill you,' and then we laughed until we cried some more."

Bethany turned her flashlight on Grandma's grave marker.

"I miss her so much. I just wish she could—" She swept the light back around to him. "Hey, why isn't *she* standing here talking to me?"

"Did she kill herself?"

"Oh, no, not Grandma. She wasn't the type. She just kind of fell apart, I guess. Diabetes, bad heart, kidneys, liver, veins, and old age. It was her time."

Nodding, he said, "Exactly, her time. She was at peace. She moved on. I committed suicide. My life wasn't over. I interrupted it with all kinds of life left to live, and now I'm stuck here until *my* time comes. Turns out that's how it works. All that stuff about heaven and hell? You can ignore that. Dying is more like going to the Department of Motor Vehicles. And it's like I tried to cut in line, or something, and they don't like that. At all. So here I am, waiting for my time to move on. They won't tell me when that'll be, so I just wait. That's why you shouldn't kill yourself." That smile again. Very charming.

She did not know what to say. Finally: "The flashlight in your eyes doesn't bother you?"

"No. Not much bothers me. What's your name?"

"Bethany. You didn't know that? Can't you, I don't know, read my mind?"

He laughed with that smile lighting up his face. "Don't be ridiculous."

"Bethany Schwarzkopf. Nice to meet you, Gary Bell. You just . . . wait here, huh?"

He nodded. "Most people go when it's their time. And everybody has their time. But some of us . . . you know. We decide to go early, for whatever reason. There are a couple of other suicides here in Hillside. And there are a few people who were killed before their time, but through no fault of their own. One guy was shot in a hunting accident. He's pretty, um, cranky. A woman over by the angel statue didn't know she had some bad wiring in her house and she was electrocuted in the kitchen. If that hadn't happened, she would've lasted until her time came."

"Why aren't they wandering around here?"

"Oh, nobody shows themselves. Normally, I don't either. I never have. But this was a special case, you know, an emergency. That's how I saw it, anyway."

"Have you made friends?"

"Here? Nah, they aren't like that here. I don't think any of the dead are, tell you the truth. They're not a friendly bunch. Not the ones waiting their time out in some cemetery, I mean. Those are the only ones I've met because everyone else has moved on. We say hi now and then, but nothing more. Everybody's just . . . waiting."

"Does it ever get lonely?"

"Sure. Sometimes."

"It sounds . . . depressing."

"It *is*, that's what I'm saying. You wouldn't like it."

"You don't . . . *seem* depressed."

"I'm not. But that's just me. I've never been the depressive type."

"But . . . you killed yourself."

"Yes, true, but it was a big mistake. Really stupid. It was over a woman, can you believe that? But I was doing a lot of drugs at the time. Not because I was depressed but because I really liked the way drugs made me feel. And I guess I got addicted. I mean, yeah, of *course* I got addicted. Then things turned bad and I just wasn't thinking straight. Or at all. Drugs changed me and I wasn't myself. But I did it and now I've got to live with it." He laughed, and she found herself briefly laughing along. "Well, not *live* with it, but you know what I mean. I'll wait however long it takes. In the meantime, I like to people watch and eavesdrop. I like to watch the birds. Those cypress trees are full of nests in the spring.

Right now, in fact. Mostly finches and sparrows. I like to see how many chicks come out of each nest. It probably sounds boring, but it passes the time. Nights are the loneliest because I don't sleep. You're done sleeping when you die. Then it gets so quiet at night. I usually just watch the skies. You see some weird stuff in the skies at night sometimes." He smiled again. "This is the most I've enjoyed a night since I got here. Talking to you, I mean. It's more fun than the orgy."

She laughed and blushed a little. "You don't ever talk to the people who visit during the day?"

"No. And freak them out? None of us here want to do that. Sometimes ghost hunters will show up at night and wander around with their gadgets until they scare themselves and run off. We ignore them. If we showed ourselves to them, they'd just keep coming back, and, really, they're kind of annoying."

"What if someone comes to visit your grave?"

"Nobody ever does. I was kind of, um, a family problem. With my drug addiction, you know? Couldn't hold a job, kept getting in trouble with the law. I'm a page they've turned, if you know what I mean. And my girlfriend, the one I killed myself over, got married and moved away. I knew she was going to, which is why I killed myself. She sprang it on me suddenly. I didn't see it coming." He shrugged. "That's the way it goes. I've just got to wait out my time here and see what comes next."

"You don't know?"

"Nobody does. They keep a tight lid on that stuff. Let's stop talking about me, though. You're the one I'm worried about."

"You're worried about me?"

"Well, you said you were going to kill yourself and I don't think you should. It's a bad idea. I'd like you to do me a favor, OK?"

"What?"

"Go home and go to bed. Sleep on it. Then come back here tomorrow night and tell me you've changed your mind. Can you do that?"

"I don't know if I *will* change my mind."

"I think you will. Just do that for me, OK? When you come back, we'll talk some more and you can tell me you've got things to live for after all. And if you still don't think so, we'll talk about why."

Bethany thought about that and wondered if it would be worth another night trying to sleep and crying into her pillow as she dreaded tomorrow.

Gary gave her that smile again and said, "Do it for me."

She slung the bag's strap over her shoulder and wiped her still-damp eyes with a knuckle. "You promise you'll be here?"

He laughed. "I'm not going *anywhere*, believe me."

"Well, is there anything you'd like me to bring?"

"I can't think of anything I could use. I don't eat or drink, and I can't hold anything. I miss reading, but I can't turn pages or operate one of those things, what are they called? Ereaders? I've seen people carrying them around."

"Would you like me to bring something for you to read? I could turn the pages. Or I could read to you."

His eyes widened again. Like most guys, he had long, thick lashes. Women had to use mascara while most men had gorgeous lashes. Even their *ghosts* had gorgeous lashes. The universe was a mess.

She said, "What do you like to read?"

"I used to read a lot of science fiction and fantasy."

"How about Harry Potter?"

"Harry who?"

His response gave her a surge of pleasure. She loved the Harry Potter books and enjoyed talking to other people about them. "I'll bring the first book in the series. You're gonna love it."

"Good. I'll see you then."

Bethany went home and cleaned her kitchen.

Being a nervous cleaner meant that her apartment was always spotless and never needed cleaning because she cleaned it so often, but she kept cleaning it, anyway. She cleaned to distract herself from her own nagging thoughts and worries and insecurities. Lately, she had been distracting herself from the pangs of missing her cat, Baxter. She had gotten him when he was a kitten and she was eleven years old, and four months ago she had him euthanized because liver cancer was killing him and she could not let Baxter suffer. Those pangs had kept the apartment extra-squeaky clean.

She was thorough, washing and scrubbing things and vacuuming and dusting and sweeping and polishing. When she exhausted herself, she went to bed and slept until it was time to get up and go to her job at the only remaining brick-and-mortar book store in town, store number 7483 in the only remaining nationwide chain of same. The store was classic Poe because it had a deadly blade swinging pendulously overhead, lowering just a bit with each sweep, getting closer and closer to severing Bethany's employment, because it was only a matter of time. That frightening inevitability was always good for a bathroom-scrubbing or closet purge.

That night as she lay in bed with some soothing Beethoven playing quietly in the dark, all she could think about was Gary Bell and his gentle voice, the brilliant smile that spread all the way up to his dark, expressive eyes with their beautiful lashes. The more she thought about him, the more convinced Bethany became that she was unforgivably gullible and had stupidly fallen for a prank. A harmless prank, yes, but still humiliating. Not simply harmless — it had distracted her from ending her life.

She would, Bethany decided, return to Hillside Cemetery the next night to see if Gary Bell—probably not even his real name—showed up, and if he did, to give him a piece of her mind. And to thank him.

───

"Do you *really* believe that I made all of that up on the spot just to keep you from killing yourself?" Gary said the following night. "Are you sure you didn't see that in a Hallmark movie?"

Bethany surprised herself by laughing. "It might sound like one, but you *aren't* a ghost."

He opened his arms and said, "Hug me."

After hesitating briefly, she stepped forward and tried to wrap her arms around him. Instead, she passed through a column of icy-cold air and nearly fell on her face. When she turned around, he was standing in the same spot, facing her, and smiling.

"See?"

She stared at him.

"You look horrified. Don't worry, I didn't feel a thing."

All she could do was laugh.

They sat down at Grandma's grave and Bethany placed her bag in her lap. When she reached in, her knuckles bumped the gun tucked in the outside pocket. "I brought snacks. I stopped at Popeye's for some popcorn shrimp and Taco Bell for some Nachos Bel Grande, and I have a bag of M&Ms and a box of Fiddle Faddle in case I'm in the mood. I was going to bring some — " When she saw him watching her closely and smiling, she said, "Why are you looking at me like that?"

"You look happy."

"I do?"

He nodded. "If you killed yourself, you wouldn't be able to eat. You'd have to wait all that time with no food."

"Maybe it wouldn't be so long. I'm pretty fat. Maybe I die early."

"A lot of fat people live a long time."

"Well, how do you know the food is the reason I look so happy?"

His smile vanished and he blinked rapidly several times. "Really?"

"Why not? I enjoy your company."

"If you killed yourself, you couldn't come here and visit me. You'd be buried somewhere else, stuck there to wait alone."

"No. My grandparents raised me. My mother was alone and she died having me, so they took care of me. Grandpa died when I was only seven. But before he did, he bought all of us plots right here. One for himself," she said, pointing to the grave marker beside Grandma's, "one for Grandma, and," she pointed to the patch of lawn next to it, "one for me. I'll be buried right here. We can visit a lot."

He turned away for a moment, frowning and chewing his lower lip. Then: "You'd get tired of me. I'm not very interesting, really, and you'd get bored with me pretty fast. But we probably wouldn't talk very much, anyway. Like I said, the waiting dead tend to keep to themselves."

"You don't know that. We've enjoyed talking tonight and last night."

"Even so, you'd be *stuck* here. Think about it, being trapped in this place for who knows how long. People wouldn't see you, it would be like you didn't exist anymore, but you would."

"People wouldn't see me?"

"Not unless you *wanted* them to, but you know how most people would react. They'd run away screaming. Except for the damned ghost hunters and paranormal investigators. They want to talk, but they're a pain in the ass." Changing the subject, he gestured toward her food and said, "Go ahead and eat. All of that looks so good. That's one thing I've missed, eating. I think it'll be fun to watch after all this time."

"You're sure it's not rude?"

He shook his head. "I'm not hungry, believe me. I can't remember what it feels like. Tell me about this Harry Potter."

Bethany told him of the rich fantasy world J.K. Rowling had created and the phenomenon the books had become, then read to him the first chapter of *Harry Potter and the Sorcerer's Stone* from her ereader. The soft glow from the screen illuminated her round, freckled face as she read.

An owl hooted a couple of times from the hillside and the insect-like chatter of a distant helicopter sounded briefly, but otherwise the night was silent except for her voice.

"Your popcorn shrimp is going to get cold," he said, so she paused occasionally to snack.

When she finished the chapter, they talked about it as she continued to eat. Bethany noticed that both of them were smiling.

She ate the last cheese-dripping tortilla chip, the last crunchy piece of popcorn shrimp, the last candy-coated piece of Fiddle Faddle, and even the last M&M.

"When you told me that no one would be able to see me unless I *wanted* them to, did you mean it?" she said.

"Of course."

She nodded, finished off her Diet Dr. Pepper, and said, "That's when I decided. When you told me that."

"Decided what?" Gary said as Bethany reached into the outer pocket of the bag.

"That I still wanted to kill myself." She removed the gun.

Gary's eyes widened. "B-b-because no one will be able to see you then? Why?"

"Because it . . . it hurts too much."

"For other people to see you? But they're not doing that to you, Bethany. *You* are. You're hurting yourself. All you have to do is stop doing that."

Her head nodded slowly as her shoulder sagged as if beneath a sudden weight. "I've been told that. I've read it, heard it. And maybe it's true. But it doesn't make any difference, because even if it's true, I don't know *how* to stop. I've *tried*. I've been trying since I was a little girl. I don't know how."

"You don't *really* want to do this."

The gunshot sent a cracking echo through the night and flurries of small birds rose from the cypress trees in a storm of relentless cheeping and chirping. They were swirling dark spots against the moonlight that performed a brief, impromptu ballet in the air. The fluttering of their wings sounded like polite applause. The echo died somewhere in the darkness and the chirping and applause diminished as the birds resettled in their trees. The night once again became silent and still.

Richard Christian Matheson
ABUSED

Moans.

Echoed; helpless.

"He's begging me to stop."

No response.

"I'm going for the eyes. He's calling out your name. Can you hear it?"

She drew breath. Heard the screaming. Pulled the phone from her ear. Shuddered. Made herself listen again.

"He's begging for you to help him. He wants you to make me stop." Amused. "Can you hear it? *Tell me.*"

"I can hear it . . ." She could hear him screaming out how much he loved her. Could hear him shrieking her name.

"Good connection?"

She didn't answer.

"I thought so." Informing sarcasm. "I'm going to *really* hurt him now."

" . . . what do you mean?"

"*Listen.*"

She closed eyes. Could imagine him, naked, tied down. Fingers clutching. Eyes bloody; blinded.

". . . what are you . . . ?"

"Listen."

"Please…"

"I'm going to cut him up."

She imagined the shiny blade. His unguarded veins. Him carved. Squirming, pleading. She felt faint, heard clothing ripped open, flesh slashed. His screaming made the earpiece distort. She saw herself in the hall mirror. Fearful, gaunt. Bowing her head in revulsion.

"He's bleeding now. You should see it."

"I want you to stop . . ."

"No, you don't." A merciless pause. "I'm peeling him." Sounds of sharp steel on skin. "Can you hear?"

Her soft weeping drew her to the floor.

"I said can you hear?" The man's voice was low; hypnotic and cruel. "Can you hear the skin being curled back over muscle?" He waited. Breath steady. "Press the phone closer to your ear. You'll like this."

She was sweating, mouth dry. Her hand trembled as she heard what was being done.

"Are you enjoying this?"

"No," she answered.

"I asked you if you were enjoying it?"

"NO!"

"*Liar!*"

She could hear the skin being slashed apart; the tortured screams. Her eyes widened.

"Tell me you love it . . ."

"I . . ."

"*Tell me you love it.*"

"I . . ."

"Tell me how much you hate his fucking guts! How much you've waited for this. Waited to hear him tortured like he's tortured you . . ."

"Please stop . . ."

"TELL ME YOU LOVE IT!! GET EVEN WITH THIS *PRICK!!*"

She felt like throwing-up as the man began to chuckle in his deep voice.

"I'm going to cut his throat. Wanna hear?"

She could hear hideous, trapped screams in the background.

"Listen closely . . ."

She couldn't put the phone down and just as the man was about to cut, all sound stopped.

A woman's calm voice came on the line.

"Your ten minutes have expired. The cost of your *Fantasy Abuse* call will be discreetly billed to your monthly phone statement as *Pleasure-Comm, Ltd.* Please call again."

The dial tone blocked anything further; a slammed door.

She hung up. Lay on the couch in exhaustion. Relaxed for the first time in days.

Until the phone rang.

She watched it, finally picked up on the sixth ring. Waited. Fear gathered in unblinking eyes.

"I've been trying you for ten minutes, bitch." The voice was ready to hurt her. "Who the fuck were you talking to?"

She said she'd accidentally left the phone off the hook but he wasn't convinced. Said he'd be home soon and was in a bad mood. She knew what it meant; last week's bruises still a sick lapis.

She stared at the phone, as he hung up. Trembled helplessly. Dialed *Fantasy Abuse* for the third time today and asked for him to be gutted, hung upside down, bled to death.

She listened carefully and fixed coffee, waiting for her husband to get home.

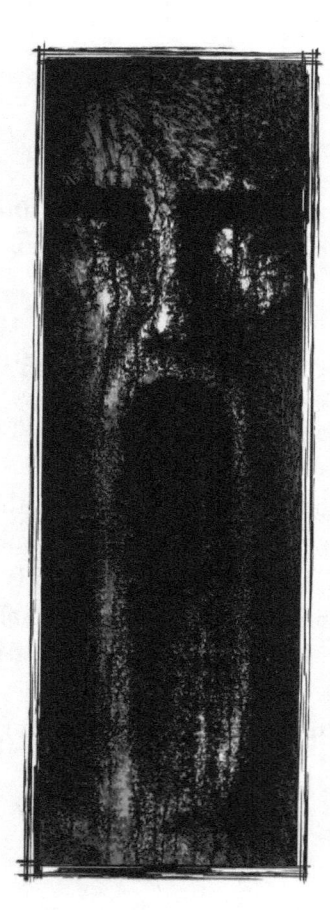

Hal Bodner

CHILDREN'S HOUR

The procession was a small one. Just the hearse, followed by a single town car, presumably for the immediate family. A few compacts and an SUV trailed behind—relatives and some friends, maybe even a teacher or two from the grade school. When this part of the cemetery was first used for burials, the plot density was greater and big, showy tombstones were still in style. Large funerals tended to be cramped and unpleasant. In this weather, a heavier turn-out would have been a recipe for disaster.

My lower back and shoulders ached from digging. Elsewhere in the cemetery, I would have used the backhoe. But not here. When I first came to work at Holy Acres, I didn't realize how impossible it was to steer the thing through the thicket of headstones in the Children's Graveyard. Though the backhoe escaped damage, I accidentally chipped one of the monuments. My boss, Sidney Kippling, wasn't happy about it and I was summoned to the administration building to account for my carelessness.

"Respect for the dead, Adam," he told me, and sneezed lustily into a handkerchief.

During the three and a half decades I've been employed as a care-
taker, I can count on the fingers of both hands the number of days that
Kippling wasn't suffering from some ailment or other. Not that the man
was a hypochondriac; he wasn't. He was simply one of those people
whose constitution seems to put out a WELCOME mat for everything
from ragweed allergies to typhoid. I've often speculated that the main
reason Kippling chose to work at Holy Acres was because he expected
to need its services at any moment, and he didn't want to burden his
relatives with the trouble of carrying him very far to his grave.

"That is the foundation of Holy Acres. Respect." He paused, both to
hawk phlegm into the handkerchief and to make sure I appreciated the
gravity of his words. "I hardly think it respectful for our employees to
be taking the machinery for joyrides across the grounds. . ."

"I wasn't. . ." His fit of hacking coughs cut short my protest.

". . .And getting into head-on collisions with tombstones, is it?" he
finished with a gasp. "No," he said when I decided that remaining
quiet was probably my best defense. "I thought not."

He looked at me sternly for a few minutes to make his point. Then,
his expression softened.

"Adam, Adam, Adam," he shook his head. "I know your employment
with us is probably only temporary. A way for you to. . ." He searched
for the right words to express himself in a tactful manner. ". . .recuper-
ate from the awful tragedy you suffered."

He's talking about Patrick, I remember thinking with a kind of dull
surprise. I tensed the muscles around my eyes, widening them slightly;
I knew that if I allowed myself to blink, the tears would come again.

"I also know how terribly, terribly overqualified you are for the
position. But. . ." He punctuated the last word with a raised finger and
paused to inspect the nail. I'm not sure what he saw, evidence of a
potentially fatal nutritional deficiency, or perhaps just a tinge of fungus.
". . .in spite of my friendship with your wife, I will not hesitate to ter-
minate you should there be another...incident."

Over time, there had been several such incidents, none of them
major, and an equal number of similar lectures in the office. Thirty-six
years later, Kippling had not yet succumbed to any of the various plagues
he'd been infected with. And I was still employed.

The storm had been a bad one, and the ground quickly became over-saturated. Any bit of earth that wasn't covered with grass was a muddy soup. Beneath my oilcloth slicker, I was soaked and cold. Nevertheless, I took care to dig the grave a full three feet deeper than normal. I knew what it was like to lose a child. The family was traumatized enough without having to watch the floral tributes atop the casket slowly befouled by oozing muck as their loved one was lowered into a watery pit. It was not a memory I'd want even my worst enemy to take away from a funeral.

I always went the extra mile when a child was buried. And, though I wasn't strictly required to be present during the ceremony, I usually waited nearby at a respectful distance. Not too long after Patrick died, at the urging of my then-soon-to-be-ex-wife, I tried therapy. The psychologist, a New Age Herbal Lesbian type, urged me to admit that abandoning my career to take a menial job at the cemetery, and my insistence on attending the funerals of strangers' children, were morbid attempts on the part of my subconscious to expiate my feelings of guilt. What little chance I had of actually *hearing* what she had to say was quickly banished when she also suggested that I burn sheaves of sage on the beach near the spot where I failed to rescue my son.

Given that Patrick was only eleven, I suppose it was only natural that I was drawn to the Children's Graveyard. Even if I was doing nothing more than pulling weeds and wiping the granite markers clean of bird shit, working around the graves of those whose lives had been cut short gave me a measure of peace. When I looked at the tombstones, the short span between the dates always reminded me that I was not alone, that I was not the only parent who had suffered this way. I found strength in what I thought of as a macabre solidarity.

I remember that the ditsy therapist also suggested that I try prayer. But it brought no solace, not for me anyway; I had never been particularly devout. Instead of easing my mind, it made me uneasy to imagine the souls of children ascending to heaven, there to reside in some celestial Day Care Center, watched over by haloed guardians who gave them ambrosial milk and cookies. Instead, though it may sound a bit gruesome, I drew comfort from the idea that decomposition and decay inevitably lead to rebirth.

I don't think it at all ghoulish to reflect that the earthly remains of the children who are buried here will eventually pass on their youth and vitality by way of the mulch and detritus that nourishes every new blade of grass and each spring bud. There is a low stone wall that separates the Children's Graveyard from the rest of Holy Acres. Much of it is obscured by tendrils of an ancient climbing rose bush, with vines as thick as my forearm. From the chopping I have to do when I'm digging graves in the wall's shadow, I know how deeply the roots penetrate the soil. I do not doubt that they invade some of the nearby plots.

In every rose that blooms, I fancy I can glimpse a hint of a child's smile.

I used to visit the sea. I suppose I was looking for a sign that some essence of Patrick still lingered or that, like the remains in the graveyard, his loss somehow contributed to the cycle of things. While I could admire the beauty and the majesty of the waves, the ocean always seemed sterile and unforgiving. A child can be irrevocably lost in that endless expanse of roiling water whereas, in my little burial ground, he would be sheltered by the canopies of leaves in a cradle of stalwart roots.

When he could divert his attention from his battles with psoriasis or his struggles with dysentery, I think Kippling may have tried to hint there was something odd about the Children's Graveyard. But I never picked up on the cues. In retrospect, I'm surprised it took me as long as it did to come to that conclusion on my own.

It was the toys of course. It always came back to the toys.

In every cemetery, the living bring gifts for the dead. Most often, they leave bouquets of flowers. Some of the foreigners are partial to leaving food, which makes Kippling crazy. He's convinced it draws raccoons (which it does) and that they all have rabies (which they don't) and that he'll be infected (which is inevitable, given his medical history, with or without the racoons). The Jews place pebbles on the tombs, a kind of calling card to remind the deceased that they have had visitors. Often, family members bring holiday or birthday cards, even though they know that what they have written inside will remain forever unread. Nowhere are the mementos more abundant, more elaborate, or more touching than where children are buried.

People are often surprised by the plethora of stuffed animals, dolls, crayon drawings, faded photographs of birthday parties and vacations, tin soldiers, model cars and other favorite toys decorating the graves. Often, I've overheard casual visitors commenting on the quaintness of the Children's Graveyard. While I certainly understood why they'd find it charming, I didn't always share their sentiments.

There were times, I'll admit, when it was all I could do not to go on a rampage through the place, smashing the toys with my shovel, shredding the stuffed animals with the rose pruners and ripping up the birthday cards and letters left on the graves. Some days, every memento seemed like a slap to my face, like the universe joyously drove a rusty blade into my soul and maliciously twisted it. I gazed on the lovingly decorated tombstones through a veil of jealous hatred. For a time, I forgot why I had first taken this job and the foolish notion I'd had that, by tending to the graves of children who were complete strangers to me, I could somehow reach a catharsis. I seethed with resentment at how tenderly the graves were prettied up and surrounded by flowers and toys.

Where were Patrick's toys? His fire truck with the ladder that extended when he turned a little crank? The blue dragon with the googly eyes that he insisted had to be positioned–just so!–next to his pillow to protect him from imagined monsters lurking in the closet? The clay snowman he made for his mother and me one kindergarten Christmas? How could they serve as his memorial unless I was willing to toss them into the sea where they would simply be swept away in all directions? What would be the point?

In spite of my conviction that the dead return to the earth to be in turn renewed, there were moments when I could not help but doubt. I wanted so desperately to believe that Patrick was not lost forever, that some part of him remained. But I could not. And sometimes, when I was feeling particularly vulnerable, the toys left on the graves of luckier children seemed to rub a healthy measure of salt onto my spiritual wounds.

Ironically, it was those very same toys that changed me. Eventually, they gave me hope but, in the beginning, I was troubled by an eerie phenomenon.

After months of exposure to the weather, even the jauntiest of stuffed animals would be expected to look worse for the wear. And they did. But in spite of how much stuffing oozed from torn seams, no matter how matted or soiled the fur, a good laundering and a few minutes with a needle and thread was all that they needed to be cuddle worthy once again. Yet some of them, I came to realize, had been leaning against the same tombstones for as long as I could remember.

The dolls were even spookier. Constant exposure to the elements slowly leached the pigment from their bright and cheerful outfits until, in time, even the prettiest dress was a pale grey shroud. Porcelain expressions cracked and faded; plastic ones simply wore away. Yet their features were never fully obliterated, and none of the miniature outfits were ever quite reduced to rags. A wind up river boat, its metal paddle wheel pitted and rusted, still looked seaworthy after a decade. A trio of wooden cars also defied entropy; though the rain stripped them of paint and caused the wood to swell, the little wheels stayed firmly attached to their warped axles and spun freely.

Somehow, deterioration never became decay. Until I uncovered part of the solution, new funerals only added to mystery. Now, with what I'd learned, I made it a point to be present for every burial in the Children's Graveyard. Kippling worried that his clients would object to the grave-digger lurking in the background. To keep him happy, when a funeral took place elsewhere in the cemetery, I made myself scarce during any obsequies at the grave. But not there.

My mud spattered slicker made it difficult for me to fade entirely into the background, but I did my best. Fortunately, the absence of very many cars in the procession accurately predicted a dearth of mourners. Even among the tightly packed plots, there was room enough for me to watch without being too intrusive.

Only three people emerged from the town car; a tired-looking man in his thirties, a smartly dressed woman, and a small boy of six or seven. The child was a lively little poppet dressed in a tiny three piece suit that should have made him look like a midget banker but, instead, made him even more adorable. He waited in the car, clutching a paper sack, until his father helped him down and took his hand to guide him across the rain-slicked grass.

The woman followed behind, awkwardly. Her footwear was not designed with such marshy terrain in mind. She caught her heel in a mud-filled pothole and her shoe stayed behind, leaving her precariously balanced on one leg to avoid plunging her stockinged foot into the muck. Before the man could come to her aid, she stooped with a grimace to retrieve the errant shoe. At the expense of a handful of mud, she slipped it back on, while the little boy did his best not to giggle. As they drew closer, I could see a strong resemblance between the two adults. She was an aunt then, not the mother. I found myself wondering if the loss of a child was not the first tragedy to befall this particular family.

A mere four pallbearers hoisted the tiny coffin with poignant ease. Not more than another dozen people got out of the rest of the cars and joined the procession. The solemn little parade followed the elderly priest as he made his way across the berm with jerky steps, wary of the slippery brass ground plaques poised to trip him. Fastidiously, he lifted his cassock so as not to drag the hem through the mud, unintentionally exposing corpse-pale ankles and calves. He looked like some exaggerated cartoon wetlands bird, an egret or stork, leading its chicks through the marsh.

The child laughed aloud and pointed at the cleric before his father could hush him. The older man's cheeks reddened as if he, too, feared a reprimand for making fun of the priest. He looked at me, as if I was the arbiter of what he was allowed to do at his own child's funeral, and I shrugged as sympathetically as I could, hoping he would understand that I, at least, had no intention of judging him. The father shifted his grip on the little boy's hand and said something to the aunt. She moved to take the child by the other one. But the boy shrugged her away, unwilling to relinquish his grip on whatever was in the bag.

The little group zig-zagged its way past the obstacle course of monuments and treacherously slick grass. When they reached the grave, I stepped forward and wordlessly offered the woman the rag I used to wipe away the sweat while digging. Though it was none too clean, she accepted it gratefully and used it to wipe the muck from her hand. When she tried to return it to me, I shook my head slightly and was rewarded with a sad and sweet smile of thanks.

Curious, the little boy watched the exchange. He held up one grime besmirched finger for her inspection. But when his aunt tried to wipe it with the bit of cloth, he saw how dirty it was, wrinkled his nose with distaste and snatched his hand away. She heaved a visible sigh, rolled her eyes and shot a wry look my way. Now, it was my turn to smile and to silently reassure her that I wasn't offended.

The priest stood awkwardly, unable to put more than a foot or so between himself and the open grave for fear of tripping over an established monument. As he began to speak, the rain resumed pelting down with fury and, by the time everyone fumbled open their umbrellas, they were all drenched. The father stooped to offer the little boy the chance to hold the umbrella over them both. The child refused, again preferring to hang on to his paper sack.

The weather wasn't the only reason the priest kept the eulogy short. With bland and innocuous words, he praised the dead child—the little boy's twin, as it turned out—as fun-loving and attentive at school. Lacking the conviction of any details, he painted a picture of a kid who was well-liked and popular. It seemed obvious, to me at least, that he hadn't known the dead boy well, if at all.

The surviving twin was remarkably well behaved. When Patrick was his age, I'd have exhausted myself trying to keep him from running wild between the tombstones or worse. This child gave me pause only when I saw his eyes flickering curiously toward some of the toys and, involuntarily, all my muscles tensed. I caught the boy's eye again and shook my head firmly to let him know the toys were off limits.

I shivered, but it wasn't because the rain was cold. Though it was twenty years since my eyes were first opened, the memories of one particular burial were still fresh. Before then, it was inconceivable to me that any family would not be devastated by the loss of a child. But *that* funeral was far more about ostentation than it was about grief.

The parents spared no expense. The coffin, lacquered pink with real silver fittings, was carried from the chapel in a fully restored antique hearse drawn by a quartet of magnificent white horses. The sheer volume of the flowers could have filled a grave of their own and, though I'm unsure of his exact rank, the clergyman who officiated was no mere priest.

Predictably, the ceremony was a long one—never a good idea when the deceased has four or five under-aged siblings. The kids restlessly poked and pinched each other. One whined about wanting ice cream while another threw a tantrum until a nanny was able to haul him away. Throughout, only one little girl of about nine showed any signs of true bereavement, weeping quietly and casting desolate looks at the coffin.

Midway through the eulogy, the child just snapped and began to keen. I was no stranger to what grief is like; I'd spent many months living with my own. As if her parents weren't horrified enough by her lack of decorum, she snatched a tattered princess doll from a nearby grave. Sobbing uncontrollably, she buried her face in the doll's dusty hair and, in spite of her parents' fury at being embarrassed in public, she refused to give it up.

Naturally, since this was a funeral where money was no object, Sidney Kippling was standing by, inhaler in hand, to make sure everything went smoothly—which it obviously wasn't. But my boss' normally unctuous charm had the opposite effect. The minute someone official objected, however tactfully, to his daughter having taken the toy, the father's attitude underwent an abrupt reversal and, to save face, he insisted that his daughter be allowed to keep it.

It was an uncomfortable situation for everyone. Worse, the father arrogantly flung a few bills in Kippling's face with imperious instructions to "just buy another doll and keep the change." Kippling, to his credit, left the money where it fell and, with admirable tact, backed down. As for me, I was hard put not to deck the guy with my shovel and dump his rotten corpse into the hole I'd dug for his daughter.

That night, I lay awake for hours. They had lost their *child*, for pity's sake! Bereavement can take many different forms, I know. Though it was not my place to judge, I couldn't help it. To me, it seemed that they were no more traumatized by their loss than if they had discovered one of their cars' fenders was dented. Yet they'd been blessed with six while mine was gone. Was it any wonder that, when I finally drifted into an uneasy slumber, I was plagued by dreams of an empty plastic sand pail slowly being washed out to sea?

The sobbing woke me.

I'm not sure why I didn't pick up the phone. I live in a small apartment above the mortuary so I can be on site in case of maintenance emergencies. Kippling has strict rules about how to handle those sorts of things. Usually, my biggest challenge is a broken sprinkler, but there had been a few incidents with trespassers and, once, I tangled with a group of drunken would-be Satanists looking for mischief. After that last run-in, Kippling made it very clear that he wasn't paying me to take those kinds of risks; he had a security company for that.

Yet that night, it never occurred to me to make the call. Instead, still groggy, I slipped outside in my bare feet and I lurched across the lawns, following the weeping which led me to the Children's Graveyard. What I saw jolted me wide awake.

The children had come out to play.

For long moments, I was paralyzed by what I saw. My stomach churned, but it wasn't from fear. The scenes before me were too innocent to inspire fright.

A toddler held a teddy bear, one thumb crammed into his mouth. Two boys wearing old fashioned sailor suits raced wooden cars back and forth across the top of their headstone. Next to them, a girl with long hair used her tomb as a makeshift table to host a tea party for a few dolls and a sepulchral stone angel. Toward the back of the graveyard, a boy bounced a rubber ball against the vine covered stone wall, over and over. And all of it went on in absolute silence but for the faint rustle of dried leaves on the rose vine, and the weeping.

Odder still, I saw that most of kids seemed completely oblivious to their neighbors. Unless they were siblings buried in the same grave, none were truly playing together. It was like I was watching several movies being projected onto a single screen. Each story was layered on top of the next, occupying the same space but never actually merging and no one within it made contact with anyone outside it. A boy with a stick rolled a hoop through a game of jacks, but the little girl continued to bounce her ball without pausing. Another child with a whirligig on a string ran incessant rings around his headstone, swinging the toy through the bodies of several others, none of them even winced.

It was chaos, just like on any earthly playground, but even in their isolation, the kids seemed to be enjoying themselves. In that tumult of silence, I felt calm and centered for the first time in a long while. But the tranquility could not last.

While part of me was soothed by this proof that something lived on after death, there was another part that was furious at the unfairness. My body trembled with the urge to run through the tombstones, screaming and waving my arms to drive the children away like flies from an open wound. At that moment, I despised them and I wanted to see them miserable. At the same time, I was horrified at the thought of giving in to such vindictive pettiness. It would only compound injustice for me to blame them for having what my own son did not. With that thought, my rage evaporated and left only a melancholy depression in its wake.

The charm, the innocence, the joy—all were spoiled. My heart hardened to even scenes of ineffable sweetness.

Two girls propped themselves against a double tombstone, their attention fixed on a tattered picture book. It was obvious to me that the older sister was teaching the younger one how to read. It should have been as charming as a Normal Rockwell painting but all I could see was the pointlessness of the endeavor. Not too far away, a boy barely into his teens guided the hand of a child with a grotesquely large and misshapen skull as it struggled with a broken crayon. I was shocked when a vicious voice in my head suggested that it was kindness that a child suffering such horrible deformities was already in its grave.

They were unworthy, ignoble thoughts and I hated myself for having them. But I couldn't help it. I tried to recapture those first moments of wonder, that fleeting instant of peace, but the weeping I'd heard earlier demanded that I pay attention to it.

Emily Cooper was the name carved into the headstone; there was no date.

Emily looked about Patrick's age though, from the tight curls in her hair and from the frilly bows on a dress that no modern child would wear, I guessed she had died long before I was born. She sobbed as if her entire world had been shattered; in the clear moonlight, I could see that her kewpie doll cheeks were blotchy and her eyes were swollen.

Every so often, she stopped crying and raised her head sharply, as if at a sudden sound. With sad longing in her eyes, she searched the shadows. There was hope there as well, as if at any second she expected to find something she'd lost. But as the minutes passed and she found nothing, her lower lip started to quiver again and she burst into fresh tears.

I was angry, angry at the arbitrariness of any universe that could allow the wonders I was seeing and still deny me another glimpse of my own son. But even more so, I was angry for little Emily. It wasn't that I didn't understand how much pain the living girl must have been in to do what she'd done; I'd been in that kind of pain myself. I empathized with her and yet, at the same time, I couldn't quite forgive her. In time, the pain of her loss would dull, even if now, she was too young to realize it. But Emily's pain, like my own, would just keep on.

I blocked the other specters from my mind and squatted next to the tomb. I knew it would do no good to try and hug the girl to my chest but I tried anyway though my arms closed on empty air. I called her name, softly at first, but she didn't hear. The sharp pebbles digging into my knees brought me to my senses. I hadn't realized that I'd collapsed, sobbing and screaming, on top of the grave and that I'd abraded my hands by pounding my fists against Emily's headstone.

I must have waited with her until she, with the others, vanished at sunrise. I don't remember much about waking up that morning except that I was filthy from sleeping on the grass and dew-moist earth. And that I was alone.

I went and bought the biggest princess doll I could find. It seemed to do the trick. For many nights afterward, Emily and the other children stayed in their graves.

In the years that followed, I saw them from time to time, though I never completely understood the mechanism for rousing them. Obviously, moving a toy was one sure fire way to do it. If one of the day laborers knocked a stuffed animal onto the wrong grave, or if a crow flew off with a toy soldier, I'd hear crying in the night until I could figure out what was missing and set things right. Yet there were other times, when nothing had changed, and the children rose anyway. On those nights, there was no crying and, if it hadn't been for insomnia, I never would have known that the kids were back.

Often, when I couldn't sleep, I found myself drawn to the Children's Graveyard. It was peaceful there, even relaxing when the children weren't at play. But there were times when it was terribly lonely too. There were times I was tempted to steal a toy or two myself, simply to summon company. But I never did. It would have been a spiteful, vengeful thing to do and, I knew that if my own son were buried here, I would be horrified at the thought that a selfish stranger would cause him distress.

Mostly, I waited. I did my best to make sure they rested peacefully. And that is why, while I listened to the priest finish his prayers and I saw the little boy looking curiously at the toys, I frowned to warn him off. As it turned out, I need not have worried.

Though the drizzle hadn't ceased, the sky seemed to take the end of the service as a signal to renew its own weeping in earnest. The mourners struggled with their umbrellas while the rain pounded down. Slowly, because the rope was soaked clear through and might jam the winch, I turned the crank to lower the top of the coffin to just below ground level. One by one, the mourners stepped forward to cast a handful of dirt upon the casket. After they took their turns, they slogged cautiously across the slippery lawn to the gravel road where their cars were parked. When it came time for the aunt to add her measure, she motioned with the rag I'd given her and shot a quizzical look my way. I spared her a sympathetic smile to let her know it was okay. I had other handkerchiefs. With a nod of thanks, she scooped up some earth, squeezed it to remove as much water as possible, and let it fall onto the coffin with a plop.

Next, the father tried to help his son but the boy shook him off and wriggled away. Evidently no stranger to playing in the mud, he eagerly snatched up his own handful and flung it enthusiastically into the grave. I tried not to grin when he grabbed a second handful, before his father stopped him and pointed in my direction. From the disappointment on his face, it was clear to me that the kid had been naively been hoping to pitch in and help fill in the hole.

The aunt thrust my grimy rag at her brother, burst into tears, and turned to stumble blindly across the berm toward the road. Patiently and with sad dignity, the man used it to clean his son's fingers as best he could. When the worst of the mud was gone, the boy dipped into the paper sack and took out a stuffed animal, a bright orange tiger wearing a jaunty green bow tie. The toy was well worn, obviously not new.

With great solemnity, the child kissed the animal's nose. Then, with his father holding tight to the back of his jacket to keep him from tumbling onto the casket, the boy carefully nestled the tiger among the bouquets that would shortly be buried with his brother. Once the tiger was settled to the boy's satisfaction, the two of them stood, waiting. With a pang of dismay, I realized they intended to stay while I finished lowering the coffin and filling in the grave. I'd never had that happen before and wasn't quite sure how to deal with it.

"Um . . . we like to wait until after the family is gone," I said, as gently as I could. "It can be upsetting for some people and . . ." I gestured at the little boy.

The man smiled with a bitterness that I recognized from my own bathroom mirror.

"Eddie will be all right. He understands . . ." He stopped, at a momentary loss for words before he sighed heavily and began again. "Eddie understands that it's okay to be sad that his brother is gone. At the same time we can be happy. Because he's in heaven."

"Michael is with Mommy now." He said it very seriously, as if he was sharing a great and terrible truth. "When Mommy is busy," he continued, "Tiggy can play with Michael until me and Daddy get there for company."

I gripped my shovel tightly while I struggled to get my feelings under control. It would be so easy for me to reach out to this father and to share with him what I knew. Even if he didn't believe me and thought I was just offering platitudes, just knowing that I was also a father who had lost a son might comfort him a little. But then I asked myself if I had been in this mans' place—*when* I had been in this man's place—would I have wanted to know, and I repressed a shudder. No, I pictured my own boy sunk in the blackness of the deep sea and I thought how much easier it would have been had I never known of an afterlife.

I spoke to the child instead.

"But Tiggy will get dirty," I told him.

"I know," he said. "But we need to make sure Tiggy stays with Michael and doesn't get lost. That's what Daddy said."

"Fill it in, please," the man said in a low voice that cracked with emotion. "With the tiger on top.

I avoided meeting either of their eyes while I lowered the casket into the grave. I slipped the canvas cradle from underneath and disengaged the winches to retract the cables. Then, against my better judgment, I began shoveling earth into the grave while they watched, the one with barely maintained stoicism and the other with an innocent certainty that everything was happening just as it should.

It took me close to an hour. Throughout, the child watched with a quiet dignity that belied how young he was while the rain pounded down and the father held the umbrella to shield them from the worst of it. There was nothing he could do to prevent the ricochet from the puddles against their trouser legs but, even after he was drenched from the knee down, he seemed unconscious of the splashing.

Slowly, the level of the dirt rose. For their benefit, I pushed myself to work as fast as I could, even though mud is much heavier than dry earth and my lower back didn't appreciate the effort. When I was finished, the father awkwardly balanced the umbrella so he could reach into his breast pocket, presumably for his wallet. I smiled to let him know I appreciated the gesture but, again, I shook my head. Moments later, they were gone and there was nothing left for me to do but to smooth over the dirt once again, pack up the winch and stow it in the wheelbarrow with the rest of my tools.

The rain continued into the night, becoming more violent as the hours wore on. I lay in bed unable to sleep, listening to it pounding on the roof. Either I dozed a little or the rhythm of the storm lulled me with a kind of hypnosis because, when the sobbing eventually registered, I realized with surprise that I'd been hearing it for some time. Without hesitation, I shrugged the slicker over my bare torso and headed into the night.

Perhaps it was my imagination, or perhaps it was the effect of the storm, but there was an unusual feeling of wildness hanging over the

Children's Graveyard. The kids seemed no less happy and carefree than normal, but it seemed to me that, tonight, there was a new intensity to their games; it was as if their play was tainted by a hint of desperation. Yet there was nothing specific I could point a finger at; it was only a feeling.

I recalled that the priest had mentioned that the boys were twins, but I still suffered a momentary shock at the likeness. I had the uncanny feeling that it was the living boy that I had seen scant hours earlier, who was standing by the new grave. His eyes were fixed on the ground where his body lay. He bit down on one of his fists, as if he was trying to keep from crying, but it did no good. His expression was so lost, so forlorn, so unlike the simple, trusting acceptance his brother had displayed all through the funeral.

I watched him sink to the ground. His hands scrabbled in the dirt but, when he paused, they held nothing. Still, he kept digging even though it was hopeless. After a while, he finally gave up and stretched himself across the plot, his little body heaving with every sob.

I don't remember deciding to bring the shovel with me but something in my subconscious must have known. Without hesitation, I thrust the blade into the newly turned earth and, as if compelled, I began to dig as fast as I could. My hood fell back but I didn't stop to pull it over my head again. Even with the rain trickling down my bare back, and with the sweat causing the oil cloth to cling uncomfortably to my skin, I never paused.

I'd forgotten that I'd dug the grave particularly deep and I was momentarily disoriented when I reached the point where the coffin should have been exposed, and I saw nothing but more dirt. Terrified that I would be impotent to ease the boy's pain, I tossed aside my shovel and leaped down into the grave, frantically scraping aside sodden earth with my bare hands. A few moments later, I sighed with relief when I at last came up with a handful of ragged stems and muddy flowers and knew I was close.

On all fours atop the casket, I used my entire arms to push aside the muck. Finally, I seized the tiger and held the sodden and filthy stuffed animal over my head in triumph. I laughed—I couldn't help myself--

when a strange and joyous euphoria washed over me. When I pictured what Kippling's face would look like if he should see me now, it brought on the worst attack of the giggles I'd ever had.

With the tiger tucked under my arm, I climbed out of the grave. It was tricky. The surrounding earth was so over-saturated from the storm that huge clots broke free when I tried to dig a handhold. Eventually I emerged victorious with the stuffed toy and I held it out to the little boy.

He saw me.

It was the first time that had happened. None of the children had ever shown the slightest sign that they knew I was there. But this child was different. He looked directly at me. At first, he seemed confused. But when he saw the tiger, he reached for it.

And his hands went right through it. I gently placed the toy on the ground at his feet but it did no good. The poor little tyke tried to pick it up, but he couldn't. It simply lay there as the rain formed a puddle around it, looking lonely and tragically forlorn. I tried handing it to him again but there was nothing I could do. My heart broke a little.

He looked at me with ineffable longing, pleading desperately with me. I frowned. Something about his expression was chillingly familiar but I could not quite place it at first. A clap of thunder sounded overhead and the downpour worsened. I didn't know that I was crying. I thought it was rain in my eyes, blurring my vision. But then, something inside of me broke open and, as I drew a breath for another heaving sob, I inhaled a bit of rainwater.

Michael. His name was Michael. *Not* Patrick.

The only salt in the water I coughed up was from my tears.

But the look, the look in his eyes . . . it was the same.

I gasped and involuntarily retreated a step. My feet slid in the mud and I toppled backward into the grave. Choking and sobbing, it didn't help that my breath was knocked out of me when I landed on top of the casket. I scrambled to my feet and gouged huge craters from the wall of the grave when I struggled to climb out.

Once again, I could see Patrick's face when I reached for him. The gap between our straining fingers was so small. It seemed like it should be an easy distance to cover, not much farther than what it took to place a toy in a child's hand. But it was far more vast and, after all this time, I finally realized that there was nothing I could have done to span it.

The sides of the grave, weakened by the rain and chunks I had scratched out of them, gave way and I fell onto my back once again. Great gobbets of mud landed on my slicker, weighing it down like tent posts hold a tent against the wind. Though I struggled and thrashed, I knew it was hopeless and I soon gave up. Mud crept up my sides and covered my chest while the walls continued their steady collapse. Mercifully, I didn't have long to wait and, when I tasted my first mouthful of wet earth, I was surprised that it wasn't nearly as unpleasant as I feared.

It wasn't my fault, I thought, as the dirt closed over my head.

Just before everything went dark, I panicked briefly before I remembered that the tiger was still on the surface. Perhaps, once the grave was filled in again, the boy would be able to reach it.

I saw Patrick's face, slowly fading from view. I stretched my hand as far as I could until with a groan of resignation, I knew that I could reach no farther.

There was nothing else I could have done, I told myself. For first time since I could remember, I was at peace.

"Are you here to play with us?"

I blinked. I was still in the Children's Graveyard but now, I could clearly hear their laughter and their happy squeals. I instantly saw how wrong I had been. The children were *not* isolated from each other. A new knowledge stirred within me and I began to get an inkling of how truly connected they all were. As I stood taking it all in, I sensed that the link extended over the walls of the Children's Graveyard, past the boundaries of Holy Acres, and perhaps as far away as the sea itself.

"Are you going to stay here with Tiggy and me? To keep away the lonely?"

The little boy clung to the stuffed animal. He looked at the tombstones with wide eyes, not really frightened, but unsure of where he was of why he was there. I wanted to reassure him but, even so, I surprised myself with the confidence of my answer.

"Yes," I said. "I'll stay." I paused. Then added, "To keep away the lonely."

The instant I spoke the words, I heard the echo of distant waves and, just as suddenly, something told me that I needn't wander from my own grave in order to reach far beyond it.

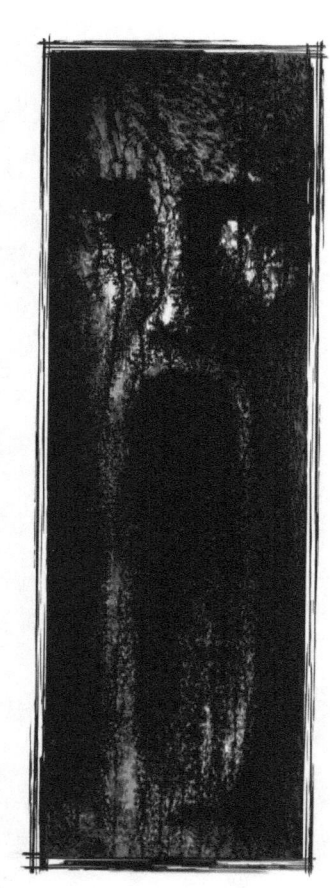

Kathryn E. McGee

CARMICHAEL MOTEL

Alana's stomach cramped the whole time she drove and she had to swallow often to keep the thoughts at bay. The thoughts that were trying to inch their way in and remind her. About Chris. About the loss. The breakup they'd had a few hours prior. She'd left her apartment and gone straight to her car, hitting the road without a plan. She'd hoped escaping would clear her mind. But all that time alone was only forcing her to think.

Something else was bothering her, too.

Not just a headache, but a migraine. The kind that pulsed behind the eyes. She plucked two Excedrin from the loose pills in the ashtray and placed them on her tongue. She chugged water and kept driving. The constant migraines were terrible, but some part of her was glad for the pain. It was a type of pain she could do something about. It was pain she could stop.

Alana drove for three hours. When she spotted the partially illuminated neon sign for the Carmichael Motel, she was ready to call it a night. She traveled several miles on unpaved roads before the building came into view. There wasn't much to it: just a two-story rectangular box. A small reception office at one end formed an L-shaped arm that reached out toward the near-empty parking lot.

Alana parked her car and went inside.

The man behind the front desk looked worn out, his facial hair greyish and too long, his gut sagging. He wore a nametag that read *Gary*. Alana caught a chill and shivered. She wanted to get out of the office and into a room fast.

"On the second floor, please," she heard herself say.

Gary eyed her a moment. "We've only got first floor available."

Alana paused. "But it looks like you're empty. There's only one other car in the lot."

"Renovating the whole top floor." Gary crossed his arms and leaned forward onto the orange countertop. "Sorry for the inconvenience."

Alana began to drum her fingertips on her thighs. She didn't like the idea of a first floor room, never had. She hated the sound of footsteps overhead.

"The motel is pretty much empty," Gary said. "You shouldn't be disturbed, but are you sure you want to stay here? You seem young to be alone in a place like this. There's a few other motels, up the road, you know."

Alana glared at him. She'd been through enough—too much—for anyone to call her young. Gary had no idea what she'd been through. Not just with Chris, but all her failed relationships prior, all those men who had been bad for her.

"I'm fine," she said.

Gary sighed and held out a key attached to a cold metal tab with the words *Room 114* inscribed in red. "Checkout is at noon."

Alana tried to smile. "I'll be out of here long before then."

Room 114 was on the first floor, at the end opposite the office, next to the stairwell door. Inside, the furnishings were simple. There was just a bed, nightstand, dresser, and desk. The wallpaper was green and there were framed prints of tulips and geraniums near the window.

She couldn't help but think about the first time she and Chris had stayed in a motel together, when they'd started dating. It had been a roadside dump like this one, but that hadn't mattered. They'd been laughing and drinking red wine in bed, stripping off one article of clothing for every sip they'd taken. The game hadn't lasted long.

Maybe it isn't too late, Alana thought, and sat down on the edge of the bed. *Maybe it isn't too late to call him, to work things out.* Tears pooled in her eyes. All she wanted was to touch him again. She wanted to slip her hands inside the warmth of his leather jacket, holding her stomach against his. She could almost feel the way he'd take the back of her head in his hand, how her lips would graze his beard just before they kissed.

She stretched out on the bed and closed her eyes, tried to tell herself nothing bad had happened that afternoon. *Just sleep,* she thought. *You just need to sleep.* But how many times had she been here? How many times had she felt the desperation of losing someone she'd loved?

For a few long moments there were no sounds and her mind started to drift. Then she heard a car, maybe a truck, driving up outside, crunching across the gravel. A door slammed shut. Someone got out and walked by her room.

Alana sat up in bed. Could it be Chris? Could he have come so far to find her?

The footsteps traveled past her room and entered the stairwell, thumping heavily up the steps. Alana sighed. Of course it wasn't Chris. He'd have no idea where she was. It was just another tired traveler there for the night. She squeezed her eyes shut. She hated herself for even considering he would have come. He wouldn't. She was the one who'd left.

The footsteps continued, loudly across the floor above.

There weren't supposed to be any guests upstairs. But apparently there was one. And now there was pacing. Heavy pacing. Back and forth. Back and forth.

Alana squeezed her eyes shut.

She told herself to ignore the sounds, to block out the noises, go back to sleep.

Just breathe, she thought.

But the noises grew louder and her headache came raging back.

She felt a rush of anger. The headaches were Chris's fault. She'd been having them for weeks now, since that afternoon when they'd argued and he'd shoved her into the corner of their dresser. She'd blacked out and woken alone on the floor, the room blurry and streaked with color. She hadn't been able to see or walk straight for days.

I'm better off without him.

That's what she tried to tell herself.

But none of what had happened had been his fault. She'd been the one who'd started the fight. She'd picked on him because of his dirty apartment and all that time he was spending out late with his friends, stomping upstairs and not bothering to come down to see her when he got home. They lived in the same building—that's how they'd met—and he couldn't be bothered to walk down a flight of stairs and see her, throwing his presence in her face when he stomped above her in the middle of the night.

But she shouldn't have picked at him. Instead of criticizing, she should have celebrated him more, told him how she loved all the unique, quirky things that made him great. He'd been good to her a lot of the time— occasionally sweet. She thought about the four or five times he'd shown up with flowers. Or the nights it had been too hot to cuddle and they'd slept side-by-side, holding hands, waking the next morning with their fingers still intertwined. There had been all those good moments, hadn't there? She'd give anything to feel his hands touching hers now. *But you can't,* a voice in her head replied, and she rolled onto her back, trying to distract herself by counting the points on the popcorn ceiling. *Maybe I should call him when I wake up,* she thought. *Maybe I'll call him and let him know we should talk again, that I still care, that I still want—*

More footsteps.

Stomping, heavy and loud.

"Why won't you stop?" she whispered, holding her face against a pillow. "Why won't you please just let me sleep?"

Alana held her hands up to her temples.

Please stop. Please stop. Please stop.

She rolled over, grabbed the phone from the nightstand, and dialed the front desk. She had to complain. There wasn't supposed to be anyone on the second floor. The line rang and rang with no reply. Alana dropped the phone into its cradle. The footsteps started to shake the room, making her head throb even worse.

Alana found two more Excedrin at the bottom of her wallet. She stumbled, disoriented, toward the bathroom, where she filled a glass of water and swallowed the pills. She made her way to the bed, stretched out on her back and stared upward until her eyes started to glaze.

She had a vision of Chris. She saw his face, the strange shape his lips had taken, curling up into a half-smile when he'd walked in earlier that day, before he'd started talking. All that talking. Too much talking. Her headache had really begun then, hadn't it? A slow, subtle pulse behind her eyes, blurring her vision. She could almost recall the precise moment when things had—

The noises from the footsteps worsened.

Alana covered her face with a pillow. It wasn't just the noise that bothered her, but the claustrophobic feeling that was mounting. The sense of being surrounded on all sides.

She couldn't stand being there anymore.

She fled Room 114 and ran out into the night. The cold blast of air felt good.

But the parking lot was darker than it had been and now there were no other cars—not even Gary's. She looked toward the reception office. The lights were off inside. Gary must have gone home or turned in for the night. She gazed out into the distance. There was only blackness in every direction for miles.

Alana had a sudden and terrible feeling. The sense she might be alone, that she *was* alone. She should go home, she decided. Back to Chris. Back to her life. All she had to do was grab her wallet and car keys, and get back on the road.

The door to her room had closed.

She tried the knob.

It wouldn't turn.

"Shit!" She was locked out. She backed away from her room and looked up at the second floor, but all the windows there were dark. Who knows, maybe Gary lived in the motel and was still there, just asleep.

She went for the door to the stairwell. That door was locked, though, and her only remaining option was to check the reception office. Maybe Gary had left it open. She walked over to it and found that door locked, too. What kind of motel didn't have at least one person on duty? Her heart started to race, panic rising. What was she going to do? Sleep curled up outside her motel room door for the night?

She walked back to her room and stared at its closed window. Maybe she could figure out how to pry the window open without breaking the glass. It was one of those old aluminum sliders. It didn't look that sturdy. Maybe she could dig her fingernails under the sash and get it to come out of the frame. She pulled at the metal and it gave a little. She pulled harder and the pane of glass trembled. Her eyes caught her warped reflection in the glazed surface. Just then her fingers slipped across a raw edge of the metal. She screamed and let go of the frame, sucking the blood from three of her fingertips, eyeing the place where she'd left a smear of red on the window. Blood dribbled down her hand, onto her wrist and forearm, staining the sleeve of her shirt. Pressing her fingers hard against her palm to stop the bleeding, she felt defeated. It was no use. She'd never get back inside this way.

A second floor window slid open overhead.

She glanced up, still cradling her arm. A light went on in the room above hers. Alana breathed a sigh of relief. It had to be Gary up there cleaning, didn't it? Or another guest, at the very least. Whoever it was must have heard her outside messing with the window.

"Gary?" she called out, but her voice sounded small. "Hello?"

There was no reply.

She decided to try the stairwell door one more time. Remarkably, she found it unlocked. The knob turned easily and the door swung open toward her, a rush of cool air from inside curling around her ankles.

The stairwell was dimly lit and the steps were rickety, squealing with each movement. There was a closed door at the top. She was walking steadily and then her hand was on the knob, turning, pushing the door open.

She walked out into the second floor corridor.

The door closed behind. She grabbed to open it again, but her wounded fingertips ached and she couldn't locate the knob. She ran her palm over the door, but it seemed to be gone—as if it had become flush with the wall. She balled her hand into a fist to control the pain. The overhead lights went dark and then illuminated again. She stared at the lights a long time, and then realized she was walking, down the hallway. She had to find Chris. Not Chris. Gary. *Find Gary. Find Gary. Find Gary.* Her thoughts repeated. The lights flickered. The air hummed.

She tiptoed along the corridor, eyeing the numbers on each door. She assumed she should be looking for the room above hers, and checked for number 214. She found it to her left. Then she found it again to her right. And again on another door to her left. Every door was labeled 214. Must be part of the renovation work, she told herself, though her heart was racing.

She felt disoriented, unsure now where the room over hers should be located. She gazed down the hallway, as if for answers, and couldn't see the end. The corridor was longer than she'd thought it would be, fading into darkness.

"Hello?" she called, as loudly as she was comfortable. "Anyone around?"

There was no answer.

She passed several rooms before she started knocking.

"Is anyone here?" she called out.

She heard a creaking sound.

A door behind her opened onto the hallway.

She whirled around.

The tall, shadowy figure of a man stepped into the corridor.

"Hello," she said softly. She squinted in his direction. "I've locked myself out and—" The hallway lights flickered again and dimmed even more. She couldn't make out the man's features. Something in his posture reminded her of someone she'd dated. Years ago. He hadn't been a man then, really. They'd been teenagers. Kurt. That had been his name. The first guy she'd fallen in love with. The first one to make her come undone. The man in the hallway said something in a low voice that she couldn't understand. It was more like a grunt than words. She would have asked him to repeat what he'd said, but she hesitated. "Sorry to bother you," she offered, and backed away. The man began to move, shambling toward her now on slow, heavy feet. A noise came from his throat. "I'm sorry, what was that?" Alana's voice was a whisper. She could still remember sitting cross-legged in the grass of her parent's backyard, realizing Kurt had stopped calling for a reason, that she wasn't going to hear from him again.

The man kept walking, his gait slow and jerky. Feeling uncomfortable, Alana turned away and continued down the hallway, away from him.

She heard a second door open behind her.

Another man stepped out into the shadows near the first one. Alana squinted, tried to see him. Something about his posture was familiar, shoulders hunched forward. Aled. That had been his name. The guy from college. She thought of the letter he'd sent her after they broke up, how she'd stood at the kitchen sink burning the paper, dropping it onto the wet porcelain and watching ink bleed into water.

The man walked toward her.

Focus on something else, she told herself. But for a while she couldn't. She was caught up in remembering that last night with Aled. How he'd stood there confessing and how after a while she hadn't been able to hear what he was saying. When she'd finally left him on the street by his car and gone back up the stairs inside, all she'd been able to do was wonder how she kept failing, again and again.

Stop thinking about all this, she told herself, and for a moment her mind cleared. *There's more to you than this. There's more. There's more. There's more.*

She looked up to see that the men walking toward her had paused. They were silhouettes—barely there. Were they there at all? Their form came and went, in and out of focus. Then one of them made a sound, mumbled something that could have been her name.

"What?" Alana said.

Another door swung open onto the hallway.

And another.

More men stepped out into the corridor, until there was a small crowd walking toward her, all of them looking vaguely familiar, but making strange noises—sounds she'd never heard. None of them said anything she could understand; they just kept coming.

She headed as fast as she could away from them, toward the far end of the hallway. Behind her, heavy footsteps sounded. She ran hard without looking back, but realized she couldn't see the end of the hallway in front of her. For what felt like several minutes she covered a long distance, until she finally saw a door at the end, labeled 214.

Please be unlocked, she prayed.

It was.

The door swung open and she threw herself into the room. She could hear the bodies from the hallway ramming into the closed door, and she backed away.

Room 214 was arranged similarly to hers, though there was something different about the space, a sense of motion about things. The sheets on the bed were undulating, rippling like water. She bent over to touch them and found herself running her hands back and forth over the material. Then she was lying down, feeling small movements beneath her back as she stared up at the ceiling. The ceiling blurred. She struggled to make out the shapes above her. And then the room grew darker, slipping away into blackness.

Then it changed.

She wasn't in Room 214 anymore.

She was standing in her apartment back home, moving unseen like a ghost. Across the room was another version of her, as she had been hours before, arguing with Chris. She had just thrown the first candleholder, the glass one, against the wall. She had watched it shatter. She had felt Chris grab her by the shoulders and listened as he yelled that final, hurtful thing.

I never loved you.

He kept repeating those words. Over and over again.

"Stop!" she said. She didn't want to hear him. Her head hurt. Didn't he know how badly her head hurt? She saw herself pick up the second candleholder—the bulbous iron one—and raise it threateningly. "You've got to stop."

Chris wasn't listening.

Alana's headache intensified.

Chris was shouting.

There was beating on the door from the things in the hallway.

Alana felt like her head would split in two.

The noises have to stop, she thought. *Make them stop.*

"Please!" she heard herself beg.

But Chris didn't stop. Not at first. He kept talking.

I never loved you.

Alana watched as her hand brought the heavy metal of the candle-holder down hard on his skull, making him fall to the floor. Blood dripped from his wound and he began to scream. The sound was high-pitched and loud. She didn't want to hear it. She needed a moment of peace, a moment to think and sort things out.

But all she could think about were the bad feelings. The ones she'd been struggling with for years. The ones that pulsed in her with constant pain. The nights Chris had forgotten to call her back. When he hadn't introduced her to his friends. All those times she'd wondered if he'd been ashamed. How she'd been the one to say, *I love you*, first, nearly every single time. She didn't want to think about those things.

The pounding on the door of Room 214 grew loud, so painfully loud.

Please, she thought. *Make the sounds go away.*

The walls trembled and it was as if everything in the room were swelling and heaving, the floor beneath her, the ceiling above—all of it in motion. And then calm. The room had fallen quiet. Alana had brought the candleholder down on Chris's skull. Six times, seven times, eight times, nine. A bright red spray coated everything. The white bedspread. The floor. The walls. But Chris's screams had stopped. The hammering in her head had stopped. The bloody apartment had slipped away. She and her former self were one.

She was back in Room 214, curled on the bed, praying the scene with Chris hadn't been real—but she knew it had. She gripped the bed sheets next to her, felt their texture between her fingers. She looked around the room. All of the surfaces were solid and unmoving. Chris was really gone now and she was really here, in this strange motel somewhere off the interstate.

She stood up and walked toward the window, sliding it open. Leaning out into the cool night air, she could see her car waiting below in the parking lot. She'd be in the car soon, by tomorrow morning, at least.

She could drive as far as she wanted, start over in another state.

A noise made her turn.

Loud crashing sounds. The splintering of wood. She breathed in sharply and whirled around to watch the door tear from its hinges, exploding into pieces. She closed her eyes and opened them several times, expecting her eyelids to wipe the vision away. But there was no vision. What she saw was real. The men—those *things*—from the hallway had rammed their way through. With groaning, guttural sounds, they walked toward her, thick-shouldered frames ever in shadow, faces without noses or eyes, obscured despite the overhead lights.

"What?" She started to say, but she couldn't deny that the group was coming closer, coming for *her*.

The window was her only way out.

She turned toward it and stuck her torso through. There was a chance she could climb outside and hang from the bottom of the frame. With only about fifteen feet to fall, she might be okay.

But the men were on her; it was too late.

Hands gripped her ankles and high up on her legs. A strong tug pulled her back into the room, where she was thrown on the bed, her arms extended out on either side.

The shadowy figures surrounded her. One lifted her wounded hand to his mouth and lapped at the blood. He sucked hard at the gash on her fingertips, snaking his tongue in and out of her dripping flesh. She cried out in pain, trying to jerk her hand away, but the others held her down. Their shadowy forms pulled at her wrists, ankles, and neck. She could hear them gnashing teeth, frenzied with hunger. One bit into the meat of her leg. The rest stabbed knife-like talons into her armpits and upper thighs. She screamed as her muscles ripped and they tore her apart at the limbs. She felt their jaws dig in as they suckled and fed.

The pain was intense and all around her; then as quickly as it had started, was gone. There was just her heart pounding and the recollection of fear. There was the sense of sadness. And then nothing. Just warm liquid pooling beneath her body—a body she could no longer feel—and the notion of something soothing and calm on the horizon. The monsters, no longer mattering, fell down on her like rain.

Chet Williamson

THAT STILL, BLEEDING OBJECT OF DESIRE

"And I will execute great vengeance upon
them with furious rebukes . . . "
— *Ezekiel, 25:17*

They were beautiful, all of them. He couldn't decide if he preferred
the blondes or brunettes most. There weren't many redheads in his collection. For some reason he wasn't particularly drawn to them, though
he didn't know why.

He tilted his head to the side and looked closely at the face and body
nearest him. It was that of a blonde woman in her twenties. She was
visible from the waist up, and nude, lying on her back. Her eyes were
open so that only the whites showed, and her mouth was agape so that
he could see her teeth. A trickle of red ran from the right corner of her
mouth down below her ear, and vanished where her hair covered her
neck.

Slash marks were in three different places on her chest. They appeared
to be deep, and part of the flesh of her right breast seemed to be drawn
back, as if a knife had incised it and laid bare the muscle beneath. For
all the perceived damage, the nipples were still erect, and the sight excited him. He turned away his gaze and looked at the next victim.

This was a brunette of the same age as the previous girl. She was lying on her back as well, but her eyes and mouth were both closed. The bruises and marks on her naked torso would lead one to conclude that she had been beaten into unconsciousness or death. Her stomach showed a number of contusions, as though the blood vessels beneath the skin had been broken by repeated blows. The purplish and yellow flesh extended to her thighs and sparsely haired pubis.

He stepped closer and sucked in a breath. Brunettes, he thought. He definitely preferred brunettes.

He reached out a hand to touch her, and his fingertips felt the glossy photo paper. Still, he moved his fingers over the entire image of the body on the photograph, imagining that he was touching flesh. He shivered at the thought of both real and imagined memories, and closed his eyes, taking his hand away. Then he opened them again and looked at the entire wall.

Forty-two photographs were pinned neatly to the corkboard that covered much of the wall, in seven rows of six each. All the images were on 8.5 by 11-inch paper, and were placed there in chronological order as to when he had printed the photos. All were of women between twenty and forty. Most of the women were white, though a few were Asian and black. All were nude or semi-nude, and all bore signs of terrible violence.

He turned from the wall and moved to a rough wooden workbench on the other side of the small room. There he examined an assortment of knives, handsaws, and metal clamps, brushing dust from their shining surfaces, or using fine sandpaper to scour off even the slightest hint of rust. He glanced from the tools to the photographs, then back to the tools again, and he smiled.

A small upholstered chair stood in the center of the room, and the man sat in it. It swiveled and rocked slightly, and he turned it toward the wall with the photographs, undid his pants, rested his head against the back of the chair, and did what he had come down to the cellar to do, among what he thought of as his souvenirs.

When he had finished, he got up, turned off the lamp that illuminated the room, pushed back a curtain of worn, heavy velvet, and stepped into the main part of the cellar. Then he slid a heavy bookcase back over the area where the velvet curtain hung, and headed toward the stairs, reminding himself to vacuum the cellar floor. Dust and pieces of detritus clung to his slippers as he walked, and he had no wish to take them upstairs. No, the only thing he wanted up there was memories, and, of course, the possibilities of making new ones.

He sat in his small den at his computer, and examined what was available for his purposes. It was time to choose what would become a *new* memory.

The 911 call had come in from a UPS man who was delivering a package to Gordon Taylor's house. He had remained until the ambulance and the police had come, and was still there when Detective Vargas arrived.

Vargas quickly examined the crime scene, then went back outside onto the back porch and asked the UPS man to tell him exactly what he had seen. With a trembling hand, the UPS man pointed to the window, which was at a right angle to the back door. The fabric of the beige honeycomb blinds, which were lowered, was soaked with a dark red liquid.

"That," the man said. "That's all I saw, but that was enough. I called right away."

In response to more of Vargas's questions, the delivery man said that he delivered packages to the house once or twice a week. Sometimes the resident was at the door to meet him, and when he wasn't, the UPS man just knocked and left it. After getting the man's contact information, Vargas allowed him to continue his route.

Vargas was about to go back inside when his partner, Detective Ridgway, pulled into the drive. "What's the story?" Ridgway asked, getting out of her car.

"This is one you've gotta see," Vargas said, beckoning her inside.

They stepped into the kitchen, then hung an immediate right. The cellar stairs were before them, and to their right the open door of a small room from which came a stench of salt and sourness. "Jesus," Ridgway murmured as she looked inside.

Even though a ceiling light was on, the room seemed dark, bathed in crimson, and Ridgway knew instantly that it was from blood covering nearly every surface. There was something sitting in a leather desk chair. It had the shape of a human being, but the details were all wrong. It seemed like one of the musculature models Ridgway had studied in her Forensic Pathology course, stripped of flesh to reveal the red, striated meat beneath.

"Interesting, eh?" Vargas said.

Ridgway nodded. "He live here?"

"We think so, though the face is as messed up as the rest of him. Name's Gordon Taylor."

"Charlie been here yet?"

"Yeah. Got his pictures. Put on your booties and take a look."

Together they stepped into the room and looked around. There was a large laptop computer on a desk with a printer next to it. The room was walled with inexpensive unit shelving, and on those shelves were rows of DVDs and Blu-ray discs. Blood spatter was all over the plastic and cardboard spines and boxes, but they could still read the titles. As they were about to start examining the computer at which the corpse was sitting, they heard a voice from the doorway.

"Uh . . . detectives? We found something downstairs . . ."

The officers looking through the cellar had been quick to see that one corner of the basement, cluttered as it was, consisted of an area with no visible door to access it. Pushing away a bookcase, they found a velvet curtain and looked behind it. As soon as they saw the photographs pinned to the wall, they alerted Vargas and Ridgway.

"I didn't think this one could get any weirder," Vargas said as he examined the photos. "Color me wrong."

"Let's get photos and prints taken down here," Ridgway told one of the officers. "And we'll want that computer upstairs cleaned and taken as evidence."

Vargas looked from the photos on the wall to the knives, saws, and other implements on the workbench. "Have we got an honest-to-god serial killer here, Ridgway?"

"Either that or a reasonable facsimile thereof," Ridgway said. "But if it's the guy who lives here, who did *him*?"

A positive ID was the first thing that was necessary, and dental records proved that the flayed and infinitely wounded body in front of the computer was that of Gordon Taylor, sole resident of the house. He was thirty-eight years old, had never been married, and worked as a shift manager at a local Bob Evans restaurant.

The medical examiner told Vargas and Ridgway that he had never come across such a case before. Gordon Taylor's body was complete, "if externally disassembled," as he put it. The body bore "uncountable" wounds, as though it had been stabbed or hacked over and over on nearly every square inch of his body, so that one wound simply merged into the next. There were even what appeared to be numerous bullet wounds in the flesh, though no actual bullets were found in the tissue.

The semblance of missing flesh on the corpse was created by the skin having been pressed deep into the muscle by whatever instruments had caused the wounds. The flesh was there all right, the M. E. told them, but it was just buried too deep to see, except on the bonier parts of the corpse, such as the hands, knees, and skull. Still, on those harder surfaces, the majority of the bone was crushed, possibly, the M. E. said, by either large caliber bullet wounds or blunt trauma, such as a hammer might make if it were continuously pounded onto the bones. Some small strips of skin had been found on the floor of the den, while others had been stuck to the walls and plastic boxes that housed the many DVDs on the shelves.

Samples of blood had been taken from the walls and floor of the room, and every sample showed that it was from the corpse of Gordon Taylor. Tests were made on the implements in the cellar room, but no blood was found on the tools, the handles, or in the joints which held them together.

The photographs of the women were copied and sent to various investigative agencies to cross check with reports of missing women. While Vargas and Ridgway waited for any positive IDs to come back, they meticulously examined the photographs themselves, in the company of the Medical Examiner, who offered his own conclusions.

"This isn't typical," he said. "You've got forty-two photos here, forty-two victims, but only a few of them—these three and this pair—seem to have the same M.O."

"Right," Ridgway agreed. "The trio with the stars carved on their stomachs. Satanic?"

"Maybe," said the M. E. "But if so, why none of the others?"

"But these three aren't together on the wall," Vargas said. "Different rows, different files."

"Maybe he did those at different times," said Ridgway. "Maybe it's chronological."

Ridgway looked at the three individual photos, then stepped back to observe the entire array recreated on the wall of their work room. "Or maybe," she said, "it's aesthetic."

"I'll leave you to it," the M. E. said, heading for the door. "And I wish you luck. I've never seen a single killer work in so many different ways. Personally, I think there's more than one guy here. Maybe they had a falling out, and the one guy killed the other, but dammit, Jim, I'm a doctor, not a detective."

The door closed behind the M. E., and Vargas threw himself down into a chair. "All right, let's think about what we actually have. We have all the photos on his computer in one file, and we've found a digital camera, but no photos on that other than some fucking birds in his backyard."

"We also have the fact that not all the photographs were taken with the same camera," Ridgway said. "So we should have found several more cameras, and we didn't."

"All the photos were printed on the same kind of photo paper on the printer that was right next to the computer." Vargas shook his head. "And the backgrounds aren't the same, when we can make them out. Some of the victims are lying on concrete, some on carpet that doesn't match anything in the house, some outside on the grass, some on a bed. And when it comes to mode of death, holy shit . . ."

"Yeah. Stabbing, hacking, gunshot, strangulation—with hands and with an assortment of ties—blunt trauma, beatings, sweet Jesus, it's like this guy was a whole murder squad by himself. Like he wanted to kill his victims in as many different ways as possible."

"So where did he do it?" Vargas asked.

"Christ, *how* did he do it? *When* did he do it? *Why* did he do it? With *whom* did he do it?"

"Think there was more than one?"

"Hell, yes. Somebody had to kill *him*, remember?" Ridgway drank the last of her coffee and tossed the cup. "I want to go back to the house. We have to check those DVDs."

Everything at Gordon Taylor's home was taped off. Ridgway and Vargas looked in the den, where Taylor's blood still tinted everything except the bare islands on the desk where the computer and printer had been. Ridgway and Vargas both snapped on latex gloves and examined row upon row of DVDs, whose spines were streaked with dried blood. One detective started at one end of a row, and one at the other, opening every case to make sure that the proper commercially labelled disc was inside each case, rather than anything that Taylor might have burned for himself.

They found no surprises, but when they had finished going through every individual case and every season box set, Ridgway said, "I'm seeing a pattern here."

"Yeah," Vargas said. "Cop shows."

"Uh-huh. Season after season of them. Recent stuff too, no old Mike Hammer or Perry Mason. Lots of cable, HBO, Showtime, stuff made for Netflix and Amazon . . ."

"BBC shows too," Vargas said. "What was that one the UPS guy brought?"

"Should still be on the kitchen table." She walked into the kitchen and lay back the flaps of the box that they'd previously opened. The picture of a man holding one hand over his right eye looked up at her. "*Wire in the Blood*," Ridgway said, and picked up the box and turned it over. "Criminal psychologist solving murders," she explained as she read the back panel copy. "'Gruesome,' it says."

"Another BBC show," Vargas said, looking over her shoulder at the box. "I haven't seen that one."

"Want to?" Ridgway asked, offering it. "Might tell us something about our boy."

"Sure. I'm a sucker for these myself."

"Fill out the form when we get back," Ridgway said. "After all, it's evidence. Maybe."

The weekend lay ahead of them, and Vargas decided he'd binge watch as many episodes as he could. He managed to get through sixteen of them, and by the time he went back to work on Monday morning a theory about the photographs had begun to form. But before he could pose it to Ridgway, she had some news of her own.

When Vargas arrived, Ridgway had already put small blue post-it notes on several of the photos on the wall. "I came in for a few hours yesterday," she said, "just to see if we heard back on anything. And we did." She pointed to the marked photographs. "These five? They're . . . accounted for."

"What do you mean," Vargas said. "Bodies were found?"

Ridgway shook her head and gave a little smile. "No bodies. These five women are all alive."

"Oh shit," Vargas whispered. "I was right . . ."

"*You* were right?" Ridgway said.

"These . . ." Vargas pointed to the five photos, then made a circle with his hand to encompass the wall full of pictures. ". . . and probably *all* of these . . . are *fakes*. Staged."

Ridgway looked a bit nonplussed, but nodded. "Yeah, these five anyway. How did you know?"

"You tell me first."

"Heard from other law enforcement we sent the photos to—cops watch cop shows. Some of them actually remembered the shows they'd seen them on. One was from *Dexter*, another one from that Amazon show *Bosch* . . ."

"Screen caps," Vargas said, sitting in a wooden chair.

"Probably," Ridgway said. "That would explain the different M. O.s, the varied settings for so many of the photos—"

"And the photos that have similar backgrounds or detailed wounds, like the three with the stars carved on their stomachs . . . those are probably from the same show, victims of the same fictional killer."

Ridgway nodded. "Well, at least we know who to send these photos to now."

"Right, what do they call them, casting directors?" Vargas's face soured. "Y'know, I'm not going to feel relieved until every one of those women is accounted for somehow. It's possible that he started as a fan-boy, but that a few of these might really be his. Why the hell would he do this in the first place?"

"Creating a fantasy without taking the risks. Imagining they're actually his kills and the photos are his trophies. The knives and other things just help to fuel it. All in his little secret room. Maybe it was a release for him, so that he'd never end up doing the real thing." She walked to her desk. "Let's start sending these out to L.A. That'll be a start anyway."

Vargas shook his head. "Christ, these could be from foreign films too—Hong Kong, Korea, Europe, who knows? We might never find them all."

"Maybe not," Ridgway said. "But at least there's one definite murder we know of."

"Right. TV freak boy. Whoever minced him up might have been doing all of us a favor in the long run. Be pretty ironic if his death is the only real one of the bunch."

The two women met in front of the coffee shop on San Pedro, hugged, went inside, sat down, and ordered lattes.

"So what's new?" PJ asked Jen.

"The usual. Mostly background stuff. Doris keeps finding me corpse actor roles now and then—did three of them last month."

PJ shook her head. "I won't do them anymore," she said.

"Why not? The money's good—about two-fifty a day with the make-up."

"I don't know, the ones I've done, and the ones I get offered . . . they're mostly nudes, at least topless."

"Well yeah, so are the ones I've done," Jen said, then narrowed her eyes and gave a mock leer. "But it's not like we're not used to that."

"I know, but . . ." PJ paused to reason it out. "When we did . . . *those* videos, it was like . . . they were kinda fun, you know? They weren't weird or kinky. And when I thought about guys—or *girls*—watching them, I thought cool. I look good, I look like I'm enjoying it, 'cause I was, and it was a kick that I was turning people on. But . . ."

The arrival of the lattes suspended the conversation for a moment. "But?" Jen finally said.

PJ lowered her voice. "It just seems . . . weirder and weirder. When I do those dead girl things, I know that guys on the crew and the effects guys and all get kinda . . . turned on when they're working with me."

"That's because they're guys, and you're naked. Nothing weird about it."

"Okay, right, I know. But what about guys watching the show? I mean, they see me, they see my boobs and whatever else, and they know I'm not really dead, even though I'm supposed to be. What about if *they* get turned on?"

"Hon, what does it matter? They don't even know who you are."

"I *know*—to them I'm just a piece of dead meat. Just another dead whore. I'm what they'd like to do to their wives or their girlfriends. And that makes them hard."

"PJ, where the hell did this come from? And I don't get it. First you say they know you're not really dead, and then you say they *like* you dead? What the fuck, girl?"

"Who the hell *knows* what they think, Jen? All sorts of things, maybe! There are probably guys out there who get off on seeing us that way, because that's what *they'd* really like to do—kill us and then . . ." She gave her head a short, quick shake. "I think about it and think about it, and when I see myself like that, on a show, it just makes my skin crawl, wondering what they're thinking. So I'm just not doing it anymore, okay? I've had it! When I think about those assholes sitting in their little man-caves, watching in their underwear, I'd like to . . ."

She trailed off, and Jen held up her hands, fingers spread. "All right, all right, I got you. If that's how you feel, that's how you feel. And I'm good with that. But, baby, what brought this on? Did something happen? Did somebody say something to you, or what?"

PJ took a sip of her latte, then licked her upper lip. "Like I said. I've been thinking about it a lot. Being uncomfortable with it. And a week or so ago, right after I posed for what's the last dead girl picture of my life I swear to God, I had a dream that night." She looked down into the liquid in her cup. "I don't want to go into detail, but it put the shoe on the other foot." Jen looked at her quizzically, and she explained further. "Turned the tables, you know? In a really . . . extreme way. All the frustration, all the . . . hate I'd been feeling about it just . . . came out in that dream. And when I woke up I said no more. I was done. I can't feel that way again."

"Okay," Jen said slowly. "I think I get it. And I don't blame you. That's pretty . . ." She shook her head and gave a little shrug at the same time. "Jesus, that must've been some dream."

PJ only nodded. She didn't want to go into the graphic details. Indeed, she'd been trying to forget them. And she didn't tell Jen that when she'd awakened from the dream and gone into the bathroom to get a drink, there was grit on her feet that hadn't been there when she went to bed. She'd also felt something sticky beneath her right breast, and, when she looked, she found what she could only assume was a small patch of nearly dried stage blood that her bedtime shower had not washed away. She took another shower, but it didn't wash away the dream.

Tracy L. Carbone

LUNCH AT MOM'S

Twenty-Five Years

Mom passed in June and was buried in her favorite blue dress, the one with daisies and a white lace collar. "I'll miss you, Mom. I'll miss our lunches." Billy leaned in and kissed her forehead; stepped back abruptly at the coldness of her once warm skin, and brushed cake makeup from his lips. Mom and he had been so close. He didn't know how he could get by without their daily lunch visits, or even if he wanted to. He gripped the inner edge of the coffin, bunching burgundy satin under his fingertips.

The funeral home director tapped his shoulder. "Billy, it's time to let her go."

Bill nodded and released his hold. *Goodbye, Mom.*

"Are you sure you won't reconsider an open casket? The cancer took her so quickly; her body is unmarred. She looks just as beautiful as—"

"No. No, I want it closed." Billy's voice broke as he talked. He'd never felt so sad, even when Dad died. Nothing even close to this. "I don't want people poring over her, talking about how great she looks, how she's in a better place." He glanced down at her one last time. "She's dead. Gone. And what's left—" He lowered the lid. "The sooner we all accept the tragedy of her passing, the better."

Five years before, Billy quit college to help the family business when Dad passed away. Since then, he'd gone to Mom's every day for lunch. It was close to work and it made them both happy. It was the one constant in all his years of change.

Dad had been a clock aficionado, or a clock nut as Billy jokingly called him. The house was filled with grandfather clocks, desk clocks, and anniversary clocks, and four cuckoo clocks from Solvang. Not a digital face in the house unless you counted the front of the microwave. Mom kept all the clocks wound in Dad's honor. The rhythmic ticking had been a part of Billy's childhood and he still enjoyed it, now that he was an adult.

Billy and Mom had a routine. Billy would arrive at 12:05, as he worked only five minutes down the road. The apartment he rented with his girlfriend was an hour away, so their lunches provided perfect Billy Mom time, as she called it. Mom would set the round metal alarm clock for 12:55. She'd make him various lunches, childhood favorites: bologna sandwiches and tomato soup, grilled cheese, or Sloppy Joes. On rare and special occasions, she'd make homemade macaroni and cheese. At 12:55 the loud metallic rattle would sound. She'd whisk his plate and bowl away, toss it in the sink. "Gotta hurry, get back to work, Billy." He'd kiss her cheek and off he'd go.

He wiped a tear from his eye as he thought of it now, as the somber organ music played a dirge. No more lunches with Mom.

It was a week before Billy visited the house again. He spent all day winding the clocks and cleaning up. He threw away the old food, wiped down the counters. His girlfriend Sandra's plan was for him to sell the "old dump" so they could buy a bigger newer house. As he walked through the place where he had spent his formative years though, memories overtook him.

He walked to the bannister and ran his hand along the smooth wood. He thought of the times he slid down that railing, with Dad laughing and Mom calling out to be careful.

The front closet still held his father's overcoat, and the hockey skates Billy wore as a young boy. Mom insisted on keeping things, said memories lived in them, and tossing them out meant saying goodbye. He shook his head at how much she'd saved. Sandra said Mom was a hoarder but she wasn't. The house was clean and orderly even if every drawer and closet was packed with memories.

He touched his father's jacket and could hear his laugh, could remember his strong scent of cigarettes and Old Spice. Behind the coat hid his old hockey stick. Fondling the worn wood brought back the feeling of cold air on his face, ice chips flying up and hitting his cheeks as he skidded to a stop on the rink. The smack of the puck hitting his stick, hurting his hands.

"I can't sell this place," he said aloud. He closed the closet door and headed for the kitchen.

He picked up the receiver from the wall phone and dialed Sandra.

"Hi. Just listen, Sandra. I don't want to sell. Coming back here, it's like—my life was here and I want to stay. I want *us* to live here. But we can do renovations and change things around, add on—"

"No," she ordered. "Billy, no. You need to say your goodbyes to that place. Sell it and we'll get a house out here by my parents."

In his head he heard his mother's voice, with her familiar words. "She's not the girl for you, Billy." For once, he didn't argue.

In that second he decided he was done with her, was going to move his things back to the old house. He'd do it today and—

"I'm pregnant," Sandra said from the other end. "I'm pregnant and I want us to live close to my family. We'll need to get married of course."

He hung up. *Pregnant. Marriage.* He looked at the fridge, covered with pictures of Dad, Mom, and him over the years. He didn't want to leave all this behind but reality had slapped him in the face. He needed to be a part of this new family. Mom was gone so what was the point in keeping the house?

Billy heard the loud clicking of the clock Mom set for lunch. It was

12:05. On habit, he set the timer for 12:55. "One last lunch together," he said, as he took some bread from the box and peanut butter from the cabinet. He made himself a sandwich and sat down.

"Forgot your milk," Mom said.

He turned around and saw her, in her favorite dress. She smiled and handed him a glass of cold milk.

"But how? You're—"

"We won't speak of how, Billy. Lunches. That's all we get. No questions, and it has to be our secret." She kissed him on the forehead with warm lips.

"Our secret," he replied.

Thirty Years

"Going to lunch at Mom's," Billy said as he left the office. His co-workers saw nothing unusual in his spending his lunch hours there. His home with Sandra was an hour without traffic so it made perfect sense to hang out at the old homestead. It was paid in full and the utilities and taxes were low. He had to miss lunch some days to visit with clients, but come hell or high water he made it to Mom's on Fridays.

"Hi, Billy," Mom said as he walked in the door. She set the clock and placed it on the table before him. She wore her blue dress as always, with the daisies and a white lace collar.

Nothing ever changed in the house, he thought with a smile. Mom didn't age. She was frozen in time, on the last day he ever saw her healthy. It was a week after the diagnosis, and the day of her first treatment.

Billy had shown up at her house that morning to drive her to the hospital. "What's this?" she'd asked when she saw his hair. He rubbed his hand over his fresh crew cut.

"You'll lose your hair from the treatment, Mom, but you won't be alone."

"You're the best son anyone could have," she said, smiling through tears.

They chatted about the upcoming July 4th fireworks, and the Strawberry Festival. The ride to her chemo session was filled with nervous chatter.

After that day, she was gone. Allergic reaction to the chemo and cardiac arrest. She never left the clinic.

Billy resolved to keep his head shaved in her honor.

"Give it a rest, Billy," Sandra said about his hair as the years went by. "Let her go already." She didn't understand. How could she when she didn't know about the lunches?

"Bologna sandwiches today," Mom said as she pushed a plate under Billy's nose, and handed him a napkin. "Do you have any new pictures of the boys?"

He pulled out a couple of photos and handed them over as he chewed his sandwich. Mom had it down pat, just the right amount of mayo, with white bread and no lettuce. Sandra insisted he put lettuce and tomatoes on everything, to add nutrition.

"They're getting so big," Mom said. "Four and five. Such fun ages. I wish I could visit with them, just once."

"You have. I brought them here a few times."

"You know what I mean," she said as she traced a loving finger across the photos. "I wish they could see me, that I could speak with them, hold them in my arms."

"Me too, Mom. Me too, but this only works with us."

"Billy Mom time," she said, smiling at him. The harsh alarm rattled and he slapped the top of it. She pulled his plate away and sent him out the door with a kiss.

Forty Years

Billy owned his uncle's company now. He was rich by some people's standards. Not bad for a college dropout with a blue-collar background.

Sandra and he built a huge house with high ceilings, a brick walkway, and immense windows with mountain views in every room. It was on the lot next to her parents' place. The land was a gift from them, and Sandra's father designed the floor plan to mirror that of their house. Billy hated the modern feel and the open spaces. There was nothing cozy in the place.

"It's so big, we never see each other," he told Sandra.

"You say that like it's a bad thing," she said.

Billy knew he'd become little more than a placeholder. A provider. He'd known for some time but clung to the memories of the girl she'd been in college, who'd loved him. Who wanted to spend her life—

"We don't feel like a family. We go out in public and play the part, and we live in the house. We've got all the trappings of a family but we just . . ."

"What constitutes a family?" Sandra stood across from him in her expensive clothes, with a photoshopped face courtesy of Dr. Stein. "Allegiance to a dead woman? Spending all your time in an empty house pretending she's alive?"

Billy slapped her face.

She stood strong. Glared at him.

"My boyfriend is twice the man you are. You want a family? You got it. I get the boys and you get your mother."

She said it coolly with triumph in her voice.

She stared at him until he relented and walked out.

"What did you do to Mom?" His oldest son Jimmy asked him when he reached the foyer. Jason came up behind his brother. They wore dark blue blazers with their prep school insignia on the lapel. Though the boys resembled him physically, they couldn't be less like him in personality.

"Nothing. We had a fight is all," Billy said.

"Are you getting a divorce? Mother told us last week that she—"

"Last week?" Billy asked. "Last week what?"

"That you were getting a divorce because she needs to trade up," Jason said, as matter-of-factly as the way they talked about the newest model of Porsche.

Billy sat on the bottom step. Rubbed his crew cut fuzz like a worry stone.

"What do you boys think? You want us to work to stay together right?"

The boys looked at each other and shrugged.

"Mom says you're rough around the edges," Jimmy said, "And that you should act more like Grandfather. You should buy better clothes, get rid of your truck. Take a job in Grandfather's company," Jimmy said.

"You work with all those Mexicans in that dirty factory. You call yourself a manager but you're still blue collar," Jason added, as if his critique of his father's life was helpful. As if the insult were an intervention.

What hurt the most was that he knew the boys' words were not their own. They were parroting Sandra.

Billy packed his bags and moved out.

Billy opened the back sliding door of Mom's house and smiled when he saw the familiar warm paneling in the small house. He smelled Sloppy Joes.

Mom approached him in her special dress and gave him a hug. He aged, but she looked the same. "Are you sleeping, Billy?" she asked. "You look so tired."

"I'm getting old, Mom. That's all."

She handed him a napkin and set the alarm clock.

"Don't," he pleaded. "Just once I want to stay. Can't I move back here? Or stay for a little longer at least? Sandra doesn't want me. The kids don't care. I want to come home."

"You know we only get fifty minutes for lunch, Billy," Mom said. "I'm sorry about Sandra and the boys. You'll be all right. You're strong like me." She patted his hand. "Eat your lunch now. You'll run out of time."

The alarm went off at 12:55 and Billy rushed out before Mom transformed. He'd exceeded his time once, stood by after the alarm rang, and watched. Before his eyes she grew older, withering and drawing into herself, decaying. It broke his heart and he vowed never to witness it again.

Fifty Years

Billy offered Jimmy a job when he finished college but he refused. Now it was Jason's turn. He brought him in for the afternoon, walked him around the plant. When Jason was very young he'd enjoyed the work tours. He'd smile at the women and men hunched over their work tables, as they assembled parts.

"So what you do think?" Billy asked Jason as they stood in his office.

Jason was tall and handsome in his dark blue suit. He was out of place in Billy's office in the factory where the managers wore short sleeve shirts and the rest of the staff wore smocks.

"I know you've got a job but I need to hand the company over eventually and it should be someone who knows the business. If you start now, by the time I retire you'll be—"

"You can't be serious. Me? Here?" Jason looked with disgust at the floor of workers below them, men and women huddled over parts tables assembling product.

"Well, why not? It's a good company. Our family business," Billy said.

"You asked Jimmy and he said no. Why should I be the schmuck who gets stuck out here, working with *these* people?"

Billy tried to hide his disappointment, hide his shame in raising such a shallow person.

Jason stood and began to leave. "No offense to you but I'd sooner work in Wal-Mart. You-you build little things all day, insignificant things that will be obsolete in five years. I need a future."

Billy didn't reply, just stared at his son who, he realized finally, he didn't know at all.

"George got me a job at Intel. Now that's a company." Jason didn't notice the disappointment in Billy's face. If he had, he probably wouldn't have cared. Sandra's second husband George was Jason's hero.

"There's a whole world out there, Dad, but you live in the past. Bad enough you won't see this dead end company for what it is but you're obsessed with Grandma's house. It's creepy, keeping her house all these years. Mom says you're mentally ill and I don't think she's wrong."

"She *is* wrong. Your mother is wrong." Pain shot through Billy's head. His headaches were rare but boy when they hit—

"Why would you keep a place like that? It's an old dump. It's embarrassing."

Billy sank deeper into his chair. "I'm not crazy. Your mother doesn't understand the bond I had with my mother. She never has and never will."

The two men stared at each other, worlds apart.

"You know," Billy said, "You and Jimmy are greedy little buggers who have never seen past your own wants. You're Sandra's kids through and through. Go on, get out of here."

He watched his son leave.

⬤

"So you're done with them then," Mom said as she set the alarm and handed Billy a crunchy grilled cheese sandwich. "Made you a root beer float," she added as she kissed the top of his head.

"It breaks my heart. I had such hopes for my boys, that we could be a family like you and me and Dad were. We were great, weren't we? What a family is supposed to be."

"Still are, Billy." She squeezed his hand. "We have the perfect family." The clocks surrounding them ticked their melody, soothing him.

"Wish Dad was still here too," Billy said.

"He's moved on without us, but I'm here for you. Someday we'll catch up with him, don't you worry."

"I don't know how my life went so wrong, how my wife—ex-wife—and I could be enemies. She hates me, the kids do too. All I ever did was love and provide for them."

Mom patted his hand again. "Maybe they'll come around someday, when they've got kids of their own. Till then, you know I'm always here for you."

Sixty-five Years

Billy smiled as the movers carried the last of his things into his new home. It was small and run down and he'd greatly overpaid, but it was right beside Mom's house. Living in her house was not an option, because the fifty minutes of life with her was all he got. But now he could walk over each day for lunch. Seven days a week.

At 12:04pm the movers pulled out and Billy walked across the lawn. He waited until 12:05 then turned his key.

Mom greeted him with a hug and waved him into the kitchen.

"Happy retirement! Did they throw you a party?" she asked.

Billy took his seat at the table, happy to see his entree. "Mac and cheese!"

"It's a special occasion. You live next door and no more work meetings to keep you from our lunches."

He held up his shiny new watch. "The guys at the plant got me this as a parting gift. Permanently set to 12:05pm. No battery. They said now it's Lunch at Mom's all the time."

"I wish that were true but I enjoy the time we do have."

"Me too. I brought a piece of cake from the party." He opened a container and exposed a wedge of yellow cake with blue frosting. Mom didn't eat but pretended to smell it.

"I'll get you a dessert fork," she said.

Mom handed him the fork and then sat across from him at the table. "So what are you going to do with all your time now that you sold the plant?"

"Not sure. Hopefully I can spend some time with Nick. He's the only grandchild worth a damn out of the five of them."

"I'm sure they all have their good points."

"Maybe, but Jason and Jimmy keep the others close to their vests in their snotty little dream world. If Nick wasn't a sickly child that slowed them down they probably wouldn't let me take him either."

Mom rose and took a picture of Nick from the fridge. A skinny five-year-old with dark hair, and sad eyes as big as an Anime character, smiled in a studio picture. He had a severe cleft palate so his grin was deformed. She set the photo on the table.

"He's my favorite," Mom said.

"Mine too," Billy said. "Last time I saw him I asked him what he wanted to be when he grew up and you know what he said?"

Mom shook her head. "What?"

He said, "Come on, Grandpa. We all know I'm not going to grow up."

Mom took Billy's hand. "What did you say to that?"

"What could anyone say? I said nothing. Just hugged him."

Mom stood and busied herself with the dishes, facing away. Billy knew she was crying.

Billy looked to the fridge where pictures of other very attractive boys and girls at various ages were displayed. "You know it's nice of Jason's and Jimmy's wives to send pictures and allow me to visit the others on occasion but you know they're just doing it to stay in my good graces, to get my money when I die."

"People do what they have to do, what they learn to do," Mom replied, her back still turned.

"But this little guy, they'd probably let him live with me if I asked," Billy said. He looked again at the picture. The handle of a wheelchair peeked out behind Nick's shoulder. "He doesn't fit with their image of the perfect family."

Mom turned around and smiled. "He fits with mine," she said.

◆

Billy rolled Nick's wheelchair through Disneyland, toward the *Pirates of the Caribbean* ride. Though the sun was shining bright, the boy wore a hat, a long sleeve shirt, and long pants. "It's hot out, Nick. Why don't I get you a short sleeve shirt and shorts at the gift shop? You must be sweating in that."

The boy stiffened. "Mother said I have to wear the hat so I won't scare people with my face. And she said my arms and legs are funny and no one wants to come to Disney to see *that*."

Billy knelt beside the boy and removed his hat. His face was ghostly pale. "That's the craziest thing I've ever heard in my life. I love your little face. And your arms and legs. Come on, let's get you some new clothes."

A few minutes later, the two emerged from the gift store.

The boy was clad in shorts and a tee shirt. He carried a large plastic sword. The sun beat down on his frail crooked body in the chair and he smiled. "This is way more fun than white water rafting with them. I'm glad Father said I would slow them down and couldn't go. Today I'm glad I'm different, because this is awesome!"

Billy smiled. "I'm glad too."

◆

"I thought we could do something fun for lunch," Billy started. It was the second day of their weekend together. Nick was a little sunburned from Disney but happier than Billy had ever seen him.

The boy sat on the couch next to him. "Sure!"

"You want to see the house I grew up in?"

The boy didn't answer.

"What's wrong?"

"Father said I'm not supposed to go in there. He said, well he said some bad things. Some mean things. About you. About that house."

"Well, Nick, I'm your father's father so I get to make the decisions. Maybe your father doesn't like the house, and he's never let the other kids come see it, but you're special. You've always been my favorite, you know that right?"

The boy beamed and nodded. "You're my favorite too."

"Then let's go. It's just across the yard."

He set Nick into his chair and pushed him across the grass.

"Now when I walk in, we're going to play a game of pretend okay? When I talk to someone, just play along."

"Do you talk to your mother? Father said you do and that means you're crazy."

Billy nodded. "Yes, your great grandmother. I'm not crazy though. It's just a game."

Billy checked his phone for the time then walked through the back door. "Mom, I brought Nick along."

Mom walked around the corner in her blue dress with daisies and a white lace collar. She held a plate of warm chocolate chip cookies and their aroma filled the room.

She put the plate down and set the alarm. She hugged Billy then got on her knees in front of Nick. "Well aren't you about the cutest little boy I've ever seen."

"Thank you," the boy replied. "No one ever says I'm the cutest."

"You can see her?" Billy asked.

"Why? Can't *you* see her?" Nick asked back, scrunching his face. "She's right there. Are we supposed to pretend we can't see her? Is that the game?"

Billy sat down hard on the kitchen chair.

"Would you like a cookie?" Mom asked. "I always make my Billy eat his lunch first, but you are a special little boy, aren't you?"

Nick smiled. "I'd love a cookie, thank you." He joined his grandfather at the table.

Mom walked to the counter and returned with two bologna sandwiches and steaming bowls of tomato soup. "Yay!" Nick shouted, grabbing at his lunch. "Father says I can't have bologna but I get it at school sometimes. You're the best great Grandma ever!"

As always, the alarm sounded too soon and Billy and his grandson had to leave. "Can I visit again?" the boy asked. Mom hugged him good and tight. "Anytime you like. Remember, this is our secret." She kissed them both on the cheek.

Seventy Years

Billy was dying. Stage-four brain cancer. Inoperable. He sat at a wooden table beside his lawyer.   Jason and Jimmy and their wives sat at the other table, all facing a judge.

"He's clearly not competent to make financial decisions," the boys' lawyer said to the judge. "He's got a trust set up to pay utilities and a clock winder for the next ten years on a house no one lives in." Jason whispered something to his lawyer and the man spoke again. "Right, and he donated all the rest of his money to charity. We ask that his sons be placed in charge of the trust once he passes and—"

The judge, an old friend of Mom's, put his hand up to stop.

"I think cutting his sons off was probably the most sane decision Mr. Osborne could've made. I've listened to testimony from Billy and the boys and the attorneys and all I see here is a man whose sons have veered so far off course from what matters that he has no choice but to cut them off."

Jason and Jimmy stood shocked, as did their lawyer.

"Mr. Osborne worked hard his whole life, gave jobs to hundreds of citizens in this town. He did volunteer work at the Vets shelter." The judge flipped through a stack of papers.

"Jason, your father spent more time with your handicapped son than you did. You didn't see fit to question his sanity when he was helping you with the boy's expensive medical treatments, or taking him off your hands for weeks at a time."

"But your honor, the boy—" the lawyer began.

"I find in favor of the defendant." The judge banged his gavel and winked at Billy.

Weeks passed without any word from Jimmy or Jason, or the grand-kids. As Jason said that day in the parking lot, "Fine, you want to cut us off? You're cut off." He meant it.

Billy checked the clock. 12:04pm. He walked out and across the lawn to the back of Mom's house.

Nick stood on a bright red scooter in the back yard. "Hi Grandpa!" he shouted. "Great Gram found this in the shed and cleaned it up for me." The boy ran to him. Billy lifted him in his arms and swung him around. His arms and legs were strong and firm, his face smooth and even. "She said it was yours when you were little."

Billy eyed the scooter. "I remember that old thing. She did a good job. Looks like new. How are you feeling today?"

"Feeling great!" the boy said. "Come on in. It's lunchtime."

Billy took his hand and opened the sliding door to the kitchen.

"Hello, Billy," Mom said. "Special day today. I made meatloaf and mashed potatoes." She set the tray on the table and Billy readied to dig in as Nick and Mom watched.

"Hey, you need to set the alarm, Mom. You almost forgot," Billy said. He didn't see the clock on the table.

He listened for the familiar loud tick tock of the alarm clock and all the others, always in motion, always tracking the time he got to spend here.

The clocks and Mom and Nick were . . . silent.

"Where's the clock. Where is it?" He began to rise from the table, looking left and right for it. Terrified of missing the deadline, of—

Mom and Nick shared a glance and a smile between them. They took his hands. "No need to set the alarm anymore, Billy," Mom said. "No need to set the alarm."

Jack Ketchum

FATHER AND SON

The old man feels a cool flutter like the rush of air off tiny wings against his forearm and stirs in bed. He's almost awake on this warm summer night but not quite. The gin takes hold again and drags him back to sleep.

The second time he feels it across his cheek and now he's startled full awake, aware that this is *not right* somehow. Somehow a bird or a bat got into his bedroom and his heart is pounding which it shouldn't be, not after two bypasses, the latest being just two weeks past.

He reaches across the yellowed sheets for the table-lamp and fumbles for the switch. The room snaps into focus. His eyes are still fine even though the rest of him's shot to hell. He looks around and there's no bird nor any bat either. He doesn't know about birds necessarily but bats will go to ground in bright light, find someplace in the shadows to wait it out, like under the bed or in some dark corner so he gets up, woozy from sleep and booze but easier in the heart and searches behind the night-table and bending slowly and carefully under the dresser and as best his skinny legs can manage checks beneath the bed.

Nothing. The bedroom door is closed. Windows too. He's heard that even a warm breeze can kill a man his age if he lies in it long enough so he keeps them that way permanently. Which means there's no way into the room and no way out.

Now ain't that a hell of a thing he thinks. I felt something.

I know goddamn well I did.

And now he's got to piss like a racehorse.

Old prick would have woke me up anyhow he thinks, sooner or later.

He opens the door and shuffles out into the hall, passes his son Joey's room and peers in. Joey's not there. The bed's a mess but then it always is. Probably passed out in front of the TV again he thinks and realizes then that he can hear it dimly, canned laughter, some stupid sitcom, so he bypasses the bathroom for the moment and goes to the living room and there he is in the overstuffed chair. He's snoring, a two-hundred-eighty pound rumble that's nearly as loud as the laughter. There's a bottle of that cheap bourbon he drinks between his legs so that it looks like he's been jerking off on a whiskey bottle and fell asleep halfway through it.

The old man can remember real erections.

He can remember when neither of them were drunks.

It's over fifteen years now since the bright winter morning his wife Ella and Joey's wife Susan went out grocery shopping and then through the windshield of his pickup together—or in Susan's case, only halfway through. He'd been seventy by then and said to hell with it. Joey'd been only fifty-two and weighed in at a trim one-hundred-eighty pounds. Good-looking boy. But Joey'd said to hell with it too.

The old man's bladder's killing him.

He turns and once inside the bathroom closes and locks the door because Joey has been known to blunder in unannounced, they both have, and sits his tired bones down on the toilet. For all the pressure up there you'd think it would come flooding out of him but it doesn't, it takes a whole painful minute or more and once it's started he finds himself gasping, that's how good it feels.

He surveys the bathroom. It's filthy, it's desperate for a cleaning. There's something growing on the shower curtain and it seems to have spread to the tub. Whisps and balls of hair all over the tiled floor, Joey's hair mostly since his own is mostly gone. Even the soap is disgusting. They ought to hire somebody he thinks. He's too weak to clean it and Joey's too goddamn lazy.

He thinks about those wings. That breeze against his cheek.

The strangest goddamn thing.

He's almost finished, it's just dribbling out of him when he hears a crash, glass hitting the floor and breaking and skiddering across hardwood and then he hears a thud. He knows what it is, it can only be one thing. It can only be Joey. Suddenly his heart's pounding again.

"Joey! You okay, son?"

Once his voice had a bellow to it. Now it's all phlegm and gristle.

He flushes the toilet and uses the edge of the sink to help him stand and goes to the door and throws its lock. Pushes it.

The door budges half an inch and stops.

"Joey?"

Through the crack he can see him there lying belly-up on the floor. The bottom of the door in fact is pressing on what for Joey passes for a ribcage. He pushes the door again with the same results. He tries again, really getting his shoulder into it this time, his feet braced against the stained base of the toilet. He pushes with all his might, all eighty-five pounds of him, until he can't push any more.

No go.

He curses the sad silly sonovabitch who made a bathroom door open outward rather than in.

He looks around for something to wedge into the crack. Maybe he can pry the door open. No plunger beneath the sink, Joey's left it in the damn kitchen again. The toilet seat is thicker than the crack and he's got no screwdriver to remove it anyway.

There's no point yelling for help. The bathroom faces the overgrown back yard and the Mackenzies next door are his own driveway and their driveway away and they never come by. Never go near his place. It's arguable if they'd help even if they *did* hear him, the Scots bastards.

No getting through that tiny window either.

He can't count on anybody coming to his rescue. The liquor delivery was yesterday and the soda and junkfood and TV dinners today and neither is due again for another week. His friends are all dead and Joey's had nobody since Susan died and the garage closed down and he started to seriously drink.

It looks like he's going to have to stick around in here awhile. Till Joey comes to.

And then a sickening thought occurs to him. He has to sit back down on the toilet it's so bad. A thought so perfectly formed and awful it makes him dizzy.

Joey's own triple-bypass was a little over year ago. The doctors said the same thing they'd said to him.

Quit drinking.

They hadn't. Neither of them.

So that there's every goddamn chance in the world Joey might never come to. That Joey's gone for good.

It's a bathroom so water's no problem. Booze is though. When the shakes start hitting him he drinks the rubbing alcohol and the aftershave and then Joey's old dusty bottle of cologne. That staves them off for a while but then they're at him again and so is the craving. He can't do much but curse and scream and roll around on the floor holding his knees and jerking, spasming for god knows how long and by the time it's over he's pissed and shit his pyjamas and there are bruises all over him where he's slammed into the toilet or the tub or the pipes.

It's a bathroom so water's no problem. Food is though. He has no sense of time in here not going through what he's going through but he's guessing it's been a few days at least when the hunger finally gets to him so that it's like a mad dog tearing at his stomach and even with Joey's stink drifting in from the hallway he has to eat. He eats a half-full tube of toothpaste and then a full one, chases it with water. He tries a bar of soap but throws it right back up again. He shreds the toilet paper and swallows that. Anything to fill his stomach. The bottle of aspirin is tempting but he knows it's going to kill him if he does so he flushes them down the toilet against the moment they might become inevitable.

He's so weak he can barely sit up straight. He can barely shred the toilet paper and chew and swallow.

He's in and out of focus all the time now, like even his eyes are be-traying him. But it's not his eyes, it's the rest of him. He sleeps and doesn't sleep and one is pretty much the same as the other. There's nothing to do but sit or lie there thinking about the past and Ella and the place they used to have down by the river and his dead brother Henry and his dead sister Laurie and his parents both long dead but the one thing he thinks about most is how his son has killed him and when he thinks about that he often as not starts to cry thin miserable old-man's tears because he maybe could have helped him had he not been so goddamn drunk himself, a disgusting excuse for a father and then he thinks about the wings.

He *feels* the wings.

Actually *feels* them now, the tiny brush of air against his cheek. Just like before.

And just like before they wake him up again. He's been sleeping. He's startled.

He hears voices outside, people entering the house, people *having entered* the goddamn house and they're moving down the hallway toward Joey's bloated fly-blown body on the floor and he pulls himself up to tell them he's in here dammit he's not dead yet and the wings rush away with his heart.

Thanks to Dale Meyers Cooper.

Karen and Roxanne E. Dent

THE DEMON OF SPITALFIELDS

Naughty Nelly's - 1892

Naughty Nelly's was rowdy as usual, rank with sweat, stale beer and cheap gin, the scourge of the underclass.

Unseen by the crowd, a creature huddled in a dark corner, cold eyes focused on a group of young gentlemen, obviously slumming.

"You're a damn braggart," Percy muttered.

"And why shouldn't I brag. I've bedded more women than most men meet in a lifetime."

"Sheer hubris," Aubrey muttered. "You my friend, are due for a comeuppance."

"Order a bottle of champagne for the table," Shelly said laughing. "I'll be back."

Shelly pushed through the mob and headed for the back door. In the narrow alley, he leaned against the pub's stone wall enjoying the quiet, cool air. Puffing on his cigar he allowed the smoke to billow around him. It camouflaged the stink of the sewers, the stench of the gutter and the ever present, throat clogging reek of the Thames.

A sudden movement in the shadows startled him as a figure stepped out. This wasn't Shelly's first time in the East End. His eyes traveled to hands for a pistol or a cudgel.

The voice was husky. "Got a smoke?"

Surprised, since he expected to be robbed, he reached into his breast pocket, removed his silver cigar case and opened it. The unkempt creature didn't move. He felt a wave of pity. "Go on, take one."

A snarl escaped the figure before Shelly's arm was locked tight by fingers that bit into his flesh and yanked hard. Despite the frail appearance of the figure, Shelly was smashed onto the wet cobblestones, cracking his head.

On his back, Shelly was momentarily stunned.

The disgusting thing wrapped around him like a mating spider. Horrified, Shelly watched as the face hovering above him altered. He stared into blazing red eyes. Fangs slid out of a wide cruel mouth. Claws sprouted from fingers that tore Shelly's starched, pristine shirt apart. They carved through his tender white, belly flesh, ripping his intestines out. Shelly's body went into convulsions.

His mouth opened to scream, but the laughing demon jammed Shelly's steaming entrails down his gullet, choking off all sound.

The fiend clawed Shelly's face before grabbing his jaw and dislocating it, biting off two fingers to gloat over later. But by that time Shelly was dead.

⬤

Officer Deeds was new on the job and didn't relish entering the warren of unlit alleyways. Lights had been installed in the East End after the Ripper murderers. Many alleys were still pitch black.

His partner, Daniel Watkins was older and a stickler for following the rules. Holding up his lantern, he spotted what looked like a lump of clothes lying in a puddle.

When they approached and Daniel lifted his light, his partner gagged and threw up his fish and chips as Watkins' shrill whistle cut the air.

⬤

The Séance

John Hammond was reading "The Brothers Karamazov," when Mrs. Garrett, his housekeeper announced he had a visitor.

"Mrs. Langston is here for the séance sir."

John put his book down. The noise outside penetrated the thick walls.

"What's all the shouting about?"

The housekeeper shuddered. "A special edition. There's been another one of those gruesome murders."

John frowned and a lock of brown hair streaked with grey fell into his eyes. "Where did it happen?"

"An alley in Spitalfields. You don't think—"

"Think what, Mrs. Garrett?" John asked standing up.

Mrs. Garrett's voice held a tremor of fear. "The Ripper's back again?"

"It's been ten years. I doubt he'd wait that long before killing again. Give me five minutes before showing Mrs. Langston into the back parlor."

"Yes sir."

Limping down the hall, John opened the door and surveyed the room. A pentagram painted in red was drawn on the polished, wooden floor. Symbols in silver and gold glowed to ward off evil spirits.

Resting on top of the pentagram was a long, mahogany table. On it was a silver candelabra and seven, white candles. He moved around the thirteen maroon velvet chairs placed around the table as he lit the wicks.

He walked over to the tall windows and pulled the matching velvet drapes together, blocking out all light.

Mrs. Garrett knocked once and entered with his client.

Mrs. Langston was in her forties. Her pale, blue eyes were red from crying. She wore a grey wool dress and jet earrings. In her hands she clutched a crumpled, white handkerchief. It was trimmed in black, indicating she was a widow, but not a recent one or she would have been dressed in black bombazine and worn a veil.

"Please, sit down, Mrs. Langston," John urged.

"Do you do table turning or use a Ouija board?" she asked nervously.

John smiled. "None of those devices."

She shivered slightly, "What do I do?"

"There's nothing to be afraid of," he said gently. "You, Mrs. Garrett and I will simply hold hands." He held out a chair and she took a seat next to his housekeeper. "You wrote in your letter you wished to contact your father. I will enter the spirit world and summon him. He will speak through me. His full name is?"

"Josiah Turner."

"Are you ready?"

A timid Mrs. Langston nodded. They grasped hands as John blew out all but one of the candles, leaving them in murky shadows. Breathing slowly, he closed his eyes. He'd done this so many times the trance state came as natural as sleep.

"Josiah Turner, your daughter wishes to speak with you," John called out in a firm voice.

Mrs. Langston let out a little squeak and Mrs. Garrett squeezed her hand.

Opening his eyes John saw what no one else did, dozens of spirits crowded around the room.

"Josiah Turner, step forward," John commanded.

An elderly gentleman with white hair, side whiskers and a beard moved forward.

The old man tried to speak but a wrenching moan burst into the room, rattling the pictures. They all jumped and Mrs. Langston's father vanished. In his place was the slender, eviscerated body of a murder victim dressed for a night on the town. The man's agony was evident. Despite all the blood, ripped flesh and slack jaw that made his features impossible to distinguish, there was something disturbingly familiar about him.

Without warning, the ghost flew into John who stiffened and groaned, his body twitching spasmodically.

Shuddering, John struggled to expel the cold, clammy spirit. A trail of ectoplasm poured out of his nose, ears and eyes, taking shape into the gruesome corpse now visible to everyone in the dark room. Only John heard the words, "Help me."

Mrs. Langston fainted. Mrs. Garrett sat frozen, clutching onto her employer's hand afraid to let go.

John battled to gain control not just over his body but his emotions. As the icy ectoplasm finally dissipated, he tried not to show how shaken he was.

The voice belonged to his brother, Shelly.

The Autopsy

As John and Chief Inspector Banks headed to the police mortuary, the Inspector glanced at his friend curiously.

"We've known each other for eight years but I never knew you had a brother."

"We had different fathers and were never close."

"How did you know he was dead?"

"Shelly frequented clubs like Naughty Nelly's and a friend of his said he went there the night before."

"Prepare yourself. Dr. Fitzwilliam did a preliminary autopsy at the scene but we removed the body to the morgue for a more detailed examination. It's not pretty."

"I've attended autopsies before."

The Inspector was overcome with pity. He'd witnessed throats cut, bodies poisoned, deadly beatings and disease before death took them. But to see your own flesh and blood lying on a slab in such a revolting state, then dissected by a coroner, needed a strong stomach.

When John showed up at the Yard shortly after the murder, claiming the slaughtered corpse might be that of his brother, the inspector was astonished. When he insisted on being present during the autopsy, Inspector Banks tried to talk him out of it. But John had been instrumental in solving many of their most difficult cases, and he eventually relented.

As they walked along, John was thinking of the last time he saw Shelly. It was over three years ago and he'd tried to stem the tide of his younger brother's self-destruction. Nothing he said had any effect.

His mother remarried after John's father's death. Good clothes, a handsome face and great wealth hid a cold and cruel man. Shelly was born of the union. Their mother died when Shelly was six. He still bore the scars of savage beatings administered by a father whose approval he could never win and who terrified him.

Away at school, John escaped the abuse. He attributed the beatings and lack of love to Shelly's later descent into a rapidly decadent lifestyle. That he had finally met a violent end came as no surprise but asking John for help, after his death, was. This time he wouldn't let him down.

As they neared the morgue, the smell of bleach and carbolic mingled with the vile smell of decomposing flesh. It was the constant echo of water dripping from an undetected leak that always unnerved the Inspector. The drip, drip, drip reminded him of how life inexorably drains toward death whether one leads a good life or a vicious one.

Inside, the room was well lit. Dr. Fitzwilliam and his note-taking assistant, Adam Jenkins, stood around a table that contained a stout piece of Mackintosh.

On it lay a naked corpse. One terror stricken blue eye bulged from the skull. The mouth was stretched open so it nearly touched his Adam's apple. The jaw appeared unhinged. From its socket and from that wide, silent death scream, a plume of intestines vomited forth, spilling down his chest all the way to his navel, a ghastly, glistening beard of grey-white, purple and red.

Surgeons refused to wear rubber gloves, insisting their bare hands could more easily detect anything unusual, Dr. Fitzwilliam had seen his predecessor die in agony from an infection and was the exception.

There were basins, towels, rags, sponges, carbolic soap, turpentine, and buckets to hold discarded body parts. A set of implements were set out on a cloth on a side table. A stone sink with both hot and cold running water was in one corner of the room.

Dr. Fitzwilliam, wearing a stained apron, looked up at their entrance. "Jenkins, are you ready?" he barked.

"Yes sir," Jenkins said whipping out his notebook and pen. He'd been the coroner's assistant for six months and loved his job. Death, especially brutal murders, fascinated him. In his little room at Mrs. Todd's boarding house in Bethnal Green, he kept a library of books on the subject.

Inspector Banks cleared his throat and turned to John, "Is this your brother?"

Gone were the good looks and easy charm Shelly had in life.

"It's Shelly," John said unable to control the tremor in his voice. "I recognize him by his ring and the birthmark on his right thigh."

"Full name and address," Dr. Fitzwilliam asked more gently then he was wont to do.

"Shelly Theodore Collins. His address is . . . was Seventeen Half Moon Street."

The coroner began. "The time is eleven o'clock. The body is that of a man in his late twenties. He is identified by his brother, John Hammond. Mr. Collins was viciously attacked with what appears to be very sharp and pointed instruments."

"Like claws," John muttered.

Dr. Fitzwilliam looked at him in surprise, "It wasn't an animal."

"No," John agreed grimly.

The coroner exchanged an uneasy glance with Inspector Banks who looked as if he would puke at any minute. "The fingers appear to have been chewed off in a frenzy. May have been taken as trophies. His stomach was slit open, his intestines removed and . . ." Dr. Fitzwilliam paused and glanced at John apologetically, "stuffed down his throat while still alive."

Extracting the intestines, the doctor dumped them in one of the buckets and began to slice away other parts, noting their condition as he did so. "Mr. Collins' lungs showed signs of lesions from heavy smoking. His heart was still good but he was suffering from the beginning stages of syphilis."

Guilt at not playing a stronger role in his brother's life hit John hard. The chewed off missing fingers added to his suspicion it was the work of a demon but he had to know for sure.

"Open the stomach cavity all the way down," he ordered.

Dr. Fitzwilliam's face turned red. His mustache bristled and he puffed up with outrage at the command. "Who the blazes do—"

"You were going to do it anyway," the Inspector said mildly.

Grumbling, Dr. Fitzwilliam made the incision revealing a sticky, greenish substance that clung to the walls of Shelly's lower abdominal cavity. The men stepped back. The stench was so bad even the coroner grabbed a cloth and held it to his nose.

"What is it?" The Inspector gagged.

"The mark of a very special kind of murderer," John said grimly.

"Like the Ripper?" Jenkins asked thrilled.

"Like the Ripper. The murderer is extremely dangerous and he'll keep on killing until he's caught." John turned to his friend, "Let me help."

The Inspector frowned. "Not a good idea. You're emotionally involved."

John glared at him.

"Let the Yard handle it," Inspector Banks pleaded soothingly. He was afraid John would get himself killed or worse, take revenge and he would have to arrest him.

"Thank you, Adam but I don't believe I will," John said as he left.

Arriving home, John went straight to the back parlor and turned on the electric lights. Walking over to a framed watercolor of the archangel Michael, John took down the heavy picture revealing a safe. He removed a black velvet box that held a curved, steel dagger with gold hieroglyphs on the handle.

His father presented it to him on his thirteenth birthday making him swear he would never reveal to anyone the powers it contained. The dagger was no ordinary blade. It alerted him to the presence of demons and enabled him to kill them, releasing the tortured souls it captured.

He placed the blade in a specially designed pocket inside his jacket, under his right arm. Emerging onto the cobblestone street in a light rain wearing a top hat and tails, he hailed a cab.

The Hunt

John carefully examined the dark alley now empty of Shelly's battered body. The rain washed away most of the blood and smell of urine but he could still detect the odor of sulfur and rotting flesh.

The hair on the back of his neck prickled. He whirled around, yanking out his knife which blazed with light, but the alley was empty.

Carefully he stepped back, pressing his shoulders against the cold, moldy brick. He waited. *I'm getting too old for this*, John thought. He peered into the blackness. Tense, his heart raced but he saw nothing. Then he heard it.

A soft slither, a brush against the rough brick directly above him, and a raspy growl. Long experience caused John to fling himself to the side. He rolled away as a crate of empty bottles dropped from above, crashing on the ground where his head would have been. He glanced up and saw red eyes glitter in a pale, bloated face before it scuttled away, laughing softly.

John stood awkwardly, wincing when his bad knee buckled. Fear tightened a band around his chest. *It recognized me for who I am.*

Cautious, he kept the knife in his hand, concealing it in the folds of his coat. On his last hunt, the knife had been in his inside pocket and he could barely get to it in time. Though he killed the demon, he nearly died.

As he moved toward the front entrance, Naughty Nelly's was in full swing, the tinny piano hammering out a jaunty tune. John hesitated, wondering what had drawn the demon to choose his brother. If you knew the nature of the beast you sought, they were easy to spot. One of Shelly's many vices was bragging. Especially about his sexual conquests.

"Demons," he remembered his father saying, "slither into the world to steal the souls of their victims. The Braggart Demon rages to hear someone else boast of being the best. Their signature is stuffing the intestines down the throat of their prey. The demon absorbs and traps their victim's energy, often using their body to better disguise themselves."

John grimaced, remembering his brother's shade begging for help.

His throbbing knee made him pause in front of the seedy club. He was still weak. *I'm not at my peak. I should return with the Inspector and let him take charge.* But he feared by that time the demon might have moved on.

John looked around but there were no carriages in sight. He would have to walk a few blocks. He dropped the knife in his jacket pocket and started walking through the fog.

"Hey mister, buy my roses," a flower girl begged.

He turned and paused. She was ragged, barefoot and looked about twelve. She shivered with cold, looking as wilted as her flowers.

"What's your name?"

"Alice."

A pretty, young prostitute stepped out of the shadows, "Want to buy me some roses gov?" she asked, looping her arm through his. "My name's Cherry."

John pulled away, immediately alert. He could feel the blade growing hot in his pocket.

"What's wrong?" she teased. "Don't you like me?"

"Don't Mister," Alice warned.

"Beat it, kid," Cherry snapped, pulling John down the street.

"She's dangerous," Alice warned, following them.

"Shut up you little creep."

John's fingers dug into Cherry's wrist. He reached into his pocket and grabbed the knife's hilt. "Not so fast."

"Hey, that hurts."

John withdrew the knife which glowed like lightening in the dark, foggy street.

Panicked at seeing a knife, Cherry screamed, "Let go," but John held her tighter. Cursing, Cherry delivered a savage kick to his weak leg and fled. Alice edged away, her eyes big and fearful.

"I won't hurt you." John assured the child, slipping the knife back into his pocket, showing his empty hands to the girl. "Tell me about Cherry."

Alice shrugged. "Men go off with 'er but don't come back. What kind of knife glows like that Mister? Is it made of gold?"

He smiled. "No."

She edged closer, "Can I see?"

Too late, John realized the knife was burning fiercely against his hip just as she jumped him cackling with mirth, stinking of decayed flesh. He staggered, lost his balance and fell, feeling the agony of claws slash through his shirt, into his chest and rip his still beating heart out.

Alice's eyes glittered with triumph. Leaping off John's limp body, she raised her prize and shouted in the deep voice of a demon, "I, Afrit have killed a Demon Hunter."

As John expired, she licked and sucked the blood dripping from his blob of heart tissue before greedily gobbling it down.

Digging into his pocket, she removed the knife cursing as the searing heat sizzled and blistered her fingers. Snarling, she dropped the blade, kicking it into the gutter.

Twisting her head around, Alice stared at John's shell with her soulless eyes. Her body arched back painfully, snapping fragile bones as a foul smelling green smoke emerged. The demon's spirit rose in the air before it dove into John's body, leaving Alice's rotting corpse behind.

A few seconds later Afrit stood up, fastened his evening jacket over his bloody shirt and brushed himself off just as a police whistle cut through the air.

Lisa Morton

ERASURE

Linda pulled her gray fleece jacket tighter, huddling against the cemetery chill. Usually October afternoons in Los Angeles weren't this cold, but the weather was as inescapably devoid of warmth as the rest of her life.

She trudged past the mausoleums, barely lifting her head to regard her surroundings. She didn't have to; she'd come this way every day for the last three months.

Ever since Keith had died.

His headstone was just a plaque buried in the grass—Linda knew that made the lawns easier to mow (which she found somewhat ironic, since California's endless drought had left the grass yellow and half-dead). The Rose Glen Memorial Park on the edge of Los Angeles wasn't especially old or scenic, but Keith had chosen it because it was affordable. His grave at least was near a scenic olive tree; normally Linda was glad to have the shade, but today she was cold as she lowered herself before Keith's little memorial plaque, and the blank space beside it that would someday hold hers. She didn't mind kneeling or sitting in the brittle, half-dead ground cover; it put her closer to Keith, after all.

Linda was angry today, although anyone watching her wouldn't have known that. Just before she'd left the house, her sister Ally had called.

"You are *not* still going to the cemetery every day, are you?"

"So what if I am? What business is it of yours?"

Her sister's voice on the other end of the phone was taut with scorn and disbelief. "You're right, why should I give a rat's ass? Just because you've been fired for taking two-hour lunches so you could go there every fucking day—"

Linda cut her off. "I wasn't fired, I was laid off when the company restructured."

Ally ignored her. "Linda, you need help. Go to a doctor, get yourself some antidepressants or therapy or *something*. It's been three months since the heart attack . . . how long does this go on?"

"As long as it needs to," Linda answered just before she hung up.

A part of her knew Ally was right—she shouldn't be doing this, maybe a doctor could help—but the bigger part of her found comfort in the routine of daily mourning. It wasn't even so much that she missed Keith, that she refused to let him go, because while he'd been alive there'd been times—*many* times—when she'd wished he *would* go. It hadn't been a happy marriage, at least not for years.

Linda reached the small plaque set into the earth—*Keith Marshall McMann 1970-2015*—spread out the blanket she always brought, and lowered herself to the earth, her knees protesting. She was getting old. Getting old without Keith.

She looked down at the plaque and thought (again) about changing it. Shouldn't she have added *"Beloved Husband,"* even if it wasn't particularly true? All the other plaques said something—*"World War II Veteran"* or *"Husband, Father, Friend"* or *"Resting in God's Arms"*. But none of those were true in Keith's case, although Linda wasn't entirely sure of the last. If there was a God, she doubted that He'd want Keith in His arms.

Keith hadn't been an especially pleasant man. When he'd been young, when Linda had first met him, he'd possessed a sort of cruel handsomeness; he had the face of a dashing hitman, with dark eyes and sharp cheekbones. He'd taken to Linda as if she'd been a new car—something to be acquired and polished, shown off but cursed when it was too slow or a part failed. Linda had chafed under his control, and their marriage had quickly settled into a pattern of loud arguments followed by weeks of irritable silence.

The heart attack that felled him in seconds (and at too young an age) should have been a blessing for Linda; as she'd returned from his funeral to a quiet house that was now completely hers, she'd had a moment of wild exultation . . . that had soon given way to loss. Not the loss of Keith, but the loss of a way of life she'd endured for twenty-five years. Without the fights and the bitter quiet, her world felt even emptier, so she filled it as best she could with a grief that she knew wasn't entirely real.

It was still better than acknowledging what a failure her life had been.

Bastard, Linda thought as she knelt before all that was left of her husband. *You took my life, and this is what I'm left with. A house that needs more repairs than its even worth, no job, only a little savings, no friends because no one wanted to be around us, not even a child to comfort me—*

"Hello."

Linda jerked up to see a woman standing a few feet away. The woman was young, mid-twenties, slender, wearing a long dark coat that had probably been chic at some point in the past. When Linda saw the small laptop computer the woman clutched in one hand, she remembered where she'd seen her: sitting on a bench a short distance away tapping on that laptop every day for the last week.

"I'm sorry, I didn't mean to startle you . . ." When Linda didn't respond, the woman went on. "It's just that I've seen you come here every day, and . . . if you don't want to talk, I'll go away."

"No," Linda said, surprising herself. "It's okay." She got to her feet, trying not to groan with the effort, and extended a hand. "I'm Linda."

The younger woman accepted the offered hand with a grip so strong it was almost painful. "You can call me Azzie. I'd tell you what it's short for, but it's really long and usually unpronounceable."

"'Usually'?"

Azzie shrugged. "For most people. Anyway, I like Azzie." She gestured down at the grave. "Your husband?"

Linda nodded. "He died three months ago. Heart attack."

"Oh, I'm sorry. That must have been hard on you."

Linda almost answered, "Not as hard as the twenty-five years of marriage that came before it," but instead she said, "It was."

"Have you . . . have you come here every day since?"

Linda nodded again.

"You must have loved him very much."

This time Linda remained still. She couldn't lie that much, not to a friendly young person whose life was still fresh enough to be open to possibility.

Azzie took a step back. "Really, I didn't mean to intrude . . ."

Linda realized she was hungry to talk about something other than Keith, so she glanced at Azzie's laptop. "Do you come here every day to write?"

"Sort of. It's not a novel or a screenplay or anything like that. More like a . . . collection of memories, I guess."

"Oh. That sounds interesting. Are you hoping to get it published?"

Azzie laughed and rolled her eyes. "Oh *God* no! It's just for me. So I don't forget."

Linda didn't know how to respond, although Azzie seemed to be waiting for something. "You must have a lot of memories."

"I do."

Azzie peered at Linda for a second before saying, softly, "Not everyone wants their memories."

A jolt of anxiety pierced Linda. Did Azzie know something about her? Had she known Keith? Could she have been another of his little triumphs, one in the string of affairs Linda knew he'd had? Secretaries, store clerks, women met by chance in bars . . . Linda had once waited until he was asleep and then gone through Keith's phone, and discovered dozens of numbers and names—all female—that she couldn't identify. Sometimes, when he'd come home very late, she'd even been able to smell them on her husband.

"Did you know Keith?"

Azzie shook her head. "No."

Linda believed her . . . which left her again puzzling over the woman's intention. The breeze through the cemetery seemed to grow colder, and

Linda wanted to be away from here, somewhere warmer, somewhere alone. "It was nice meeting you, but I need to get home—"

Azzie cut her off. "What if you could get rid of what you're feeling?"

The words seemed so irrelevant that Linda stopped, caught between laughing and curiosity. Was Azzie some sort of guru, a new age saleswoman offering false hope and fantasy? "Let me guess: I sign up for your course at a very reasonable price, and you teach me some method that makes me a better person."

"No. I literally take away your memories. And without those . . . no more anger, resentment, disappointment."

Linda's mouth opened, but no response came out. Azzie had just revealed that she knew Linda's secret, the one she thought she kept so artfully hidden. She looked away, hoping to hide her dismay at being discovered, and said instead, "And why on earth would I believe that?"

"Because you've done it before."

Linda turned to look at her, confused. "What are you talking about?"

"Your son, David."

"Ah, now I see: you've made a mistake. I'm obviously not who you think I am, because I've never had a son. Keith and I had no children."

"Look down, Linda."

For a second Linda almost turned and walked away; she knew it was what she *should* do. But instead, her eyes betrayed her and looked.

There was Keith's plaque, in the ground, the sickly grass edging up against it, and there beside it was the empty space intended for her, and there next to it was the plaque reading:

David Patrick McMann 1999-2009 Beloved Son.

"How did you . . . what is this?"

Before Linda could react, before she could pull away, Azzie reached out and took her hand. And Azzie's touch brought the memories: Of how she and Keith had decided to try to save their marriage by having a child and they'd conceived a son, a son who was a squawling bundle of hope, who grew into a toddler who made them laugh in exasperation, memories of a smart little boy in glasses who dazzled his kindergarten teacher with the list of books he'd already read, of Keith teaching him math and showing him how to hit a free throw, of Linda watching his glee when he opened his birthday presents, of the day his eyes rolled into his head and he fell over on the school playground, of hearing the doctors tell them it was a brain aneurysm and they'd try to save him, but the operation had failed, and they'd buried David here, and Keith's heart was gone, he lost himself in a series of meaningless affairs while Linda drank and shouted and blamed Keith's DNA for the genetic time-bomb in their son's skull.

And one day Linda had come to the cemetery, anxious to escape another confrontation at home, and she'd met an attractive young woman who had offered to take her pain away, and the offer had been irresistible.

Now Linda found she was on her knees, sobbing as she clenched fistfuls of the dying grass, calling David's name over and over. She finally looked up at Azzie, desperately. "Please . . . please, take it away again."

Azzie knelt beside her, with great compassion. "Linda, you have to decide first: do you want me to also take Keith?"

Linda choked back the sobs as it hit her: this offer was real, not a hoax or a trick, not the ramblings of a huckster or a crazy person. She looked at Azzie and whispered, "What are you?"

Azzie half-smiled, and for an instant Linda saw something very old in her face. "Just someone who might value your memories more than you do."

"Why would you value them?"

"They keep me alive."

"How many times have you done this?"

"I don't know. It would be like me asking you how many times you've eaten."

Linda crouched there, over the graves, her thoughts a frantic kaleidoscope. David dead, erased from her memory, returned now, the pain so great it threatened to crush her into the graveyard dirt, and how could she not have known, she'd had a son, how was that possible—

"I don't understand. Even if I'd forgotten David, other people hadn't . . ."

Azzie answered, "That's right. Other people have mentioned him around you, even shown you pictures . . . but you simply don't hear or see them. I can't erase David's existence from the world, only from you. It'll be the same with Keith—if friends ask you about him, you won't know. Don't we all tend to hear or see only what we want to anyway?"

To never have to think about Keith again, his casual cruelties, the lies she could see through so easily, the thousand little petty betrayals—"Linda? I have to go soon . . ."

"All right. Do it."

Azzie smiled and inhaled deeply. "I just need your hand."

Without rising, Linda held out her right hand. Azzie took it, standing over her. Azzie's touch was firm, warm, almost electric.

Linda waited . . . and then she felt it: the memories being uprooted, pulled away from her, and in that instant she saw *all* of them, not just the bad she'd chosen but the good she'd pushed away, and there *had* been good, especially in the beginning, when Keith had been young and dapper, smitten with her, he'd wooed her with songs he sang under her window in a passable imitation of Dean Martin, he'd won her with the way he held her when they danced, how he looked at her, how they made each other laugh, and suddenly a part of Linda tried to cling to those memories, inwardly crying out as they were torn away. She tried to pull her hand from Azzie's grip, but the other woman—or whatever she was—was stronger, much stronger, and she nearly crushed Linda's fingers. Linda cried out, but her protests were unanswered.

I'm so sorry, Keith, I wasn't fair to you, I've wallowed in the worst part of you because it was easier than blaming myself. Now I don't want to lose.

Linda felt dry, parched grass beneath her legs. She looked around in confusion, saw she was in a cemetery. A younger woman stood nearby, her eyes closed as she panted, apparently in some kind of ecstatic state.

"I don't understand," Linda muttered, to herself, but the other woman overheard and opened her eyes. She gazed down at Linda with a strange compassion and asked, "Are you okay?"

"I'm not sure. I don't know where I am, or how I got here . . ."

"You're at the Rose Glen Memorial Park. Are you trying to find a grave, or . . . ?"

Wisps of thought drifted through Linda's mind and she tried to catch them, but they evaporated. "Maybe, but . . ."

"You were bent over this one." The woman pointed; Linda glanced down and saw the name "Keith."

"No, I don't know anyone named Keith."

The younger woman helped Linda to her feet and turned her to face her car, parked a short distance away. "Tell you what: why don't you head home, sit down with a nice glass of wine, and I bet you'll forget all about this trip."

"Yes, that sounds good . . ."

Linda staggered a few steps, stumbled on a half-buried plaque. The woman caught her elbow and held her up. Linda righted herself, said, "Thank you. I really don't know what's happened to me. I think I might have come here to visit someone, but . . ."

The younger woman said, "He was actually a very decent man."

"Who was?"

"No one."

Linda turned to look at her, curious, but saw only a shadow against the dying lawn. By the time she reached her car, she'd forgotten even the shadow.

But it didn't seem to matter.

T. C. Bennett

THE WINDOWS

Scant showers and pill-sized hail stoned Los Angeles, Orange, and Riverside Counties, leaving a fine residue of white ice and oil on the streets. None of this bothered the thirty-eight year old Elias Stratton much. He liked it when it rained, because this didn't happen much in L.A. Today a behemoth cloud seemed to follow him, hunched over villainously, with its lethargic face, almost touchable above his head. The frigid pelting goaded him to repent for all the spitefulness he'd directed toward others but repentance to Elias Stratton seemed as unnecessary as Cerberus guarding the Gates of Hell.

Elias managed to avoid several blocks worth of camouflaged potholes that would have splashed street grime across his Dodge Ram truck. A storm warning silenced the radio with news of flash flooding through-out the southland. The now-sodden Pasadena neighborhood was scat-tered with old houses in quaint architectural styles: Georgian, Victorian, Eastlake, and every nineteenth-century revival he remembered from his art history class.

He swerved to park on Marengo Street. Behind a tree stood a large Queen Anne house, a looming presence with gables and a wraparound porch. Three days ago escrow had closed, and the house was now his. He had purchased it for practically nothing.

As Elias approached the weather-beaten facade, a light wind parted his hair and toppled dried leaves across the spacious, dehydrated lawn, its thirst hardly quenched by the rain. The California drought was doing its work, sucking the life from the once lush vegetation. Time and the elements had taken their toll on the exterior of the house as well. Elias observed layers of chalky paint, whittled away in some places to the bare wood. The porch railing spindles were broken like a smile with missing teeth. A few fallen shingles littered the unkempt yard.

A day earlier, Elias had gone to the City Hall to research the history of the house. The original owner and builder, Krade Legnun Jones, had inhabited the house from 1893 until his death in 1980 as one of the world's oldest men. A few months later, a second owner named Brock Towers had bought the house, despite its well-known history, and lived there until he died in 2006. The porch groaned in protest as Elias climbed the steps. The key fit easily into the lock in the old oak door, which creaked a welcome as it swung open. He took a deep breath and entered the house. Home, thought Elias.

Eager to view the premises on the second floor, he mounted the grand staircase that rose from the entry hall. With each step, he felt the stairs sink and moan, his shoes leaving prints in two years of vacancy dust. At the top of the stairs he paused, letting his weak heart rest. Then, he turned left toward the first bedroom. A plaque on the bedroom door read "Little Johnny." A plaque on the second bedroom door read "Killing Gestation," and the next room had a blank plaque. Elias wondered what it all meant. He explored the rest of the hallway, passing more rooms, none of which had plaques on their doors.

Back downstairs Elias noticed a couple more plaques, positioned below the windowsills in the living room and dining room. But he did not linger to read the names on the plaques as he still had boxes to pack.

The next day Elias returned to the house with the movers. Halfway through the unloading, he decided to investigate the attic, where he planned to store his extra belongings.

The attic was mostly bare except, for a few pieces of outdated furniture. He spied a ragged journal smothered with dust under a rocking chair and stooped to retrieve it. The dark red leather cover was stamped with gold lettering that read: *Krade Legnun Jones 1893.*

Curious, Elias began to read the journal, and soon became fascinated by the origins of the design of the house found within the pages. Apparently Krade Legnun Jones had been a psychic who was obsessed with collecting windows from haunted houses throughout the United States. The Queen Anne house had been built purposely without half its windows in 1893, the openings gradually filled in as Jones expanded his collection. He specifically sought windows to which ghosts were attached. When a crime had occurred in front of a window, whether inside or outside, the ghosts could be seen after the windows were installed in the Queen Anne house.

"Hey, Mr. Stratton," hollered one of the movers. "We go eat. We hungry. You want something?"

"No, thank you. Go ahead and take your time," Elias answered. He went back to reading the journal.

Using his remarkable abilities, Krade Legnun Jones explained that he was able to witness the crimes committed in front of the windows he'd brought back to Pasadena, where they played out time after time on various occasions. Jones's first ghost-capturing window was from a Georgian house in Charleston, South Carolina, where a pregnant woman was a victim of a hate crime during the Revolutionary War. A mob of British sympathizers who had been her neighbors for a decade went rifling through the patriot's house, killing her—but not before cutting out her unborn child, which was near full term. The Tories had carved on her chest with a butcher knife, "Thou shalt at no time bring forth from the womb a rebel dog." Lying next to her was her toddler son, with his head bashed in. For many years Jones had seen them huddled together, sobbing, in the Killing Gestation room.

Little Johnny, whose window had been installed in the room next door, had been a victimizer and then a victim. He was a revered Chinese warlord, a leader of one of many Tong gangs. Known as the "Emperor of Chinatown," he ran a string of Fan-Tan parlors, opium dens and Chinese brothels. Five years after his release from San Quentin prison in 1897, enemy Tongs posted a ransom on buildings in Chinatown. A large reward for Johnny's death.

The prissy warlord of Chinatown let his guard down one day as he left his living quarters above the barbershop he owned. He only planned to get his long hair washed, so brought only one burly white henchman to accompany him downstairs, not the four or five that normally accompanied him making him untouchable. While in the back of the barbershop, Little Johnny was approached from behind, as the barber was unbraiding his queue so his hair could be washed in the basin. A dozen sudden gunshots penetrated his neck and back, until his body oozed blood like a strainer. Krade Legnun Jones had made a special trip to Chinatown in San Francisco, where he purchased one of the large windows of the barbershop from Little Johnny's widow, who was struggling to keep the building from warring Tongs.

Elias paused for a moment, thinking he heard something behind him. Nothing but dust, settling like fog in the dim light of the attic. He continued reading the journal. The next page revealed that Krade Legnun Jones became so obsessed with the stories playing out in his windows, that he had started killing in front of his own windows, thus capturing and enslaving new ghosts without traveling anywhere.

Krade Legnun Jones warned the reader not to remove the journal from the attic or he would chase them down to retrieve it.

Suddenly, a gust of wind swept through the attic, howling and sending clouds of dust whirling about the broken-down furniture. The pages of the journal flapped and fluttered.

"What the hell was that?" Elias said aloud, knowing all too well that he was the only one in the attic. Goose bumps formed to the size of pimples on his arms, neck and legs. He was grateful that his heart did not skip a beat, considering his heart condition. But he felt a strong wave of fear clutch his chest.

After a long wait, he heard the movers in the house. He left the attic with the journal and looked into each bedroom to choose the one he wanted. He definitely didn't want one with an engraved plaque on the door; he had no desire to share his sleeping quarters with a ghost.

Finally, Elias found the bedroom he wanted, although it had a blank plaque. As he left the room, he noticed the plaque appeared to have been scratched with something sharp, and it read: Brock Towers. How had the most recent owner of the house died, Elias wondered. Was it from natural causes, or was he murdered? Krade Legnun Jones had been dead for a quarter of a century before Towers' death. Could the ghosts in the house have frightened him so much that his heart gave out? Not likely after twenty-five years, Elias decided. He was just being silly.

Nevertheless, Elias decided to turn in Krade Legnun Jones's journal to the police the next day, to expose Pasadena's very own serial killer. He noticed that the plaque on the next door was not engraved and decided to make it his bedroom instead.

"When you finish up with the living room, I want you to move my bedroom furniture into this room, right over here," he called to the movers.

By the time all the boxes were in their designated rooms, some partially unpacked, it was nightfall and the movers had left. They would return in the morning, and by noon the next day, Elias expected they would have him completely unpacked and moved.

Elias retired to his bedroom, but he found himself wide awake. *Just nerves from the long day of moving,* he told himself. But at midnight the house shuddered and rocked, and the lights throughout the house flickered, disturbing the darkness. Appliances turned off and on. Orbs of light grazed the ceilings, floors, and walls as if examining everything in their path.

Teetering with fear, Elias Stratton walked stiffly into the hallway. The Killing Gestation bedroom door stood wide open. He stood in the doorframe looking toward the window. At first he saw the streetlight outside. Then the white haze seemed to form into a figure, he suddenly saw a young mother clothed in 18th century clothing, holding an infant above her eviscerated stomach, at the same time squeezing her toddler to her side. All three swayed wistfully, their mouths open in silent screams, gazing at him as if they, not he, were seeing a ghost.

Elias staggered away from the room in disbelief, but he kept moving, as if drawn by his own terror. With each step to each room, he witnessed another victim's fate. At the very end of the hallway, he saw a half-naked Indian warrior begin his relentless chase of a barefoot adolescent blond girl fearfully dodging the brave's manic, waving ax.

What was more, this ghostly manifestation repeated itself endlessly, and each time they passed by Elias, they ignored him as though he wasn't there.

The bedroom doors swung open and closed, slapping as they displayed the apparitions' torments. Cries, wails, moans, and screeches filled the halls, and the floor rumbled from thunderous disembodied footsteps. Elias retreated to his bedroom, shivering beneath his bedcovers, and cupped his hands over his ears. The tumult went on for hours. Then, the whole house went silent.

At five-thirty in the morning when the sky was still dark, the movers arrived as promised. They rang the doorbell several times and then stepped back at the sound of the unlatching lock. The front door swung open, and the movers tromped into the Queen Anne house. Once inside the three men followed the aroma of freshly brewed coffee, which lured them toward the kitchen. They poured some coffee for themselves into Styrofoam cups and called out for Elias. No answer.

"Mr. Stratton, you here?"

At the continued silence, the crew chief shrugged and said, "Let's look upstairs."

The movers climbed the grand staircase and walked along the hallway, where all the doors stood open. They craned their necks into each bedroom, calling as they went. At the end of the hallway, the three men saw a slipper lying on the threshold of the last bedroom. Inside, Elias, missing a slipper, had collapsed directly in front of his bedroom window. In his right hand he held a dusty old journal.

One of the movers put his ear to Elias's chest. He heard a heartbeat, but Elias was struggling to breathe. Another of the movers called 911 from his cell phone, asking for an ambulance in broken English. The third mover went to the street to direct the paramedics. Within minutes the emergency crew reached the house and raced the rattling stretcher behind the third mover toward Elias's body. They removed the journal from his hand, but by the time they had Elias strapped to the stretcher with an IV in his arm, the new homeowner had stopped breathing and died. The paramedics tried several times to revive him, but failed.

The paramedics asked the movers questions and then took Elias's body away in the ambulance. The movers went outside, stunned by what had just happened. Nervously they paced the front lawn.

They decided to leave, since Elias was gone. As they stood scratching their heads, staring up at the timeworn house, one of the movers thought he saw something moving in Elias's bedroom. "It's good we go check," he told the others, who followed him inside.

They went back up the stairs and trooped down the hallway. As they reached the doorway of the bedroom, they saw a wraithlike Elias standing erect with his back to them. He was scratching at the window with his left hand and clasping a leather-bound book in his right. A much older ghost was pulling the book out of Elias's hand. Elias spun around, dragging the other ghost with him. They floated toward the movers, who screamed and ran as fast as they could toward the front door.

Eric J. Guignard

CERTAIN SIGHTS OF AN AFFLICTED WOMAN

A dark sun climbed that morning over the crust of scorched earth known as Post Rock, but only one pair of eyes remained to watch its ascent.

Half that pair was infected, which caused Margie great torment. Her left eye swelled and leaked, and certain things she saw became slightly distorted, the constant tears overlaying a watery effect across her vision. In this way the land sometimes appeared like a mirage that wavers and blurs. It was a chronic eye infection, and Margie blamed its latest resurgence on the unnatural winds that began buffeting Post Rock three days ago. The infection always had that same effect on her when it reoccurred, being the discomfort and distortion. But although her eye was wretched, it was the reason she remained alive.

Margie was the last of the living after her sister, Pearl, succumbed during the night to the plague, enduring longer than any of the others, all the while hacking blood, gasping for air, drowning in mucus, but breathing and surviving, until she didn't. Margie prayed for Pearl, shielded her, nursed her, begged for her perseverance, but had known, even while both of them were healthy, even while the rest of the town sickened and died where they stood, that it'd be too much to hope that whatever powers brought down such pestilence would allow the survival of two sisters together.

And she'd been right. Margie had the benefit in her bad eye while Pearl ended up taking that terrible trip alongside all five hundred others.

And maybe Margie was next anyway, maybe she wouldn't be able to 'see' the germs any longer, wouldn't be able to evade them. Maybe she'd start coughing tomorrow the way the rest of Post Rock had. The year was 1918, and maybe this would be the last year of her life.

She remembered Pearl saying once that she'd always protect Margie. *I will save you in ways you cannot even imagine . . .*

Margie never made that assurance in return. It wasn't because of it that Pearl was dead, but neither did it make Margie feel any better. She bore the heartache of her sister's loss as she did the pain in her eye: a recurrent suffering that would remain forever unhealed.

On her deathbed, Pearl murmured her final words as her own vision wore down. "I see 'em, sis . . . You were right all along . . . about the clouds."

That didn't make Margie feel any better either. The clouds had been haunting her since she was a girl. She thought back to her childhood, and she shuddered at the premonitions that came true, and tried instead to concentrate on the present, which was equally dismaying.

Margie rubbed her infected eye, then cursed, then made peace for having profaned. She needed the telephone at the sheriff's office. It was the only one for twenty miles around, and she set her mind to return there for the dozenth time in recent days.

Though she knew what awaited along the way . . .

From outlying farms straddling Route Four to the clustered shops anchoring Main Street, corpses covered the land like strange leaves blown along by a horrible wind. Sometimes those leaves piled in heaps, ten, twelve high, and sometimes they were sparse scatterings but, excepting Margie, they'd all taken their fall, and they all rotted now, moldering in the trappings of their lives. It was a mortifying shame that their bodies lay as such, unburied, mounding flies and ravenous worms and other things not affected by the sickness. They were neighbors and friends of Margie's, laid waste while they shopped for sundries, toiled in the field, or groused at Tilmon's Cafe about the rest of the nation seeming intent to foxtrot its way to Hades. Each was dropped swiftly by a malady thought no more insidious than a summer complaint.

And she survived because of her infirmity.

Margie's bad eye—that sick eye—caused her to see things she couldn't observe while healthy. It wasn't a magic, not like Pearl who had imagination, nor was it a hex, but rather the watery, quivering upshot of looking through the very lens of infection. Her vision would become maladjusted (that's what Doc Stevens called it) when the world twisted before her to reveal strange carrying-ons. Of course Doc Stevens didn't believe the things she claimed to witness, but said instead that the mind played funny tricks on a person when illness got involved.

There was plenty illness now, but the tricks weren't too funny. Horrible plague floated through the air, carried along by resolute gusts that hadn't let up for three days, and Margie could see it all.

The germs were little creatures, beasts with thorny heads and wicked intent. She heard Doc Stevens call them 'bacteria,' and that sounded fine enough. She also heard Doc Stevens declare that Post Rock had caught a bug, some affliction not unlike the medieval Black Plague, but worse in terms of an accelerated incubation period. But he also said he wasn't sure of anything since it wasn't easy to tell between viral or bacterial infection, with the symptoms being so similar. Besides the plague-like traits, he'd have claimed it as some strain of influenza, a far-flung product of the Great War that still carried on in the trenches of Germany and France.

He said all that right before he died.

The bacteria were tubular, like tiny wriggling hairs crawling on the wind, softly glowing with some green luminescence of evil. Walls didn't stop 'em much, just slowed some a little until they found cracks to sneak through. When she'd first seen the things blowing into town, she hadn't known what they were, but had the good mind not to touch them.

She saw where the germs clung to people or objects, spoiling them, and she kept her distance. She saw where the germs floated in the air, great swarms like hordes of locusts, and she turned the other way. Margie even tried warning people, but they didn't listen. And those that did, it didn't matter. The plague germs came at them from all directions. Margie kept healthy by evading the germs she saw but knew there'd not be relief forever; it was impossible to remain alert at all hours, when one single bacterium could be crawling under her dress that very moment. Even Pearl, who Margie tried so hard to safeguard, grew infected.

Unavoidably the question came to mind, though it still caught her unawares: *What to do now?*

And the answer came as it had before: The phone, the phone, someone would call, someone must know what she should do. And so it was the sheriff's office to try again.

Though the germs were the harbinger of Post Rock's death, it wasn't they she was most concerned with, but rather the vehicle of their deliverance.

The damnable clouds . . . or, rather, what took their form . . .

When they were girls, Margie and Pearl loved to lie outdoors and talk of schooling and books and ponies and even boys, when then their voices fell to muffled giggles behind cupped hands. Pearl's favorite place was beside a large twisty oak tree that extended a thousand fingers as if trying to touch everything at once, and they'd lie there on their backs, holding hands. After awhile, Pearl would begin to devise stories about the clouds that languished very high above, yet entirely close, as if one could only jump just a little higher, their fingers would run through the downy wisps of dandelion fuzz. They'd lie there on the grass, and Pearl would point to the strange, morphing compositions.

"That one's a tortoise," she'd say, "and it's swimming in a sky of topaz. It's a mommy tortoise and it has eggs to lay, and it's looking for a place here on Earth to put her babies to bed."

The tortoise would soon dissipate or blow over the horizon, and

Pearl would point to the next. "That one's a prancing horse and it's been trained in a circus to do wonderful leaps and to hold its head very high."

Margie would nod and smile, though never able to visualize the whimsical things of her sister's imagination. As much as she tried, as much as she squinted her eyes one way, then the other, turned her head, blinked, or concentrated, all she made out were smeared blobs that could've been an ugly bird or a deformed foot. Margie didn't care much for the cloud game, but indulged it, as Pearl enjoyed so much to daydream of things that didn't exist.

One afternoon, lying in the shade of the twisty oak, beneath the great, great sky, Pearl asked her sister, "Margie, what do you see in the clouds?"

Nothing but daubs of whitewash, Margie thought, *but I'll try again for you.*

That day Margie was sick. Infection rose in her eye and she should not have been outdoors, but instead lying in bed covered by a warm handcloth soaked in herbs and tonic. Their parents, however, were away, and she suffered the same itch and pain of the infection's resurgence whether she lay beneath a cloth or not. So now she looked upon the clouds, comfortable with her sister, and saw through septicity what she'd never seen before.

She cried out and wished she'd stayed in bed.

"What is it?" Pearl asked.

Margie scrunched up her face and closed her eyes. "I don't want to see them."

"Why not, what's wrong?"

She shook her head and whispered in Pearl's ear, so that the clouds could not hear, "They hate us."

"Margie, that's horrible!"

"I know," she replied, quite plainly.

Above, she'd seen faces concealed within clouds, entirely unlike the jolly elves of her sister's claim. These were wretched masks of pestilence and woe, and they were alive.

The miserable visages glared upon the girls, and now Margie's imagination, previously a mouse slumbering in some dark crevice of her brain, began to wake and scurry about, gnawing on common sense, and she thought the clouds were gathering strength, accumulating in the heavens, waiting for their moment to strike. The faces were as alike, yet as dissimilar, as peering at any group of men dying a long death from starvation or consumption. Margie had an old, old uncle who fought in the Civil War, and when she looked upon these clouds, she was reminded of him: withered from dysentery, slack-jawed from a saber slash, limping from a bullet wound, angry and weary at life.

Margie had been raised on the belief that evil was all around and she must mind her tongue and her manners. The truth of such parental assertions never before manifested so apparently; the cloud faces glared not just at her, but at all the town of Post Rock, all the world. Some hung with wretchedness, burdened by icicle eyelashes, giant gray eyes twisted and weeping, cheeks hollowed and storming. Others burst with fury, curlicue lines for eyes that widened with hideous schemes. The sky was a rage, a horrible, judging sentinel, and it found fault with what it beheld.

When Margie confessed all this to her sister, Pearl said, "I don't see what you do, but I will always protect you. I will save you in ways you cannot even imagine."

And Margie was satisfied with that.

She witnessed the masked clouds thereafter, infrequently over the years, and only when her eye was sick, only when she suffered infection, and people around her spoke of fever dreams. The clouds, regardless of how alarming their demeanor appeared, proved harmless. After all, what malevolence could billows sow? And Margie wondered why she alone saw them, and she wondered why her bad eye showed so much more, shadows that walked of their own accord, ghosts of people she'd never met, reflections *inside* reflections that hinted at other things, the same as trying to make sense of shifting cloud shapes. But whether she thought them physical aberrations or madness, when Margie felt afraid, she remembered what Pearl had said.

I will save you in ways you cannot even imagine . . .

And if that were so, Margie would always remain safe. Pearl was the most inventive person she'd ever known. Pearl could image anything to save Margie . . .

But now Pearl was dead.

Margie made her way up Main Street, as she had oft before, in carriage or buckboard, on horse, or even a big-wheeled bicycle. The dead watched her pass, sightless eyes staring. Gusting winds seemed to carry whispers from silent lips: "Nice enough day, ain't it, Marge?"

There, Earl Thompson's slat-side truck—the first motorized vehicle in town—slumbered on wood blocks, its front hood popped open in display, some lever or gear in mid-repair. That repair would never be completed, at least not by Earl. He draped over the front seat, dressed in coveralls, crimson dried in rivulets across a face gone blue. Down the road sprawled Greta Chandler, crumpled as a discarded rag, dung running down the backs of her legs. Maybe she'd been on her way to find her husband, Jack, watching the dreadful occurrences all around and not wanting to face such ruin alone.

She'd not made it to him.

Margie passed Jack Chandler further up Main where he lay on the front steps of a granary, one bloated hand clutching his mouth, as if trying to keep that final breath from escaping. In between Greta and Jack lay fifty others. Around Margie hovered the green plague bugs, like floating, twitching fireflies. They seemed to be increasing in number, but still could not ensnare her.

Her mind was tired at guessing what to do next. Pearl would've known, or at least had an opinion on the subject. Pearl had said they should get out of town, but then Pearl had gotten sick, so they'd remained while she died.

There wasn't any easy means to escape. Post Rock was a prairie town, built of tarpaper lean-tos and starshine hope for the future. A railroad track was once laid down, then, realizing it didn't have anywhere worthwhile to go, slipped into dereliction. But the town had already founded and there was plenty of land for homesteading, and crops were bounteous, so people stayed. The next nearest town was Norton, forty miles away, and by then you were half way to Kearney. A good horse and a long day might make Norton, but all the horses died alongside the people, as did the mules, donkeys, oxen, and other pack animals; the saddles, carriages, wagons, and carts were all useless.

A forty-mile journey on foot, half along Route Four, then half across brush and rock wasn't an impossibility, but it begged the question of futility: *Would Norton even be safe or was it just as decimated as here?*

Margie felt more fearful of what the rest of Kansas was like, the nation, the world. 'Course, Margie was always the more fearful of the sisters. But if Post Rock could collapse so suddenly, what was to stop everywhere else? There were other towns to try at other points of the compass, further distances that, in lieu of a wagon or horse or her feet, she'd need a car, though there weren't any useable ones left in town. Post Rock was home to just three motorized vehicles: Earl Thompson's slat-side truck that was under repair, and two Model-T Fords that had absconded away as soon as the sickness began, their drivers shootin' up dust and debris from the back wheels in a rush to cut across the prairie.

She arrived at the sheriff's office, its door held open by Deputy Morgan's bowed corpse. The metal star on his shirt was covered with a sticky substance that also covered his mouth and chin. She wondered if he'd been coming or going from the office when he dropped.

Margie entered, stepping carefully over him. On a back desk was the town's singular telephone, installed only months prior. It was a strange wood box with corded cylinders for the mouth and earpiece, and brass bells that supposedly knocked against each other if someone called.

How many times had she tried to figure it out? The contraption was infuriating. All she wanted was to hear another voice, to know if outside Post Rock the world went on, or if everyone else had fallen to the plague.

There was a crank on one side that spun, though she had no idea if that was part of the telephone. A receiver hook held the earpiece, and when she removed that cylinder and pushed the hook up and down, again and again, nothing occurred. There was a button on the stand and a latch on the box, but when she began fiddling with it, a wire fell off.

Margie hurled the telephone off the desk.

"Useless devil-trick—" She covered her mouth so the germs wouldn't attract to her cry.

Her head ached from fever, and she was wary from guarding at all hours against the disease, and she chastised herself for cursing aloud. Pearl had understood mechanical devices, but Margie found them baffling. She half-believed that If Pearl wanted the phone to ring, she could have thought it, imagined it, and it would have happened. Margie wondered at what she expected now, the ghost of Pearl to call and tell her what to do?

She left the office, stepping carefully again over Deputy Morgan, and trudged back down Main Street and three miles south to her parents' house. She still called it that, though her folks passed a long time ago, and only she and Pearl had remained living there, spinsters to the end.

Overhead the sun lifted high, and she guessed it to be noon. So too overhead were the vicious clouds; their haunted gusts growing stronger, as if to blow Post Rock back to the open prairie land it once had been.

She wasn't brainless and she wasn't deranged. Margie had only schooled through the third grade, but she knew that clouds didn't cause wind, didn't have nothing to do with spreading hematic death to the land. She knew clouds were just so much water vapor rising and falling in the sky, knew they didn't give two hoots about what folks did far below, knew they certainly weren't mechanisms of genocide. . .

And yet now they were.

One time when her eye turned sick, she'd seen a creature bounding from behind Yeddi Jameson's barn, keeping within a dusking sun's long shadow. The creature was small and slight and quick, sized like a goat standing on forelegs, with a head that was much too big for its form, as if a man wore a giant wheel around his skull, looking ready to topple over any moment from the imbalanced burden. But the creature did not topple; it instead leapt easily into the air and sailed upward. Its head that she thought so large and cumbersome was but a weightless orb, glowing like a great star. It was vaporous, and its rays of light shifted many ways. The creature travelled upwards until entering a cloud, and then the cloud opened its eyes and stared back at her.

Perhaps the clouds were just as tainted as herself by some affliction. . .

The wind picked up, and a wild shrub uprooted and blew past. Margie quickened her pace, fighting through the gale until she arrived at her parents' house. Sod buffeted away, and a fence post leaned into the ground, and the shingle and tar roof danced a ragtime against the building's frame.

Margie froze, suddenly sensing a change in her surroundings, sensing that while she thought of other things, the swirling air lost its edge. The yard around her parents' house was mysteriously free of the bugs.

The scrabbling, floating germs hadn't relented yet in three days, and her first thought was that her infected eye simply healed so she couldn't discern the horrible things any longer. At this, an unexpected relief arrived that at least it would all be over soon, one way or the other. Looking upwards though, she saw the cloud faces, and the sight remained terrible. Their images were those of cruel children finding new joy in ripping the legs off spiders. Whorling cheeks billowed and they blew the wind around her in tantrum, picking up dry earth and crops and a chicken coop, hurling them in loose twisters.

But the bacteria were not around . . .

She went inside her parents' house with its shades and shutters kept perpetually closed. A faint glow came through the wallpapered-halls, and there Margie did see a few stray germs pulled along, like being sucked down a slow riptide, to the furthest room where Pearl lay. The house wasn't big, and she could see across it to her sister's shut door. The glow seemed brightest there as it slipped out the cracks of the doorframe, a throbbing cloud in its own right, green as pond scum and radiating wisps like uncombed hair.

Pearl's in there, she thought.

Of course Margie knew Pearl was in there, as that's where she'd left the body. But it was a different sense; something *else* about Pearl was in there.

The flooring was made of slat wood boards, and they squeaked as she stepped on each, moving slowly, pulled toward that shut door as inexplicably as the germs. She passed portraits of mother and father and Pearl and herself, all smiling, all outdated. The door glowed brighter, the luminescence behind it pushing to escape. When she reached it, her hand felt the knob to be cool and she wondered briefly if it were an illusion. But then she opened it, and Pearl lay in bed, mottled hands crossed upon her breast, head angled to look out the window, just as deceased as when Margie left her. Only now, she glowed ablaze. The germs covered her, piled atop each other rows and rows high, countless even if she tried.

The dead of Post Rock—when they first died—all held this faint glow, a color like the pulp of a ripe lime, the color of the plague bugs. But the glow diminished as the body cooled and grayed. Pearl was the opposite, her radiance was increasing until it became hard to look at her. Her corpse attracted the germs in the area; the plague bugs were amassing on her. But what did it mean?

I will save you in ways you cannot even imagine . . .

Pearl was drawing in all the sickness to herself so that Margie would be less endangered. Like fluttering gnats caught on flypaper, the bacteria stuck to Pearl in mounds, and Margie thanked her sibling for so much, so much for this relief!

But the more she looked at this miracle, the more she saw, too, that the germs did not perish, nor were they purposeless. They clung to Pearl, and they seemed to be eating her, to be *rotting* her. Pearl's weathered frame was already decomposing much too fast for normal putrefaction. And more germs floated into the room, joining upon her with greater and greater weight. The corpse shifted, and it was like a mushroom shriveling in the sun; Pearl was breaking down, slowly imploding within herself.

No, no, no, Margie thought; it was a lure, not for the bugs, but for herself. Once the body decayed into bone fragments and dust, she'd be next sought. Margie turned and fled Pearl's room, fled her parents' house, fled the property, not knowing if her sister had tried and failed to save her, or if something else conspired against them.

Now there was nothing holding her in Post Rock, surely no fears lessened by the unknown; the unknown still confronted her even where she lived. For Margie, it was back up the three miles of road, back up Main Street, and she'd be out the other side where crossed Route Four toward the long footpath of chance. The wind blew at her, and she tripped, and she ran, then coughed and rested, and she heard a distant 'poof' and looking back, her parents' house, far in the distance, fell in on itself, just as Pearl must have, and a sky-high wall of plague rose from the remains of all she loved.

She wished now more than anything for a vehicle. *Someday*, she and Pearl had mused, *they'd get a car and drive away from Post Rock.*

The world seemed to spin faster now, the sun bolting in getaway. The ghosts of Doc Stevens and Earl Thompson and Jack and Greta Chandler and all the others lined the road, shaking their heads in silence, as if disappointed in her, as if she'd done them wrong. Maybe 'cause she resolved to leave, maybe 'cause she was the last one standing and didn't deserve to be. Maybe a lot of things. Her infection was getting stronger though, that was sure. What Margie saw appeared more vivid, more substantial. She felt déjà vu as she passed Earl's slat-side truck and the granary, and then appeared the open door to the sheriff's office.

From there, she heard the telephone ring.

Margie's heart leapt almost as much as she herself at that sound. It rang a second time, a jangling blare cutting through the whoops of wind. She ran into the office, this time leaping over Deputy Morgan.

There was the back desk, but the phone wasn't on it. Margie's eyes widened and she made a noise like stepping on a thorn. It rang a third time, there, on the floor in the corner where she'd earlier hurled it. She shot to it and picked up a brass cylinder in each hand, placing one to her ear, one to her mouth.

"Hello! Hello!"

Silence.

She flipped the box around and switched the cylinders. "Hello?"

Nothing but silence. The cord to the mouthpiece hung loose, and Margie stared at it. The telephone wasn't connected to anything, and she remembered before that a wire fell off. *It was broke.*

Outside, the biggest gust yet tore through town, and she heard glass shattering in the distance, and buildings squealed as their attics stretched from basements, like grabbing someone's hair and twisting upwards 'til that person stands on their tippy-toes. A mighty roar thundered along Main Street and she saw through the Sheriff's window, a tidal wave of germs breaking along where she'd just walked.

She would have been contaminated for sure. 'Crushed' might be the more appropriate term. It was the wall of plague following from her parents' house.

The germs flooded the street, then rose up from the ground and dispersed through the air, searching for her. They could seep through buildings, sure, and they'd soon enough make their way into here, but Margie was safe for a moment.

She looked again at the busted phone, the mystery ring that called her inside.

I will save you in ways you cannot even imagine. . .

Was it Pearl all along, leading her, protecting her? Margie knew she had to get out now, before the multiplying germs reamassed.

She stepped over the deputy and went through the door and hugged the walls outside, making her way north up Main, from building to building, trying to stay beneath overhangs, in alleys, wherever it was dark, wherever she was sheltered from the sky. The town's clustered shops petered out quickly to a few lean-tos. The wind caught her and pushed her out into the open, and it roared, and the plague bugs sallied forth.

Away in the distance she saw a sparkle that was sunlight striking metal. From its location, it appeared to be on Route Four, snaking around the bend that broke away from the road to Norton. But with the wind whipping debris and grit across the sky, it was hard to tell.

She squinted her eyes. Her left eye immediately hurt and teared up, but she focused through her right and, *yes, it was a car!* It really was on Route Four and it was coming toward town. It was difficult to make out, but there were great billows behind the vehicle; it must've been shooting up dust from its wheels as it sped along. She thought she'd be rescued, and she thought she had to warn the driver not to get any closer, because surely he'd catch the death that swirled amongst Post Rock.

And the winds blew greater now, the clouds moving in, the things that they were, the faces of goblins, blowing and blowing with spewing mouths. The bacteria spread and bred, disease marching across every gust, every building, every corpse.

They were swarming and turning frenzied, and Margie thought: *Was it because their sole captive might finally have found means to liberation?*

In an instant, she was running.

Where before the germs lingered and wafted, they now hurtled toward her. The clouds huffed and exclaimed and blew billions of the things around in maddening squalls, trying to infect her, but they worked against themselves in that regard, too. The germs were blown so rapidly and irregularly about, they could not latch onto the escaping woman. Those tubular forms of pestilence brushed against her and then slipped past, swirling in wild loop-de-loops.

Margie was never a fast runner, such is the life in small prairie towns that excitable actions were discounted, and folks grew accustomed to meandering when they needed to get from one point to the next. But she strained every muscle in her legs, charging with untested velocity out and along the road, sliding on loose gravel, dodging around the worst of the spinning germs, climbing up the paved incline and stumbling down the decline, gasping and waving her arms wildly above her head.

If only she could get to the car, and the driver would turn tail and ferry her away. But still, she realized, she knew not how far the plague had spread. The winds of woe may blow across all the world.

I'll take the chance, she thought.

Weaving and bobbing, Margie continued, clawing into the storm, occasionally looking up, and if the flying rubbish happened to part at just the right moment, to see the car ahead. It seemed impossible, but the distance between her and it had hardly lessened. Whatever minor piddling advancement she made, surely the vehicle should have travelled ten times that amount in half the time. She should be near, but the car was still so far, dust continuing to billow out from behind its back wheels!

Blasts of hot summer air assaulted her, exhalations from the clouds trying to check her flight. Their shriveled, hateful faces realigned and, instead of gusting in wild maelstroms, they blew together now, against her, so that Margie had to lean forward, like the slope of a roof to the ground. But she progressed, one foot after the other, shouting over the storm's vehemence for the car's aid.

And the germs sought her still, but they now numbered less, by chance blown backwards as the clouds railed against her. This angered the shapeshifters further, for they had thwarted themselves again, and still Margie advanced, one foot after the other.

She was gaining ground, drawing closer, closer.

The sky began to darken unreasonably for a summer 'noon. As if realizing their quarry might chance away, more cloud people blew across the heavens, coming in from far behind the car, where rose another wave of heaven-high wriggling, flying, heralds of disease.

Margie reached the car.

It was a Model T, once gleaming black as polished ebony, but now scuffed and dented from wind damage. The driver's door hung askew, sometimes swinging closed, sometimes swinging open. A dead man lay on his side in the fetal position about ten feet away on the ground, his long tongue like a pink snake, extruding from behind desiccated lips. The car was cold and lifeless and appeared not to have been driven for some time.

The billows of dust she'd seen from behind its wheels were merely the work of the wind; little dust devils spurted up, giving the illusion of it speeding along.

Margie's spirits collapsed, and her body nearly followed suit. The goblin clouds roared in laughter at their trickery; she'd be going nowhere. The germs circled all around, a rising flood, on which her island was receding. They'd saved her last, she who had dared espy them, she who knew their true form.

If she closed her sick eye and gazed out through her right, she was only caught in the midst of a nasty little squall. If she looked out only through her infected eye, however, she saw masses of glowing microbes converging on all sides. Weariness surged, and Margie remembered it'd been a long time since last she slept. She took a step, then another, climbed the car's running board and swung into the driver's seat, closing the door after her, though the effort was negligible. It was an open-air vehicle and there were no side windows. She'd never been inside one before and hadn't that been a dream of hers and Pearl's, to someday drive?

The winds blew crossways, and the car shook. The nearing disease landed where it wanted and advanced upon the metal hood, then reached over the lip of each door. She was entirely surrounded. If the germs were a cyclone, she was in its eye, protected in a convulsing, spinning pocket of safety that gradually narrowed and faltered. Either by momentum or their own volition, the plague bugs lurched over the frame and that safety was no more. They fell onto her legs, and they tickled as any stray hairs would, then she felt their clawing under the bodice of her dress. She threw her hands out by instinct to brush the wriggling things away, but wherever she touched them in flailing, sweeping motions, the germs stuck to her fingers like so many parasites caught upon flypaper. They scuttled under the beds of her fingernails and soaked into the knuckled folds of her skin.

The winds screamed, the clouds howled, the sky broke apart in millions of cracks that spread from horizon to horizon.

Margie coughed. She coughed again. The fever throbbed between her temples and she wondered how long it'd been rising, wondered if it was her eye infection all along. She leaned back and the leather seat made a sound like crinkling paper. The bacteria—or was it a virus? Even Doc Stevens hadn't been sure—washed over her in silence. The clouds had won.

It wasn't as bad as she expected, though she wished her breaths weren't so difficult to take. Margie wished a lot of things, not least of which involved seeing her sister again. Her eyes drooped, closing slowly on that wish.

"You tried, sis, as I tried," Margie whispered, "but there ain't no saving either of us." She hoped for, but didn't expect, any reply.

And then a new wind—gentler than the plague winds—took hold of the car's front grille and began to push the vehicle in reverse. The Ford rolled effortlessly back up the road, back past fields of wheat and hay, past dead horses laying in their pastures, past other Model T's, motionless and forgotten like children's lost toys, back past Route Four that led to Norton and Kearney, past the Oak tree with a thousand fingers, past the dreams of hers and Pearl's childhood, and then the car began to rise up into the air, still in reverse, sailing, sailing high amongst the clouds, and these were regular clouds, scoops of ice cream and twists of vanilla taffy, not the cruel shapeshifters filled with hate and disease. Margie looked through the windshield and out onto the land far below and thought nothing about being turned loose upon the skies, carried away on Pearl's promise.

But what she did see, so very far down, were pale faces of two pale little girls, so like clouds themselves, looking back up at her as they talked of schooling and books and ponies and boys, and she wondered why they showed such different expressions, one of amazement and one of joy.

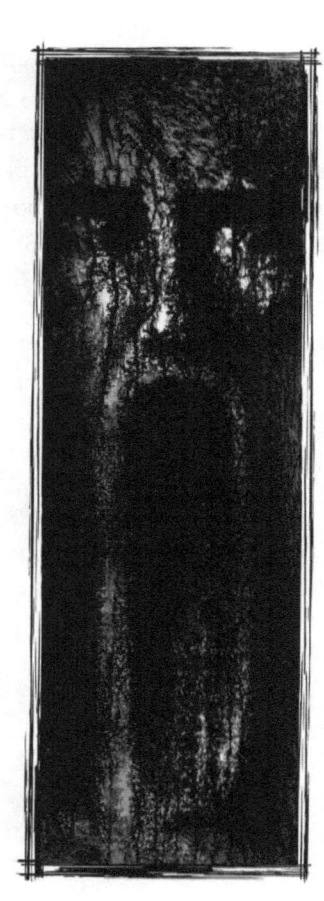

Dennis Etchison

THE MAN WHO KNEW WHAT TIME IT WAS

"This one's reserved."

The voice was close, like a breath on the back of your neck.

"I don't see a sign."

"She always sits here." The other man wheeled a suitcase to the rail and turned, blocking the view of the pool below, where children slapped water with their small hands and pink feet. Then he began texting, his head cut off by the umbrella above the table. He could have been anyone. It wasn't worth fighting about. There were plenty of places to sit.

"Sorry."

A chair scraped cement as the other man positioned it, glanced up and waved his arms.

"Over here!"

A slim, attractive older woman with round John Lennon glasses stood under the awning at the rear of the hotel. She located the voice as the other man hurried to her, took his wrist and allowed him to lead her across the sun-drenched terrace.

"Why, hello." She squinted and extended a graceful hand as she sat. "We've met before, haven't we?"

"I don't believe so."

"Pity." Her long fingers lingered. "I'm Lee."

"David."

"He was just leaving," said the other man.

"Oh, please, not yet. Are you here for the Convention?"

"Just for the day."

"Lucky you. They've got me booked solid, all the way to the Dead Dog Party." Her eyes narrowed, trying to focus. "Forgive me, but I'm blind as a bat in this light."

"I brought your other ones." The other man placed a pair of dark glasses on the table and sat next to her.

"Tom, I don't know what I'd do without you." When she switched glasses there was a quick flash of clear, wide-set eyes. "Will you be at the signing, David?"

"What?" With the late-afternoon sun at her back, her hair was flecked with gold. Her eyes, too. "I mean, yes. So they tell me."

"You *are* a writer. I knew it. And are you famous?"

"Only one book. And a review in *Locus*."

"Congratulations. I remember my first—a tiny print-run from a small press in Chicago. No one took much notice, of course . . ."

"Sure, Lee," said Tom. "It won the Spectre."

"That was years ago."

"Wait." She was not wearing a name badge but there was something familiar about those pale, transparent eyes, the color of robins' eggs. It wasn't possible. "You're not—"

"No?" She smiled demurely.

"Not Lee Crayne."

"Sometimes I don't believe it, either. If I listened to what people say about me, I'd envy myself." She turned her head. "What time is it, Tom?"

The other man consulted his phone. "Six thirty-seven. Plus a few seconds. Leaving us almost exactly twenty-three minutes."

"Is it far?"

"The Mission."

"I thought that was closed."

"Not all of it."

"Ah. Then I suppose we should be on our way."

"We have to wait till the Monitors come for us."

"Mmm. I don't like the sound of that, do you, David?"

"I'm not sure. This is my first time."

"Then we must do something to make it special. Are you free for dinner?"

Tom checked his phone. "After the signing, you have drinks with an editor from the U.K. Nine-thirty."

"Oh, that blowhard. All he cares about is posh editions for collectors. Tell him breakfast tomorrow, the Cantina Deli. As late as possible. Now then. Where should we dine, David?"

"Hmm. Cactus Jack's isn't bad, I guess. Across the bridge, behind the hotel. I had a nice lunch there. With mariachis."

"Sounds exotic."

"It's off-grounds," Tom told her.

"Then you may stay here and scrounge up something in the Con Suite. I'm sure they have an endless supply of raw vegetables and Triskets."

At that moment a frantic clanging came from the pool enclosure. A cook in a colorful sombrero banged a triangle with an iron horseshoe, smiling proudly as a barbecue ignited behind an old-fashioned covered wagon. A cloud of black smoke rose into the sky. Children cheered and parents captured the moment on their phones.

"What am I missing?" she asked, peering over the frames of her dark glasses.

"The Friday Night Chuckwagon Grill," said Tom dismissively, as the aroma of sizzling meat wafted up to the terrace. "All you can eat."

"Lucky devils!"

"It's for the Mundanes."

"Smells heavenly."

Children dragged themselves out of the pool, dripping inkblots on the concrete. One boy stretched the back of his T-shirt up over his head like a wet caul. On the horizon the trunks of tall, skinny palm trees might have been contrails in the brassy sky as sparks flew upward. An orange sun blazed behind the spiked tops as though the fronds were afire, while a half-dozen monks in robes emerged from the foliage next to the enclosure, heading this way.

"It's time," announced Tom.

They followed a path around the pool, away from the dying sun. The smell of barbecue grew fainter, and the chirping of distressed birds was only the wheels of Tom's suitcase rolling over cobblestones. The red letters that spelled EXTENDED STAY atop the hotel grew fuzzy in the distance. One of the Monitors turned and lowered her hood. She had bobbed red hair with green streaks.

"Am I walking too fast?"

"Not at all, dear," said Lee. Then, in a whisper, "How old does she think I *am*?"

The girl, who was barely out of her teens, flashed a shy grin. "Can I tell you a secret?"

"By all means."

"I read *Queen of the Red Mist* when I was in middle school. It changed my life."

"What a terribly sweet thing to say."

The girl blushed. "Anyway. If you need help with your stuff . . ."

"I think we can handle it," Tom said, steering the suitcase past her.

"Lovely costumes," said Lee. "Like something out of a Hammer film."

"I know!" said the girl. "Aren't they amazing?"

"Did you make them yourselves?"

"Yeah, no. I mean, Brianna—she's in charge of cosplay—she found the pattern and everything. She's awesome."

Ahead, the chirping slowed.

"I see it," called Tom.

Lee blinked behind the dark glasses. "*What* do you see?"

"The Mission."

Lee lowered her glasses and focused past the monitors. "My eyes are getting worse. Where—?"

"Don't worry about it." The girl touched Lee's elbow for support. "There's nothing to see."

"Isn't it the main attraction?"

"It was. The stained glass windows were crazy. It's closed for repairs now, except for the dungeon."

"Since when do missions have dungeons?"

"Well, that's what we call it. It used to be a Spanish word. I forget."

"*La cárcel*," muttered one of the monitors.

Ahead, the path ended at the replica of an early California town square, with wooden sidewalks and quaint storefronts. In the center was the original Mission San Encino, one of many founded in the 18th century by a Franciscan priest. Three sides were now roped off for repairs and covered by tarps and scaffolds. An endless line of fans with wristbands snaked between period tourist shops laid out in forced perspective, like an Old West set on a Hollywood backlot. *Trinity Beauty Spa* read the sign on one, next to *Mario's Eyeglass Hut* and *No-Name Neopolitan Pizzeria*. Only the fourth wall of the original structure was exposed. A large arrow with the words *This Way Down* pointed straight into the ground.

The girl raised her hood and walked them the rest of the way.

"Watch your step, okay?"

—

The sky winked out as they descended worn steps behind the Monitors, who carried LED flashlights instead of torches. They entered a passageway under a low adobe ceiling reinforced by rough-hewn crossbeams. The brick arches were strung with electric lightbulbs.

"David?"

"Here."

"Would you mind holding my hand?"

"My pleasure."

"Tom? Where are my other glasses?"

"I have them." The wheels of the suitcase bumped on over an uneven dirt floor. "As soon as we get there—"

"Get where?"

They entered a long room with a low vaulted ceiling.

"Dealers Row," said Tom.

Judging by the heavy wooden tables, it had once been a dining hall, the rows of small doors in the walls the monks' sleeping quarters. Several dealers had set up partitions for makeshift booths displaying genre movie posters and books for sale. Almost a dozen science fiction and fantasy authors were already seated behind placards. Most of them greeted Lee warmly as she passed. A gentleman with a stiff back and a neatly-trimmed white moustache rose to kiss her hand.

"Lee, my dear. How wonderful to see you."

"And you, Bob. Why weren't you at the Living Legends panel?"

"Apologies," he said wearily. "Too much time away from my work. You know how it is."

"I did, once."

"Got to keep the books coming. That's what they tell me."

"They? Don't listen to *them*. They'll suck you dry. With my backlist, I never have to write another word. Except for autographs."

"In that case, love, you have a full evening ahead of you."

The red-haired Monitor held out a folded card with Lee's name printed on it.

"Here you go, Mrs. Crane."

"Thank you. Oh and it's *Miss*."

"My bad." Again the girl blushed. "I sure hope you win."

"I didn't know it was a competition."

"Well, not exactly. But there's WesternCon and LostCon and a bunch of others—and this year they're all gonna be at the same place. It's a whole lot easier that way. I'd *love* it if you could stay."

"Wouldn't that be convenient. But I'm sure it's up to the Con committee."

"We're trying something new, to give everybody a fair chance. After all, it's books that count, right? Books that people want to read."

"I couldn't agree with you more."

"Go for it, Miss C. Good luck!" The girl winked. "You can sit anywhere you like . . ."

"Come along, Lee," said Tom, taking the name card. "I see a couple of spaces."

"I'll have to take your word for that."

He claimed the end of the longest table.

"Here, David," she called, patting the bench. "With me."

"Are you sure?"

"I insist on sitting between my two handsome gentlemen."

"There's not enough room," said Tom.

"Of course there is. Put your case under the table and scoot over.

Friends are the best thing that can happen to anyone."

The Monitor returned with another name card.

"Are you Mr. Matthews?"

"Afraid so."

She turned to Tom. "And you, sir?"

"Dr. Yost."

"I don't see a place card for you."

"Don't worry. I don't need one." Tom began unpacking the books from his suitcase. As he finished, the Monitor stepped to the middle of the room and took a deep breath.

"So welcome, everybody, to our group signing, sponsored by the Western Specialty Press Concurrence! Ready? Remember, every book counts! Three, two, one, and . . . *the game is on!*"

The ceiling thumped and creaked and scuffling fans swarmed down the earthen steps and into the dining hall. Some paused to purchase books from the dealers, while others toted armloads of well-preserved hardcovers and lurid paperbacks in plastic wraps and old convention programs and dogeared magazines. The Monitors checked wristbands as a line formed in front of Lee.

"Glasses, please."

Tom patted the pockets of his jacket.

"*Now*, Tom. I can't see what I'm signing."

"Oh no."

"Now what?"

"I'm so, so sorry, Lee, but I must have left them on the terrace. Not to worry. I'll place the books in front of you. All you have to do is sign your name."

And so he did, from time to time replenishing a stack of the latest title from his suitcase and selling them directly, writing receipts and banking the money in a cashbox, as respectful collectors shook her hand with nervous fingers and hunkered behind the bench to pose for pictures.

"Hard to believe I wrote all of these," sighed Lee during a brief pause. "So many lives ago. I advise you to work at your own pace, David. Otherwise they'll eat you alive."

"Point taken."

"And where are *your* books?"

"At one of the booths. Nether Regions, I believe." Yes, that was it. "My publisher was supposed to send them a carton."

"Ah, Mal and Chris. Good people. They handle most of mine, as well. Shouldn't you confirm that they received the shipment?"

"That's all right. I signed a couple. I'm not a big attraction here."

"There's no rush. You will be one day. Remind me to buy a copy."

"I'll give you one."

"On the condition that you add a personal inscription."

"It's a deal."

More books were arranged in front of her by the next in line. The paperbacks bore vivid, expressionistic covers, carefully preserved in Mylar bags, as were the old hardcovers, all valuable first editions from quality small presses. Lee held one close to her face and squinted to make out the title.

"Do you have this one yet?" said Tom, holding up a hardcover. The suitcase was almost empty.

"Is it new?" asked the fan.

"Brand new," said Tom quickly. "There's a special Con discount. Ten percent off."

"Save one for David," Lee told him. "Gratis, of course."

Tom hesitated. "We only have two left. I brought twenty-four, and—"

"Take it out of my royalties."

Reluctantly Tom handed over the last copy. It was a trade paperback fresh from the printer, with the classic painting of Lee by Ed Emshwiller on the cover. She still had the cheekbones. And those eyes. *Tales of Futures Past: A Study of Lee Crayne's Mist Chronicles, Edited by Thomas Yost, Phd.*

When the other man leaned across her with the last copy, his jacket opened far enough to reveal what poked out of his inside pocket: the top of the frame and one of the clear, untinted lenses of the round glasses she had removed on the terrace earlier. The pair he said he had left behind.

Now, as Monitors moved between the booths, recording numbers, what was happening became all too clear. They were tracking how

many books by each author were sold. This was a competition to determine — what? Who was the most popular? Of course. The winner
would qualify for an extended stay at the resort; that was what the
Monitor said. Tom was determined to win at any cost. He had brought
a case of his own self-published title, moving copies like hotcakes right
under her nose. And she had no idea what she was signing.

"Excuse me, Tom. I need to stretch my legs."

It was good to slide off the bench and away from the other man. The
Nether Regions booth was near the entrance.

"Hi. I'm David Matthews."

"Hi!" said Chris. "We were wondering if you made it."

"Over there, next to Lee Crayne."

"Wow," said Mal. "Nice work if you can get it. We haven't sold a
whole lot of yours yet."

"How many of hers?"

"New editions? Let's see. Ten *Red Mist*, six *Green Loreleis*, plus three,
no, four *Voyage to Nocturnia*. For a grand total of . . ."

"Twenty," said Chris. "If she signs the rest of the stock, they'll mail-or-
der super-fast. Her readers are hungry."

"I'd like to pick up a few while I'm here. For Christmas gifts."

"Sure. We'll give you a professional discount. How many do you
need?"

"How many do you have?"

⸻

As the autograph session wound down the Monitors made a final
tally of the dealers. The authors remained in place while the fans dispersed. The red-haired Monitor leaned over the long table.

"You did really, really well, Miss C."

"I must have signed a hundred paperbacks."

"We're only allowed to count new," said the girl sadly. "That's the
rule. You were a close second, though. Very close."

"Nether Regions sold some at the last minute."

"Did they, David?" said Lee. "And how many did *you* sell?"

"Not many. But they just moved a few more of Ms. Crane's. Better
double-check."

The Monitor brightened. "I will!"

"No need." Tom said impatiently. "We sold twenty-four *Tales of Futures Past.*"

The Monitor was puzzled. "That's not on the list."

Tom patted his jacket pockets again. This time the glasses rattled so that he could not pretend they weren't there. He reacted with surprise and set them on the table. Then he showed the Monitor his receipt book and unfolded a sheet of paper.

"I'm distributing on the West Coast. See? Here's the shipping invoice."

She revised her total. "Well, if we add those—it's a new record, actually!"

"How kind of you, Tom, to count your sales with mine."

"Why wouldn't I? *You're* what they came for. They're your stories. Without your name I couldn't have sold a copy to my grandmother. Well, could I?"

The other man spoke the truth.

He accepted the handshake. "Thanks, uh, David. What kind of shyster did you think I was?"

That was a hard one to answer.

"Congrats, Miss C!" said the girl.

Tom stepped aside as she helped Lee to her feet.

"Now you'll have so much more time."

"For what?"

"To write!"

"Dear," said Lee, "I'm afraid I'm all written out."

The Monitor walked her toward the ancient wall, where several doors were already open. The man with the white moustache returned to one of them, glanced back at Lee and gave her a tired thumbs up before he pulled his door closed behind him.

"Just think," said the Monitor, "no more flying around from Con to Con. What a waste, huh? Well, now you have all the time in the world! How about a sequel to *The Green Lorelei*? That's one of my favorites. Or whatever. You must have so much inside, waiting to come out. Your fans have been waiting, too. They *need* you! After all, the books are what counts. Isn't that right?"

Tom stepped forward. "What are you saying?"

The girl reached under her robe and held out a long, folding key, hinged in the middle. It had been made centuries ago. The girl used it to open the one door that had yet to be unlocked. The other Monitors were already leading the remaining authors back to their small cubicles.

"Here's her key. And don't worry. It works from the inside, too."

"Wait," said Tom. "I think someone's made a mistake . . ."

Someone had. First about Tom. Then about the contest. Which someone else—no, the both of them—had wanted to be sure she would win. But win what?

"Tom's right. A misunderstanding."

"Lee?" Tom said tightly. "I think it's time to go."

The Monitor laughed nervously. "What's wrong? I mean, it's not like you're a prisoner or anything. You can go out any time you want. Just be back for the vespers bell, 'cause that's when they lock the building. Okay? Ms. Crayne?"

"And what do *you* think, David?"

"I think it's time for dinner."

"That sounds divine," she whispered. "Are you quite certain?"

Her words were a warm breath against your neck.

"You don't owe them anything. You've given enough."

"But without them, who would I be?"

"May I make a suggestion?"

"By all means."

"Let's find out."

She looked up at him, her eyes sparkling again in the incandescent light. "Yes, dear boy. I think that's a splendid idea. Let's." And, turning to Tom, "Shall we?"

The other man slipped a pair of clear glasses onto the bridge of her nose. And then you and the other man walked her up the stairs and into the blue night.

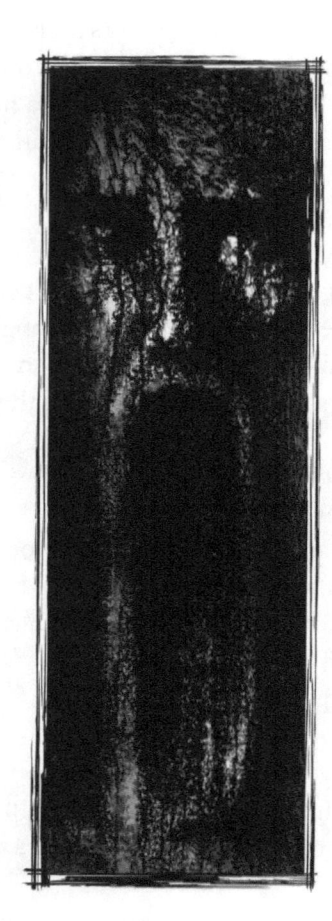

James Dorr

THE RE-POSSESSED

It was our Immortal Bard who stated, through the lips of his Danish Prince, that there are more things in heaven and earth than may be even dreamt of in our philosophies. Of this I have no doubt. Nor would I now question so much either the words of that American poet, E. A. Poe, concerning Life and Death, that "who shall say where the one ends, and where the other begins?"

I had myself a few years past, perhaps twenty some years after that same Mr. Poe's death in 1849, been on a mission for the sake of an aunt of mine to go into London to make certain arrangements. And as it happened, I and the gentleman who I was dealing with, a Daniel Higdon, having to wait on some assistant or other of his to determine some matter concerning the churchyard, fell into conversing.

"I see," Higdon started, an elderly man yet large in stature and, judging from his voice, seemingly still quite enough filled with vigor, "that you are a squire, a gentleman by your dress?"

I suppressed a chuckle then, I must allow, in that his own dress—the worn, black frock coat; the black, crepe-hung top hat—left no doubt to anyone what it was *he* was. So, instead, I nodded.

"You must understand, sir," Higdon went on, "the reason I ask, that I will deal only with gentlemen these days. I mean with *true* gentlemen, those that will keep their words and not renege on agreements afterward. I mean no impertinence; rather, I say this because of a happening some years ago that, had it turned otherwise, might have left me in ruin. And yet, as it fell out, it, may have been worse for me in the long run, in terms of peace of mind."

Well, I thought, this was, despite his denial, certainly at least *some* sort of an impertinence, yet this Higdon was one I had sought out because of a reputation for honesty—scrupulous honesty—which is always a consideration in arrangements of the sort we discussed. So for my aunt's sake, for sake of her bereavement, I bade him go on.

"I have been," Higdon said, "an undertaker for nigh these fifty years, going back even before the Warburton Act of '32, that which permitted the bodies of those died in paupers' hospitals, provided no relative should state objection and that they be, afterward, interred in hallowed ground, to be used by surgeons for their instruction. For mind you, sir, there was need enough for that—especially here in our own King's College—for how is a doctor to help preserve life if he does not know, first, the workings of that which the soul inhabits?

"But I get ahead of myself on this. The thing was, in those days, the profession I follow was different from these days, and sometimes attended with danger to boot. Gangs of criminals sometimes calling themselves 'resurrectionists'—they 'raised the dead,' you see—sometimes called 'sack-em-ups' for their method of carrying off their prey, hovered near churchyards awaiting burials, so, at night, they might reclaim the corpses to sell to anatomists. It was a trade, as mine, but one opposed to mine in that, you understand, it is my duty to see the deceased at peace. Not cut apart on some lecturer's table."

I shuddered, I think. I had heard of these things, of course, but many years ago. How indeed—I realized what he was getting at—there were sometimes even what one might call practically pitched battles between these resurrectionists and the men paid by undertakers like Higdon to stand guard by new graves. By graves with "inhabitants" still "fresh" enough to be useful to surgeons.

Higdon nodded. "You do understand, then, that this was at some expense, paid from the pockets of men like me—we ourselves sometimes joining those that we hired—to see the graves of at least the wealthier, those whose patrons might then reimburse us as part of our fee, warded from those who would thus desecrate them. And, as we have discussed already, there are other fees, coffins, winding-sheets, tips for the sexton, not to mention the labor we do ourselves for the deceased, to make them presentable for their funerals.

"Now, sir, are you squeamish?"

I shook my head, no. I did not think that I was. Yet I did not know, not yet, what this tale would be. How it would end up.

Higdon smiled. "Good," he said. "Now I must say I was just starting out in this trade on my own, having formerly been an employee of others, and it was all important to me that I should establish a good reputation. You understand that, sir, not just in the work I did, of highest quality and, yet, discretion too—ours, for reason, is called 'the dismal trade'—but also as a man versed in the business side. Honesty, after all, cuts both ways, does it not? And thus I jumped at an early commission, this from a wealthy man, a man of business, whose young wife had just passed on, one who was younger than he by a score of years. One who was beautiful, lively, charming, from all that I heard of her, and much in love with *him*— that is important, that she *did* love him well. Though, as I learned soon, he did not deserve her.

"For he was no gentleman for all his riches, this John Andercost. Yes, I may state his name—it does not matter. At least not any more. He disappeared, some say he went mad first, shortly after this story I tell you, leaving no descendants one knows of.

"While as for his deceased wife, Calantha Andercost. . . ."

Higdon paused then and reached into his frock coat, drawing forth a flask. Passing it to me, the air being chilly I took a small tot as well, as he continued: "This John Andercost had many business friends, clients and the like, which could mean future referrals for me and my services should what I did for him prove to be wholly satisfactory. So I spared no expense, having steadfastly agreed with him as to the particulars. There was to be a laying out, for instance. A viewing. Which meant I must hire a woman to wash the corpse. There must be also a casket of the best—not some temporary affair, mind you, but one to go into the earth with her. These things all add up, you know.

"And then the sexton's costs. Warders for the grave—the year this took place still being no later than 1830, and sack-em-ups roving the streets in profusion. Gravediggers' fees. Ice to keep the corpse fresh before the viewing.

"And it was all worth it. To me. To him, I *thought* —I, of course, had also by then seen the young deceased's beauty, her worthiness of his care. Of all we did for her. And, for the viewing, several came afterward, friends of this Andercost, to compliment me on the skill of my work. On my demeanor, my comforting words, my sense of propriety, remaining at all times well in the background, yet available at the gravesite to assist any who needed assistance. A handkerchief. Nosegays. Yet always discreetly.

"And so, a week later, I had my bill sent to him—*and he refused it.*

"I thought then it must be grief. That or some problem, perhaps, with the families, in settling estates perhaps. These were things that could always happen. And so I waited—one must be discreet, of course— to give him time to gain back his composure.

"And yet, a week later, when I sent my bill again, once more it was returned.

"And then I started to hear the rumors. Rumors that I hoped were certainly false, but that, if true, could destroy my hoped for success for the future. These were not rumors that my work or conduct had in any way been unsatisfactory—indeed I had witnesses to the contrary, anyone who had attended the viewing, or been to the gravesite, even now still guarded, as it would be for a week to come until that which was in would be far enough gone so as to be of no further interest to those who might steal it—but, rather, that in a *business* sense I had been made a gull of. That John Andercost had never had any *intention* of paying.

"And so I allowed just one week more to pass—it still *could* have been grief—before I dismissed my men at the churchyard and, making some pretext, made my approach to my client in person. It was, after all, an important matter: If it were borne out that Andercost cheated me, and got away with it, what chance would I have with even more clever, wealthier clients who might take example from it in the future? In short, Andercost's friends—those that I counted on. Those that, in one or two instances, had already passed hints in my direction that, in time, my services might be desired.

"Thus, receipts in hand, I confronted John Andercost— and once more was rebuffed. 'Let this be,' he said, 'a lesson in business. That one does not get as wealthy as I by paying expenses when one can avoid 'em. I had to see to my dead wife's burial, and all that went with it, because those I do business with expected it—you, of all people, should know about proper form—but now it's over. It's finished, you understand?'

"No, I did not. I played on his guilt—I tried to play on it. His guilt and his grief both. 'But sir,' I protested, 'you did love your wife? I know— I've been told— that she certainly loved *you*. How would she feel if somehow she knew that you had refused to pay for her burying? That her good memory meant so little to you. . . ?'

"Andercost laughed—he was, sir, *no* gentleman. He even *leered* then. I blush to tell it: 'Warm,' he said to me. 'Warm for her bed again, and me between the sheets. She was insatiable, Higdon, a young woman— and, yes, she did love me. But, as for me, well, I loved her beauty, her slender form on my arm when we dined out or went to the theatre with business acquaintances—she had her uses then—but she is gone now, and that is an end to it.'

"Again I protested. I tried to protest. 'Still, Mr. Andercost,' I began, but again he rebuffed me.

"'Still, Higdon,' he mocked me, looming now over me—I am a large enough man, as you can see, but he was larger yet—holding his stick aloft as if to strike me, 'there's no need at all for me to throw good money after bad, is there? The funeral is over. What's done has been done. What's in the ground lies there. If you raise a squawk, let me remind you I have enough money—because I *don't* spend money unnecessarily—to overcome any action you might attempt. So I'll put it to you as a businessman to a fellow businessman: What do you think you can do about it, re-possess my wife's corpse? Sell her yourself, perhaps, to the sack-em-ups?'"

Once again Higdon paused, drawing his flask out. Passing it to me when he'd had a swallow. "God help me, I thought on that, after I'd left him. Of digging up Calantha Andercost's corpse *myself* to get at least a part of my costs back, except, as I've said, it would have been far enough 'turned' by then that I doubted I could have found a taker. So, instead, I wandered—it was afternoon by then, *late* afternoon—walking my own grief out. Not caring too much where I might be going. Until, by chance, I happened to find myself near the dockside.

"And here I must tell you that, when I had been an employee of others, I often took on poorer sorts of clients. Some of them near here, where I had wandered now, and so, by chance, I met with an acquaintance. This was a Negro-man, a Haitian sailor who had seized his freedom during the time of Henri Christophe's rebellion there and never gone back, living in London somewhere in the East End when he was not at sea. And, as you see that I am a large man, this man, who I knew only as Georges-Michel, was even larger. Larger and stronger than even John Andercost.

"So I told him what brought me there, wandering, thinking perhaps—I do not know for sure —that, with night nearly fallen, we might accost this Andercost in his home. Maybe, disguised, to take from him my money. I *was* not thinking well.

"But my friend calmed me—I call him my friend now. He bought a drink for me. We discussed my troubles, how what was really needed was that Andercost not only not get away with non-payment of his bill, but that it be done in a manner that could be plainly seen to be completely just. And, more than even that, if rumors of it should later get out, it might serve as a warning to others who might try to be less than honest in dealing with men like me—men who, after all, did perform a most *necessary* service.

"Thus Georges-Michel said to me, 'I understand, *mon ami.* This *Jean* Andercost, he is a bad man, yes?'

"I answered that he was, adding to that, though, perhaps because I feared what Georges-Michel might do—still thinking, you see, that we might yet assault him—'They say his wife loved him. . . .'

"'And yet it is she, the wife, who this cochon insults. She who has been sullied thus in one's memory. You see, it is simple, yes?'

"I did not see. No. Yet I followed him into Limehouse to where he was staying to retrieve his sea bag, then, taking a carriage, to my own establishment. Then, changing my clothes, at his insistence we went to the churchyard where Calantha Andercost had been interred and, setting our canvas sheet down at the grave's side—this to receive the dirt, you see, so it could be put back when we were done with our work— proceeded swiftly with short wooden spades, a kind that makes little noise, by shaded lantern-light to play at sack-em-ups.

"Except we did not just break off the coffin end when we had reached it, to hook the corpse out and up as sack-em-up men do, always in haste you see—after all, one does not wish to be caught at it—but rather climbed down into the grave ourselves and pried the whole lid off.

"'My friend,' Georges-Michel whispered, 'you *have* spoke truly. I see she is beautiful, or at least that she was. You can see here, though, how some of the rot has already taken her—to be expected, of course, in this length of time. How the grave beetles have burrowed *here* and *here*. And yet, still, some *shadow* of her beauty.'

"I nodded, as I recall, then at his order I scrambled back out to act as a lookout while Georges-Michel worked. I passed down his sea bag. While Georges-Michel spoke on of what he was doing.

"'The *ti bon ange*—what we call where I come from the "little good angel-soul"—it is the thing that is all important. These powders I use now, they will tempt it back. These words that I will say. You see, *mon ami*, insulted so by the one she so loved, this soul, it cannot rest. So there is time yet . . .'

"'Is time,' I echoed him. Well I remember still even the slightest detail of that dark night. 'But time for what, Georges-Michel?'

"'Ah!' Georges-Michel whispered. Sprinkling more powders, he scrambled up himself out of the grave. 'For this, *mon ami*,' he said.

"And at that I shrank back. I nearly ran from there, I will confess it now, except that my friend, Georges-Michel, grasped me by the arm. Because another form, that of a woman, had just climbed out, too, from that yawning, open grave. A woman half-decomposed, one entire side all blackened with it, yet recognizable. One with long, curled, blonde hair, on half its head anyway. Half its face still intact.

"'*Le corps cadavre*,' Georges-Michel whispered. 'In Haiti, where I was raised . . . but wait! The moment comes.

"'Calantha!' he shouted.

"The corpse looked up now, its dull, glassy eyes opening wide. It turned then to gaze at *him*. At Georges-Michel who held something out to it.

"'It is the shouting of the *name* that joins them together, the soul and the body. The *ti bon ange* and *the corps cadavre*. That makes it remember. That and what I feed it now, that which is used by *bokors* on the island I dare not return to. And yet can be found, if one looks hard enough, even here in your London.'

"He turned again to the corpse, speaking in more of a normal voice now, while I, responding to motions his hands made, crept behind them to fill the grave back up. 'Calantha, tell me this. How do you feel this night?'

"The corpse grinned at us both first without speaking, a terrible grin, as, with crumbling hands, it adjusted its grave-clothes. Flicking the worms off as it pirouetted, *then* turned back to Georges-Michel.

"'Warm,' it answered.

"Georges-Michel nodded. Whispering to me he said, 'She can no longer be a *gentlewoman*. That much has been stripped from her, forever lost now. But she *will* remember that which is important. A woman, she knows her needs.'

"She gave a moan then that I will not forget, never until I die. That of an animal—a sound *inhuman*. As if of some beast in rut. While I, trembling, finished the refilling, scooping the last of the earth back onto the grave. Folding the canvas up, the shovels inside it, into a bundle. Blowing the lanterns out, save for the one we would use while walking home. Finally speaking:

"'What now, Georges-Michel?' I asked.

"Smiling, he answered, taking the corpse-woman's arm on his as he led us out to the street, 'In simple justice, my friend, I should say that it is our duty to restore this poor woman to her husband.'"

Michael Sebastian
CLOWN ON BLACK VELVET

For decades, the Joke Joint had stood at the top of Sunset Boulevard, a beacon drawing ambitious dreamers from all over the world in hopes of being endowed with its magic touch.

For a novice like Drew—stuck doing coffee house open mics— landing a bussing job there was a way in, a backdoor to its secrets, and it made up for the shitty pay.

He'd only snagged the job because the previous employee had gotten trashed the night before and didn't report for work the morning Drew first knocked on Heidi's office door. Now he saw every show for free, and studied the comics for ways to improve his own act while waiting for his shot.

But his favorite part of the job was right now, the silence before opening, when he'd steal a chance to stand onstage, the iconic brick wall behind him, and stare out at the empty seats under the glare of the spotlight. So many of his heroes had gotten their start right on this spot: Cliff Stoltz, Russell Barton and his favorite—

"Jackie Elling had your job, you know," a voice said, as if reading his mind.

Drew turned to find Heidi standing in the doorway.

He mumbled an embarrassed apology, then hopped from the stage and over to the nearest table, from which he lifted a chair, flipping it over to stand upright on the floor.

Heidi smiled knowingly. "Rod needs another margarita mix. We got a bachelorette party coming to the first show."

Drew frowned. "They know this is a comedy club, right? Not like hunky firemen?"

"Oh, I didn't tell you? New policy: busboys wear thongs."

"Then they're going to need a lot of margaritas."

Drew finished with the chair arrangements, then headed down the cramped staircase into the basement.

As much as he liked the pre-show silence, the club also gave him the creeps when he was alone. So far, he'd yet to experience anything weird, but his coworkers always joked about ghosts haunting the place.

Drew flicked on the basement's single overhead bulb, and the room burst with hard shadows. He searched the crammed storage racks for the margarita mix, trying to ignore the dark contours in his peripheral vision, scraping at his imagination.

The mix was nowhere to be found. Rod must've forgotten to place an order for more, but somehow Drew knew he'd be the one catching flack for it.

A distant echo of laughter froze him in place.

Drew stood there, straining to hear. He peered around the rack to a rusty steel door. The laugh had come from the other side—male, full-bodied, but with an underlying taint of cruelty in it.

You're acting like a superstitious kid, Drew told himself, glancing up at the heating ducts running overhead.

Just the guys in the kitchen.

He turned, empty-handed, and hurried up the steps.

⁂

Drew watched the opening act from the dimly lit nook beside the curtained showroom entrance.

He glanced at Sandra Kendrick, the night's host, huddling over the mixing board while jotting notes on a card under the small lamp.

Heidi squeezed through the curtain and spoke into Drew's ear. "Tucker cancelled, so we don't have a feature. Can you do ten?"

A jumble of conflicting emotions fought for control of Drew's mouth. This was the chance he'd been waiting for, rehearsing every night and day. Of course he could do ten minutes, he could do thirty!

And yet, as he glanced at the stage, the crowd erupting in laughter all around, he suddenly felt paralyzed, his heart thundering toward its bursting point.

"Hello?" Heidi snapped her fingers.

"Yes," Drew blurted.

Heidi gave him a dubious look and leaned to whisper to Sandra. The host's brow wrinkled. Her eyes flicked to Drew. Then she flipped over her card and crossed something out.

"What's your last name?"

"Szczepanski," Drew said, then when she just stared at him, added, "Shuh-pan-ski."

"Jesus," she said. "Might want to consider a stage name there, buddy."

The crowd burst into applause and the opener left the stage. Drew just stared at the spotlighted stool and mic awaiting him. His hand shook as he realized he couldn't remember the start of his act.

"You're up," Sandra said on her way to the stage. She grabbed the mic, telling the crowd to keep it going for the first act, then added, "Well, you're in for a treat now. You may have seen him bussing your tables, please welcome Drew 'I'd like to buy a vowel' Szczepanski!"

Drew found himself floating toward the stage and taking the mic. He turned to look out at the silent, staring faces, waiting for him to make them laugh. His gaze caught on a figure standing in the shadows at the back of the room.

The guy stared back at Drew from under the brim of a fedora—which wasn't unheard of in Hollywood—but what riveted Drew was his grin. There was something unnerving in it, like he was privy to a joke Drew wasn't in on.

Finally, Drew broke eye contact, but when he glanced back to the front row, he knew he'd already lost them.

The next morning, Drew awoke sweaty in a tangle of sheets, his head pounding. He shuffled downstairs to find his mom in the living room, folding laundry while she watched *The Price Is Right*.

"I got to go up last night," he said.

"Oh," his mom replied, "that's exciting."

Drew waited for her to ask how it had gone, though he knew she wouldn't.

He hadn't bombed—at least, he didn't think it qualified as bombing. True, the bachelorette party began talking halfway through his set, but there weren't any heckles, and he'd gotten a few laughs.

His mom added, "I just don't see why you can't go to school in the daytime and do that at night."

Drew rolled his eyes. *Of course you don't*, he thought, watching his mom align the corners of a towel. She and his dad went to work, came home and spent the night in front of the TV with barely a word to each other, then got up and did the same thing again the next day. They didn't have friends. They'd hardly even left California.

Drew decided long ago that, whatever it took, he was never going to be like that.

He left his mom to the laundry, heading into the kitchen to grab a banana before he went back up to his room to work.

Reclining against his pillow, notebook propped on his knees, Drew labored over polishing his set for when he got another chance to go up—assuming they ever gave him one.

After an hour, he looked at what he'd written and heaved a sigh. He knew it was falling short, he just didn't know how to fix it, how to make it great.

He put the notebook away, stuck in earbuds and brought up Jackie Elling's *Live at Carnegie Hall* on his phone. He'd long ago worn out his VHS copy, but he bought the CD, then the DVD, and always returned to it when he was looking for inspiration. It was Jackie's first special where he really became cynical and cutting, and it was brilliant.

Drew laid back and listened, laughing and marveling at Jackie's genius.

A couple months later, Drew was at work, watching the show from from his usual spot when Heidi burst through the curtain and over to Sandra, huddled again over her mixing board as host.

"We're bumping Lee," Heidi told her. "Jackie Elling just showed up!"

Drew's heart skipped a beat.

He felt the curtain move as someone else stepped through and stood next to him.

Drew snuck a glance. Despite the further receded gray hair, lanky frame and slightly hunched shoulders, Jackie Elling projected the same unmistakable confidence he exuded onstage.

The comedian turned to him and gave a little nod.

Drew realized he was staring, and smiled as if he'd forgotten how.

Sandra announced Jackie, who took the stage to rapturous applause and instantly had the audience eating out of his hand. Even more impressive, the material—Drew realized with giddy excitement—was all new. Jackie must be getting ready to go out on the road and was trying out the new stuff here first.

Drew's eyes were glued to him like Jackie'd stepped out of a dream.

About five minutes into the set, Jackie spotted something in the audience that seemed to make him lose his train of thought. Drew could almost see him start to sweat. Jackie covered it well, filling the gap by taking a sip of water, but Drew knew Jackie.

Something had thrown him.

Drew glanced at the audience, searching for what it could be, and stopped on the man in the fedora, once again watching the stage from the back of the room, that same sardonic grin on his face.

The man turned his head to look at Drew, and the candlelight caught his eyes, making them reflect green like a dog's.

Drew shuddered and nudged Heidi, who was arguing in hushed tones with the night's headliner, Greg Lawrence.

When Drew turned back, the man was gone.

Lawrence's voice was getting louder. "I'm not following Jackie Elling."

"That's real professional, Greg."

"Give Shit-Pants the mic." He flicked his chin at Drew.

Drew'd never heard that particular perversion of his name. One of the benefits of working with comedians, he guessed: more creative insults.

Heidi looked pityingly at Drew, who could only glance between the two like a frightened rabbit.

"He's not a headliner," she said.

Lawrence hooked a thumb inward. "And I'm not suicidal."

"Really?" Heidi said. "'Cause you're not getting booked here again."

"Don't flatter yourself, Heidi. This place ain't what it used to be." And with that, Lawrence stormed through the curtain.

Heidi cursed, looking angrily off into space.

Drew reached awkwardly for her, but stopped. There must be a ton of pressure on her to live up to the legacy her parents built, the evidence of it in the superstars' portraits covering the walls.

Drew hoped it was enough to make her forget Lawrence's suggestion. He turned back to watch Jackie. The whole thing felt unreal. He could envision it as a moment that would seem like fate looking back at the end of a long and successful career, but right now the weight of it was just too much. He wished he were bolder, the kind of person who made their own destiny, seized every opportunity they were given.

Heidi's voice came from behind. "Well?"

Greg Lawrence had been right.

As soon as Drew took the stage, he felt the audience's resentment. The few charitable chuckles soon gave way to silence, which grew into mounting hostility. He sweated through ten minutes of material before he left the stage to anemic applause and headed straight to the bathroom. He threw the lock on the door and leaned over the sink, his heart racing, stomach churning acid. He stared at himself in the mirror through blurred vision, thinking how he never wanted to feel this way again, as some metallic echo filtered up through the drain. It sounded like cruel laughter.

Later, after the crowd had emptied out, Drew went to collect the dirty glasses from the bar and mount the chairs back on their tables.

Something made him pause inside the doorway.

Jackie Elling sat hunched over the bar, flicking a knotted cherry stem around.

Without turning, Jackie said in his gravelly New York accent, "Pull up a stool, the view's better."

Drew hesitated. The last thing in the world he wanted was to face Jackie Elling right now.

"Sit down," Jackie said, more insistently. "You can say you had a drink with Jackie after his last show."

Drew glanced around the empty bar and climbed onto the stool beside him.

"Last show? What—"

Jackie ignored him. "You know why you're not getting laughs? You got no confidence in what you're selling. Your material"—he shrugged—"it is what it is, you're young."

Drew winced.

"You want to be good at this," Jackie continued, turning to look at Drew. "You have to know that you know something they don't. You have to learn to see."

Jackie stared at him intently. His eyes flicked past Drew's shoulder to the showroom entrance and back. "But that don't come free."

Drew nodded. It sounded like sage advice, he just had no idea what it meant.

Jackie must've read it in his eyes, because he gave a silent chuckle, then took a pull on his glass. "You want a real tip? Go to college."

Drew's expression fell to hear his mom's harping come out of his hero's mouth. This wasn't how this was supposed to go.

"It's the only thing I care about," Drew said.

Jackie looked like he was considering saying something, but before he could, Drew felt a cold ripple run over his skin, and he knew they were no longer alone.

"Now now, Jackie," came a smooth voice beside Drew. "Don't want to spoil the joke."

The man in the fedora stood behind the bar, wearing his crooked grin.

Drew recoiled off his stool, as if a snake had just plopped down on the bar, and looked to Jackie.

Jackie just sipped his drink. "Brought you something."

Fedora cocked his head. "Yes, it has been some time for you, hasn't it."

Jackie sighed, shook his head. "I got nothing left."

Fedora slowly turned his head to Drew and Drew's jaw began to quiver under the cold gaze.

"We have observed the boy."

The voice scooped out a hole in the core of Drew's being.

Drew looked to Jackie for help. "Me? Jackie, what—?"

The comedian tilted his glass back and forth, watching the ice shift around in the last drops of alcohol. "Ever wonder why the ones who stick around all seem to lose the magic? Well, congratulations, kid. I'm giving mine to you."

For a moment Drew was dumbfounded. "You can't. I mean, why?"

"It wears on you." Jackie turned to him. "You take it as long as you can. Some guys, that's not very long."

A dozen names and faces flashed through Drew's mind, brilliant comics who'd buckled under their genius, succumbed to addiction, driven themselves to an early grave.

"But you want a shot at greatness," Jackie continued, "this is it."

Drew retook his seat beside Jackie, leaning close. "What is it?"

Jackie looked to Fedora, as if asking permission, then to Drew.

"You know what this place used to be, right?" Jackie asked. "The basement's where Mickey Cohen took care of business. There was a guy, they called him the Jolly Butcher. Tortured people for fun. His signature was to carve smiles into his victims' faces. He did something, opened a wound in the world." Here he studied Fedora. "Something came through."

Drew shot a glance at the figure, who just grinned, unblinking, at Jackie.

Jackie leaned close to Drew, growing more animated. "Ever heard of genius loci?"

"That will suffice, Jackie," Fedora said. Then, turning to Drew: "We offer a gift."

Drew swallowed hard, forcing himself to meet those eyes. "Why?"

Fedora gave an almost imperceptible shrug. "Why put a castle in a fish tank? It amuses us."

"They like to watch what we do with it," Jackie said. "Artists, serial killers, tyrants—everyone else bores them."

Serial killers? Drew could feel his pulse in his throat. "Is it worth it?"

Jackie focused on Drew, and Drew saw for the first time just how old and tired the great comedian looked.

"Kid, he's not asking."

⬤

It was pleasantly warm under the lights at Carnegie Hall, and Drew had worked up a nice sweat as he prowled the stage, mic in hand, launching finely wrought phrases that detonated in laughter, one after another.

Once the initial shock of the Gift had worn off and he'd been able to just watch them—bustling from here to there, always in such a hurry, screaming obscenities in traffic one minute, declaring undying love the next, as they chased some elusive sense of completeness—he finally got the joke.

With it had come success.

It was only here, in the warmth of the stage, when he could listen to the roar of laughter and, with the lights in his eyes, look out over the thousands of happy corpses and almost remember why he'd wanted it so badly.

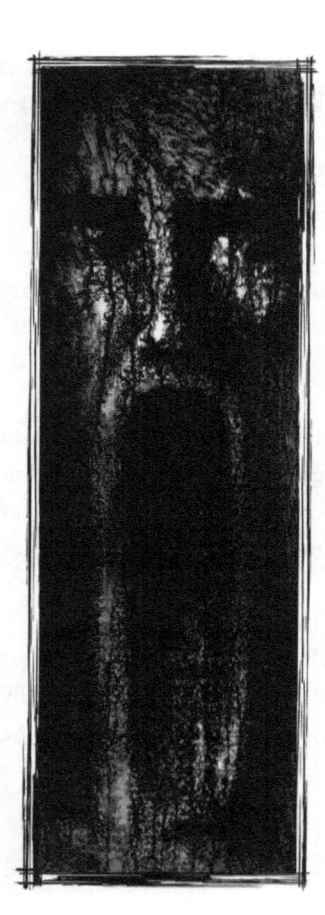

Kelly Kurtzhals

THE CELLAR

The old woman's handful of keys jangled in the blustery February wind, her wispy white hair blowing around her head like a frazzled cotton swab. Her frail body was dressed in denim-on-denim, a major faux pas which Maya noted to herself. Maya believed bad clothing was on par with body odor, and she disliked the woman instantly.

Nate smiled at his girlfriend's pretty downturned mouth as she stared at the offending outfit. He glanced up one last time at the sad tan stucco building before following the woman up the crumbling cement steps.

The woman, who introduced herself as Ida, led the young couple over dingy green carpeting down a long hallway toward the back of the building where it was nestled against a tall hillside. A feeling of dread spread in the pit of Nate's stomach, growing with the certainty that this apartment's low price would be directly proportional to its dreariness.

Landlords charged high rates for what basically amounted to prison cells with kitchens, so he didn't hold out much hope.

"This room has a bonus space, which I technically can't advertise," Ida told them with her crackly voice, motioning them toward the entrance of Unit 7. "Because it's not to code. You probably don't want to use it but it's worth mentioning."

They stepped inside. Maya's pale hazel eyes brightened and she released her breath. The apartment was not terrible. There was an outdated galley-style kitchen to the right of the entryway; the tan carpet had visible stains. The living room had a view of the city squall complete with strings of laundry strung from some windows and up-tempo Latin music streaming out of others. Nate and Maya had already seen every shithole in Los Angeles. One felt like a dungeon, with its only two black-barred windows facing a cement wall. Another had been advertised as having a loft space, which turned out to be a rickety bunk-bed type structure that dominated the miniscule living room area.

This place was still kind of a shithole. But it was a shithole that felt like home.

They followed Ida to the apartment's second bedroom, where a small useless window grazed the hillside it faced.

Nate and Maya stepped across a threshold of peeling paint onto the weathered wood-planked floor.

"I like the hardwood floors," Maya remarked.

"Last tenant tore up the carpet," Ida said. "The owners don't like coming in here, so it won't be replaced."

Ida stepped over to the farthest corner of the room, and only then did Nate and Maya notice the trap door in the floor. Ida bent her skeleton frame slightly, to point to the handle. "There's the bonus space, down there. But like I said, you'd be best to lock this door and keep it that way."

Ida clearly had no plans whatsoever to even touch the trap door handle, so Nate grasped and pulled with both hands. Maya stepped in to help when he struggled, pushing the farthest edge past the halfway point. They peered over the edge at a rough wooden ladder leading down into the dark. Ida clicked a nearby wall switch and fluorescents flickered to life, illuminating the underground room.

Through the gaping hole they could tell it was a large space. Smooth grey cement lined the walls and floors. As far as they could see, the cellar was windowless but the florescent lights seemed to obliterate any creeping shadows that might lurk. It was clean and cool and undisturbed.

"Is the ladder safe to walk on?" Nate asked.

Ida shrugged. "I wouldn't trust it."

He tested a foot on the top rung. "Seems fine to me."

Ida's eyes flickered. Maya put her hand on Nate's arm. "Maybe we could replace the ladder," she said. The way Nate confronted people when he was challenged always made her uncomfortable. "Before we try to go down there."

Nate looked down once more. He could already picture keeping Maya's mountain of fabrics down there. Her aspiring fashion designer lifestyle was already close to drowning him, ever since she moved into his current hovel. But this was just what he needed. He could invite friends over again. He would serve margaritas to go with the Latin music blaring from the neighbors.

"Why would we want to keep out?" he asked Ida.

"Because when you put something in there, the size of the opening to get back out gets smaller."

Nate and Maya laughed at the same time. Ida did not join them. Her sour face insinuated she had seen this reaction before from prospective tenants. A little chill snuck up Nate's spine, but he shrugged it off.

"Very funny," he said.

"Laugh if you want to. But if it was me, I wouldn't put nothing down there." Ida backed out of the room slowly, shaking a wrinkled finger at the couple. "I don't know why it is, but it is."

Nate and Maya didn't believe in the supernatural. Maya believed in square footage, and Nate believed in cheap rent. They signed the lease on the worn white tiles of the kitchen counter, and made plans to move by the week's end.

Though neither of them admitted it aloud to the other, Ida's warning crept into their thoughts. Nate noticed that same chill gripped his spine when he found himself absorbed in his work, plugging away freelance coding for the developers he hoped would soon hear his pitch for a new traffic app that was going to blow all the big guys away. He'd gotten the idea while performing as a street-side sign spinner. A job he never left since it helped put him through online college.

He felt the chill on Melrose on Wednesday, when a white Camaro honked. And again Thursday on Robertson, for no reason at all.

The night before the move, Nate awoke with a start in the middle of the night. He blinked twice and rubbed his eyes and looked around at the boxes filling his soon-to-be-former studio apartment, echoes of his nightmare reverberating in his brain. He was trying to come up the cellar's wooden ladder but couldn't open his eyes.

On the day of the move, Nate didn't say anything when Maya instructed the movers to put her sewing machine atop the rope-braided rug she'd placed over the trap door.

Nate put down his weapon.

He couldn't concentrate on his X-box with the incessant Latin music seeping through the walls and windows. He regretted taking this apartment. Thinking he'd just vanish into a cellar space for quiet. A space that his chills and his dream convinced him to postpone using, to the point where he realized he no longer had any intention of using it.

Maya came out of the kitchen carrying two margaritas, swaying her hips to the beat. Her funky red floral skirt swished out like a fan when she twirled. Nate laughed.

She handed him a glass. "If you can't beat 'em, right?"

He took a sip of the salty concoction. And another. He finished off the full glass and finally admitted, "I had a bad dream about that room."

Maya nodded. "I did too. I went down and there was no door to get out."

"Have you had it again, since we've been here?"

"No, nothing."

"You let that old lady spook you."

"You did too! Look at you, sitting here like el chupacabra is down there waiting to bite you."

Nate handed her his glass. "Get me a refill first."

With his second margarita down, Nate pushed Maya's sewing machine aside and curled up the rug. He grasped the handle and pulled, then leaned the open trap door against the sewing machine. Maya flipped the light switch. A stale breeze wafted up through the hatch.

"You go first," she said.

Nate felt an icicle rake up his spine when his foot touched the first rung. He paused, looking up at Maya. She looked calm, even slightly bemused.

It was his imagination, he reasoned. What harm could possibly come to him in an empty room?

He lowered his other foot to the second rung and let out a piercing scream.

Maya's face twisted with fear as she raced over to help him. He grasped her by both arms. "Oh my God I can't feel my legs!"

His mouth turned up at the corners, and she whacked him on the arm. "You're a damn fool," she said.

"You should've seen your face. Come on, there's nothing down here."

Nate lowered himself all the way inside the room's four grey walls. It felt cool but not clammy. He noticed for the first time the ceiling was bare wood like the floors, and it gave the cellar a rustic feel. It was more comforting than if the ceiling had also been cement like the walls and floor. Almost inviting.

There was an electrical outlet on the innermost wall. It had no cover, only two grey receptacles that made four little dimples in the otherwise smooth surface.

Nate stretched his arms wide and spun himself slowly around.

"Why would we waste this space? This is all ours! Nobody has basements in L.A. This is nuts!"

Maya was still peering down from the top of the trap door.

"Try and come up now. So I can see it's safe," she said.

"Just get in here."

She made her way down slowly and tentatively until she was standing by his side. Tiny icy fingertips of fear brushed lightly against her skin.

"Listen," Nate whispered. "Do you hear that?"

The icy fingertips reached up and touched Maya on the throat. "No, what?"

"Shh." Nate craned his ears to all four walls. Maya listened too, hearing only her heart beating furiously inside her chest.

Nate breathed out a sigh.

"Listen to that quiet!" He laughed and his voice rang out. "You can't hear the neighbors down here!"

Nate jumped gleefully and did a little celebratory dance around the perimeter of the cellar. Maya laughed, and joined him.

Nate and Maya slowly started to fill the cellar. Two rickety folding chairs were first. An upturned apple box to set drinks upon. Then a small television to occupy one of the plug's receptacles. Once the television survived without any indication of the trap door swallowing it and sealing it forever with what Nate imagined would be a big slurping noise, they both relaxed enough to squeeze down two armless easy-chairs they'd picked up off the street to join their other meager furnishings. Their thrift store rummaging turned up a used stereo system where they could play music – anything but Latin. And never too loudly, because though neither of them discussed it, they never closed themselves below with the trap door.

When a fabric store downtown went bust and left reams of unused material in a dumpster just outside Santee Alley, Maya fought off the bums and the aspiring designers to score free goods. She decided the most logical place to store the bulky bolts of loud prints, soft quilting cottons, and a full rainbow of scraps and remnants, was of course, the cellar. Maya had formed something of an unspoken trust with the room. But she reasoned that if the room did mysteriously disappear, these fabrics were free anyway and would not be missed.

Resting in the cool dark quiet of the cellar, the fabrics blossomed. Inspiration struck Maya as unexpectedly and as easily as the bolts of cloth had come into her life. She whirred away on her sewing machine in the room above, the rhythmic snap-snap of the needle keeping Nate up late in the night with a new noise that filled their spare room. A noise of progress. Nate began to think of himself as the benefactor of an artist in residence. His mounting dread that she was never going to be more than a financial burden to him slowly washed away with each new stroke of the needle.

Moving the sewing machine down into the cellar was the most logical progression. Maya needed to continue her work late into the night, free of urban soundtracks. And Nate needed his late nights for sleeping. The old woman's warning had become a mildly amusing encounter with a crazy person and was deliberately cast aside.

Except, the feeling wasn't entirely gone. Nate and Maya hadn't invited any friends into the cellar. They hadn't thrown the parties they originally dreamed about together. The cellar was their secret, sealed even tighter when the room above was converted to accommodate weekend guests. The rope-braided rug was tossed casually over the trap door, never revealing the bonus room to anyone else.

⚬

Nate met a man called Vincent outside some newly renovated townhomes in Larchmont, where Nate was spinning signs to draw customers.

"Don't your arms get tired?" Vincent asked between cigarette puffs.

"Sometimes," Nate replied, not missing a beat in his spinning. "But I like it. Keeps me in shape."

Vincent watched for a while until Nate started wondering if he was being propositioned. Had he not been on the clock, he might've punched the guy right in his goofy man-bun. Instead Nate said, "My *girlfriend's* got strong arms too. She makes clothes. Really cool ones, actually."

Vincent raised his salt-and-pepper eyebrows. He pointed across the street. "I own that shop."

It was a specialty-clothing boutique.

Nate set down his sign and held out his hand. "I'm Nate."

⚬

She was in the cellar when they arrived. Vincent was impressed by the extensive collection that had amassed underground. He offered to purchase three of his favorite pieces for more money than Maya had held in her hands in as long as she could remember.

Two handshakes later, Vincent took one more look around the cellar. "I just have one question," he said with his deep voice that held only a slight trace of an Armenian accent. "How did you manage to get these chairs down here?"

Nate and Maya looked at the chairs, then at the trap door opening. It had been an imperceptible shift, and they realized instantly with a gut-dropping panic that neither of them remembered how or when they stopped checking for it to change.

But the opening was indeed smaller than the chairs.

Nate laughed tightly. "It was quite a squeeze! But somehow we managed."

Maya's face turned a chalky pale. She couldn't help but whisper the truth. "The opening used to be bigger."

Nate hustled Vincent up the ladder as quickly as he could without seeming rude and blowing Maya's deal. Maya was so quickly on his heels she threatened to send the whole ladder tumbling.

"What are you doing?" Vincent's man-bun whipped around mid-climb.

Maya glanced up at him, and the opening. "Sorry, I'm just . . . I need to get out of here!"

She practically pushed him up the ladder and they scrambled all together into the room. When she glanced back down at the trap door, the opening was still there. Vincent was looking at her with a concerned expression. "Everything OK?"

Nate crawled through the opening and escorted Vincent toward their front door. "Everything's fine. We're just excited, is all."

Nate returned to the room to find Maya stretching out her tape measure across the trap door's opening.

"Twenty six by thirty inches," she gasped, out of breath.

"Well, what was it before?"

"I don't know. We never measured."

"Is it smaller?"

"Of course it's smaller!" she snapped.

She sat back and looked up at Nate, fear darkening her eyes. "What are we going to do?" she asked, her voice becoming shrill. "All of our stuff's down there. All of *my* stuff."

"How could it be smaller? It's not possessed. There's no such thing as a possessed door or a possessed room or a possessed anything! It's ridiculous!"

"I think you are ridiculous," she spat back. "You're the one who forced me to go down there in the first place! Now all my stuff's down there and it's lost forever!"

"What do you mean it's lost forever? It's right there! How dare you blame me! In no way is it my fault!" he bellowed.

Bang! Bang! Bang! A series of sharp bangs rattled their walls. They both stopped in their arguing tracks and stared at each other, petrified and frozen.

The walls rattled again. "Keep it down in there!" squawked a voice with a thick Mexican accent. "You got families living here, bro!" the source of the banging emphasized his point with one final thump from the apartment on the other side.

Nate and Maya's gazes held in shock for one more moment before they broke into smiles, amused by the irony. The reality of neighbors brought Nate back to his senses. "Look," he began, "if, and I mean *if*, the opening is getting smaller - it's doing it so slowly that we can't even notice it. If it makes you feel better, let's just take some of your stuff out now. Then we'll watch and see what happens."

"I don't want to go back down there," Maya shook her head, backing away from the trap door.

Nate stopped her, putting his hand on her shoulder. "You were fine before Vincent came over. You've been going down there for months and months and nothing ever happened. It's not going to hurt you, I promise."

Her multi-colored eyes locked onto Nate's. "You do it."

He ran his hand over her thick dark hair. "We'll both do it. Together."

Slowly and cautiously they descended the rickety ladder. Maya quickly grasped two armfuls full of clothes, with their hangers, from her rack and shoved them into Nate's arms. "You take these," she instructed.

Nate found it difficult to manage the ladder with so much fabric and jutting hangers in his arms.

"Hurry!" Maya's sense of urgency was rising fast.

"I'm trying, it's not easy you know!" he snapped back.

Maya's heart raced as she stared fixedly at the trap door opening, searching its width. It seemed to be tightening right before her eyes.

"Nate, the opening!" she gasped when she could no longer see the ceiling light from the room above, confirming that the opening was indeed changing and it was not an illusion of her eyes, or of her panic.

Nate looked up from the fourth rung and saw it too.

The boards on the ceiling of the cellar were growing.

Nate threw the clothes from his arms back down to the cement floor where they scattered like oversized fabric petals, the wire hangers landing with a clank. He scrambled to the top, just in time to squeeze through before he would no longer have fit. With barely a moment to breathe a sigh of relief at his escape, he turned to see Maya right behind him at the top of the ladder, still grasping her precious three Vincent sales.

"Let them go!" he commanded.

"No!" she wept. "Here take them!"

Maya shoved one of her favorites, a floral jersey print romper, through the trap door which was now less than half of what it had been when they descended. Nate grasped it and pulled it out and threw it behind him. He reached his arms inside the rapidly diminishing hole to grasp Maya's hands and pull her through.

Her pale hazel eyes were the last thing he saw before the opening closed around both of his arms.

He felt her hands slip from his as he struggled to pull his arms back from razor sharp spliters. He grunted and howled, inching to free himself from the closing boards that clawed and scraped him and held fast. Lines of blood ran down his arms, lines of blood that gouged deeper and deeper. Too much blood.

He finally wedged out his mangled wrists.

"Fuck you!" he cursed as he fought for his life. In an instant his hands were free. The force of the release propelled him against the far wall.

He glanced at his gashed and bloody arms and grasped the only thing available – the romper Maya had thrown. He quickly tore it in half, wrapping it around his gushing arms to stop the blood.

He scrambled back to where the trap door had been. There were no more seams, no more hinges, no more handle. The floor was smooth, and clean. No trace of the cellar below remained.

Nate screamed.

He clawed at the floor with what remained of his hands. Blood smeared everywhere as he stomped and smashed the floorboards.

"Maya!" he called out as he tried to pry up the board with his hands. "Maya!"

He raced to the closet and dug a hammer out of his toolbox, wishing he had a bigger weapon. He slammed it against the floor where trap door had been. He broke the room apart in a frenzy of rage and pain.

Once he pried up several of the boards he saw what was underneath. He sat back and stared as the truth wound its way into his brain in a thin wisp.

There was nothing under the boards. Nothing but cool, grey cement. He frantically pulled up more boards, hoping it was an illusion, a trick, a bad dream. He tore and tore until there was nothing left but broken boards and a base floor made of that same cool grey cement that had lined the cellar's walls.

Nate would not be getting his security deposit back.

The police responded after the Mexican neighbors called 911 regarding the racket from Unit 7 that had not ceased. They found Nate covered in blood, staring into space as he gripped the shredded remnants of Maya's work.

An investigation was launched. The blood that covered the room belonged entirely to Nate. With no body, all the LAPD could do was keep Maya's file open as a missing person's report. One that would gather dust along with many of their most unfortunate cases.

Nate never returned to Unit 7. Living on the various couches of various friends, his former app developing aspirations vanished into the back of his mind. The great traffic apps would not miss him, or care.

Nate found comfort in the sign spinning. The activity was repetitive, which had a numbing and calming effect on him. He liked busy street corners best, where he could see the faces inside every passing car. Always searching, searching for Maya's pale hazel eyes.

Ida's keys jangled in the lock. As she showed her prospective new tenants into the second bedroom with the grey wooden floors, she told the handsome young couple, "This room has a bonus space, which I technically can't advertise," she said. "Because it's not to code. You probably don't want to use it but it's worth mentioning."

John Palisano

ETERNAL VALLEY

May we walk this Eternal Valley
May we walk this land in peace
May we find the Place We're looking for
May this Eternal Valley ever be

The railroad men sang as the first cold winds blew across Diamond Creek, carrying smells of earthy grass, leaves, and dirt. Looking out over the sunny valley, past the men working on laying the tracks, my head overflowed with memories of little Jesse and me: us diving and playing up near the mouth of the Wabash River. Mary and me brought him, day before last, us exploring our new Missouri home, the place that would save Jesse's life.

Our place in New York sold high and left us a comfortable cushion. It was more than that, though, that made us move. Our Jesse didn't much do well in the crowded city streets. Hell, none of us did, but he reacted unnaturally toxic. His throat closed so tight he couldn't breathe. Probably had something to do with the factories sprouting coal smoke all around us in New York.

Doctor Faith said Jeese probably wouldn't make it unless we moved somewhere with lots of space and clean air. Sounded good to me; I harbored no love for the City because it made my son ill.

I made my living on the shores of the Hudson with my hands unloading and packing ships. Living off the land would suit me just fine.

Work in Diamond Creek turned out to be fulfilling. My new boss Doctor Norton managed his own grape vineyard and I did everything he'd let me. Most of my days were spent training the vines and making sure the condition of the fruit remained reasonable. We worried about the grapes catching powdery mildew or black rot, although the good German Doctor earned his name as horticulturist after cross-breeding the varieties so they'd grow more resilient than their European cousins. America turned out to be a harsher environment for grape growing. The seasons, like the people, showed no mercy.

Our life was simple and good. We lived a fruitful, productive existence before our world tore apart. One moment little Jesse played the part of a healthy six-year-old, running, playing, eating, laughing . . . the next minute his skin turned gray, his lips turned purple, and his eyes glossed over. He wouldn't rise. He hardly moved. It took all we had to feed the boy sustenance. We were scared giving him water. Jesse barely swallowed and we were afraid he'd drown.

Jim Longforth, our neighbor to the south, rushed over with his case of potions. He wasn't a doctor, but he was all we had. Rubbing a whitish, oily concoction across Jesse's forehead, he said, "Scott? I think the Devil has captured his soul. This will draw the monster out."

I was skeptical. Mary nodded, said, "Maybe we should bring him to the doctor out in Hermann—ain't Hermann the nearest big town?"

We cleaned Jesse's head off and tried to move him. He moaned like a hellhound.

"He break something, you think?" asked Jim. "If you move him might make it worse: might even kill him."

Mary looked to me. "I don't know," I said. "He seemed just fine all day."

"He'd just laid down for a nap when this started." She put a hand to her mouth. Her eyes watered. "I don't know what's happening."

"Could be consumption," Jim said. All the color drained from his face as though he'd stumbled across the answer and was embarrassed about it.

I put an arm on his shoulder. "If it is consumption, you best get going. Make sure you ain't around the boy enough for it to rub off."

"What about you and Mary?" he asked.

"We're his parents. We'll do what we have to," I said. We walked to the door where Jim snuck a last long look at Jesse. "Don't stare at him like he's not going to be here next time you come down," I said. "Don't you dare."

After Jim left I sat on Jesse's bed, looked at him until I couldn't look any more. "Was Jim right?"

Mary said, "Where would Jesse catch consumption? He's not coughing."

"There's got to be a treatment for him." I looked out the window. The valley had grown dark. It'd be hours until the moon was at its highest.

"Tomorrow you can talk to the Good Doctor and see if he might know of something," Mary said.

I shook my head. "He's a doctor of plant life, not people. His skills will be no fit for this."

She said, "Still—he may have recommendations."

I turned my face to Mary's. "I will leave in an hour, soon as there is moonlight to light my way."

"No. It's too dangerous at night." Mary clutched her cross around her neck. "There are demons outside."

"Nothing will bother me," I said.

She shook her head. "The Conner boys over the hill? They hear you coming and don't see you they're ripe to shoot. They might fire just for the game of it."

I stood up. "They don't frighten me and no creature of the night can get in the way of saving our son."

"Won't you be better useful here? What if he needs you?"

I squeezed Jesse's hand; his was limp and cool and barely squeezed mine back. "He won't miss me for a few hours. If he does, you tell him his Daddy went to find him a special medicine that will make him better."

Long purple trails of light stretched across the valley. The grass seemed painted and alive as it swayed from the nighttime wind. I pulled my jacket closer and tightened my scarf. For a late September night, the weather was colder than I remembered.

Far below, stretching across the flat lands, fires from the rail workers' tents glowed. I could make out the long black railroad lines near the camp. It wouldn't be long until the big steamers raced across our valley on their way across Missouri. The peace and tranquility we had known would now be forever broken. Mary and me spoke about the trains coming through. A new century loomed. We were both concerned because we didn't want the noise and crowds they'd bring.

"It's like the city is following," Mary had said, and I'd agreed.

There was a rustle near me. I looked round and saw nothing but knee high grass. The nearest trees were still a ways off, and there were no big rocks for hiding.

I stopped and listened for a moment. Whatever it was would spot me. I was the tallest thing in the field. My mind raced because I knew some of the railroad workers liked to drink a little too much and wander the hills. I hoped it wasn't one of those boys laid up in the field waiting for something dumb to stumble on by.

"Hello?" I asked, knowing I was taking my chances. If someone were hiding they'd see me.

Something rustled behind me and I turned full on. "Hello?" I called.

Training my eye to where I thought I heard the sound, I saw only the tops of the grass swaying gently in the night wind.

I smelled something burning—reminded me of sweet natural tobacco. *Someone was with me.* Whenever there was something on fire, there was usually a person close by. I'd found that usually nothing burned all by itself.

"Who's there? My name's Scott Robertson and I'm just passing through."

"So am I."

A woman's voice—she appeared from nowhere behind me, all slinking and sure of herself like I've never seen a woman before or since. She was striking. Long hair flowed halfway down her body. Her eyes were dark and glinted in the moonlight. She held a wooden pipe. Smoke trailed from its end. With a hand on her hip, she raised an eyebrow.

"Who are you?"

She smiled. "My name is . . . Mary."

I was taken aback. "You're name can't be Mary," I said. "You're an . . . "

"Indian?"

"Yes. You need to have an Indian name like Sunwater or River, right?" I asked.

"Says who?"

"Well . . . I don't know. Ain't that just the way it is?"

She shook her head. "Does the name Mary upset you?"

I stepped back. "Why would it?"

Mary shook her head. "You know someone else named Mary?"

"Sure," I said. "That doesn't mean anything. Look, who are you and what are you doing up here? You scared me half-way back to Jesus."

She moved closer, raised the pipe and took a pull. When she was done, she handed it over. I waved it away. "I don't smoke."

She exhaled. "Fine with me," she said. "I already told you."

"Told me what?"

"That I am passing through here," said Mary. "Same as you."

"Ma'am? I don't mean to be rude, but I have a sick child waiting on me and I need . . ."

She put up her hand. "A sick child? Is that what makes you walk alone so late on such a night?"

"Such a night? What the heck you getting at?" I asked. "'Tis the same as any other night, maybe a bit colder, might be all."

Mary said, "This is the night when the animals feast. The ones on the earth. The ones in the sky. Even the ones in the water."

"Okay? You know what? I don't believe in any of that Indian smoke. I'm a dyed-in-the-wool Christian," I said. "I sure wish there was a church up here. You believe we got a theater for actors, another one for musicians, but we got no church. Not enough people would go. I guess that's what happens when you're in the business of spirits."

Mary nodded. "Business of spirits?"

"We grow grapes," I said. "For wine. Gets you drunk. Kind of like that pipe you've got there." I pointed.

"I know what wine is," she said.

"Good Christians would probably frown upon our livelihood."

Mary looked around. I guessed her smoke was playing its fun little effects on her. "This is a special place," she said. "Don't you think so?" She shut her eyes and breathed as loud as she could. "You can just hear the animals and the spirits around you. It's safe. I could live here forever and never grow tired."

"That so?" I said. "I do need to move along. My son's going to need me to get back real soon." I started walking past her.

"May I walk with you?" she asked. "Would you mind just for a little bit?"

I shook my head and put out my hand. "I don't know," I said. "That probably wouldn't look right. If anyone sees us together it could mean trouble for me."

"I thought none of the Christ-inns cared?" she asked.

"That's different," I said and stopped in my tracks. "They're all on the same page so far as God is concerned. They ain't all going to look kindly on a man if he's walking around with another woman while his wife's home tending to his sick child, are they?"

She pulled a hood over her head. "I could wear a disguise," she said, "lower my voice, pretend to be a man." Mary laughed. "What if I were an old woman lost in the fields?" Her face changed before my eyes. "And you were just being a good Christ-Man . . ." Mary looked older and slighter and her hair went grey, all in a blink. "You might be leading me somewhere warm." By the time she'd finished speaking she again looked far too beautiful for not to be a temptation.

"You blow some of that stuff at me?" I asked. "That what it is? You got a trick up your sleeve? A couple boys hiding somewhere to hit me on the head and rob me?"

Mary laughed again. "You find me very threatening," she said. "I find that touching." She stared me in the eyes, looking back and forth inside mine several times to make sure she had my attention. "I am here to help you, Scott Robertson," she said. "I am here because of Jesse."

All the blood in my body froze.

The only thing I could think to say was, "Your name ain't really Mary, then, ain't it?"

She smiled.

"How am I supposed to know you ain't talked to the Longforth clan before you found me? How do I know this ain't some elaborate trick?"

She shook her head. "I am not asking you for anything," she said. "I have no weapons with me."

"There's still something about this I don't trust," I said. "I'd feel better if I could go talk to Doctor Norton about this. I bet he's got some ideas about what we could do."

"You can do that," she said. "But Jesse is in trouble, is he not? What if it is something much worse than you know? What if he only had hours left?"

"You know something I don't?"

"I know where we can go to find him something that will take it all away."

Mary looked up and to our left, to where the hill grew steep, to the top of Diamond Creek. "There is a point where the Wabash holds magic and power," she said. "I know of a place we can find his medicine."

"The Wabash River?" I asked. "You want to head on up there at this hour, on this freezing night?" That moment I noticed something peculiar. No longer was I shivering. In fact, the air felt just as warm as a summer evening. "Well damn me—did we hit some kind of hot spot or did the wind stop blowing?"

Mary looked right through me and I sensed that she was the reason things were a lot more comfortable. How could something like that be unless she was a witch of some kind?

She must have heard what I was thinking because the next thing to escape her mouth was, "You need to let go of some things you're holding close to your heart—at least for the next few hours."

"This ain't natural at all," I said. "It's all going against God."

"Is it?" she asked. "God would not let things happen if they would harm you, would she?"

"God's a man."

"Does it matter?"

"Sure as hell does."

"Your son's life is hanging on by breaths," she said.

Bugs crawled all over me. I felt them skitter up from the grass, up through my pant legs and right up onto my chest. I pulled my shirt away from my stomach and scratched at the little insects. Only thing is there weren't any. I still felt them walking on me. They'd reached my hair, my scalp, and nose. The itching was maddening. "Excuse me, Miss," I said and dropped to the grass and started itching like mad.

"This is the disease that's befallen your son," she said, her tone serious and forceful.

The itching burned; the sensation became unbearable. I felt what seemed to be spiders creeping all over me, biting me, nipping me, burrowing under my skin. Once inside I rubbed at my skin to try to free them, but they would not come back out. I fell on my back. As I lay in the grass, I found I could no longer move my limbs. The hand that scratched at my belly froze; my fingers curled into a stiff claw. My sight blurred and the night sky felt like it might fall and smother me.

My heart slowed and I could hear its beats, which sounded to me very much like the easy tides of the Hudson River back in New York City. It sloshed in and out, steadily. With each pull, a new wave of pain surged through my veins, beginning at the soles of my feet, gathering and intensifying inside my head. My stomach tightened and I wanted to throw up, yet, I could not even move. Blinking was agonizing.

It seemed as though I might die shortly. Jesse was in bad shape if what I was experiencing was the same for him.

In my head, I willed Mary to stop what she was doing. *She might be a witch, all right. Maybe she cast this same spell on Jesse when he was outside and made it a trap to catch me.*

"No," Mary said, kneeling down and looking me in the eyes. Her lips were shut but they still formed a smile. "I am not trapping you or your son. You must believe that I was called here to help you both."

Another wave washed over me, but it was warm and lessened the pain, as if it were being cleaned from my insides. After several seconds,

I was able to move my fingertips. Soon, my hands and arms moved and I was able to lift my head. Blessedly, the itching was gone. All that remained was a numb tingle in my hands and feet. I sat up and rubbed my eyes.

"You have only felt that way for a few minutes," Mary said. "Your son has been feeling that way for much too long already. We have to be quick. There is a point where the body will no longer tolerate pain and will stop."

"What does he have?" I asked.

"The curse of the wind," she said. "Which was what called me."

"Why?"

"You are here in a sacred place," she said. "And not everyone is happy about it."

"He is a child!"

I stood.

She said, "Gods do not discriminate."

"If God has done this than how can we stop it?"

"We will ask."

<hr />

After we turned left and made it through the prairie, we arrived at the bottom of a steep hill. The hill turned into the base of the mountain. There was a path, carved out by many of the town's folks. We climbed the side of the mountain's trail, me following Mary. "Good thing the moon is high," I said. "We can see our way."

"The Gods work in our favor," said Mary. "It's of great importance. They must know what we are doing."

"I sure hope so," I said.

As scared as I was about my son's wellbeing, I could not help but find myself deeply intrigued with Mary. Of course, she was beautiful and strong, but she also possessed a kind of magnetic pull. "I don't understand why so many people hate the Indians," I said. "You look just like a person to me." Her back was turned and I was embarrassed because her curves were quite wonderful and made my thoughts race. Shamefully, I remembered that she might hear my thoughts.

"The earliest people who came to this land and met with the Lakota were our friends," she said. "They lived with us. They dined with us. Our women loved their men."

"I can see why," I said, my mouth opening before I could stop it.

She paused. "You are right to believe the things that make us human are the same."

The path steepened. We passed a small tree, no larger than either one of us. I recalled being struck by the same tree when I'd brought Jesse and my Mary to the Wabash's mouth to play only a few days earlier.

"It just seems foolish to me that people always seem to want to fight over something," I said. "Especially the color of our skins. I mean, I kind of like all the different ways people look. If we all looked the same it'd be like that field down there all covered with one kind of flower and one kind of tree and nothing else. That seems awfully uninteresting to me."

She stopped. "I believe that may be part of the reason why I was called to you," Mary said. "You see the world not like most of the men around you."

"Come on," I said. "I can't believe I'm the only one who ever thought of that."

She shook her head. "I'm sure many others have thought it, but few have said so."

High on the hill, where the grass gives way to the towering granite of the mountain, the Wabash River curls around a bend and forms a large lake right before it all rolls down toward the valley on the other side. The land is flat surrounding the lake, and large enough for several houses. Trees and brush rim the lake. The water swirls gently and slowly round and round.

"I know this place," I said. "We brought Jesse here the other day. He loved it."

Mary stood still, her eyes fixed on the water. "This is where it began," she said. "He caught it here."

I stared at the water, too, searching for some kind of sign. I saw none. "You mean the water's poison? Is that it?"

"Something in it," she said. "Something's living inside."

"A fish?"

She shook her head. "Not quite." Then she turned to me. "You must go inside. You must clear your mind and you must ask for your son to be taken back."

I was confused. "Your son's spirit was taken," she said, her eyes glanced back to the swirling water. "The spirit within needs to feed."

Mary handed me her pipe. She reached inside a pocket, found a match, struck it, and as I lifted the tube to my lips she put the flame near the opposite tip.

I inhaled. My mouth filled with smoke, its sweet flavor reminding me of nutmeg and leaves. My lungs opened and warmed. Immediately I felt dizzy. The top of the lake seemed to glisten more than any body of water I'd ever seen. Every reflection bloomed and glittered. Mary took the pipe from me and smoked some herself. We shared her pipe for several minutes. Each pull brought me deeper and deeper under its magic spell.

The earth moved under our feet. I crouched slightly to keep my balance. "What was that?" I asked. My voice sounded as though we were inside a cave. It was difficult to keep my eyes open, despite the shaking ground.

"Look inside the water," she said, and pointed.

The bottom of the lake moved. The edges of the lake grew lighter as the creature curled its sides and revealed the true bed beneath. Its body was as dark and smooth as the night and it floated effortlessly. While the waves rippled, the creature at the bottom seemed to blend in with the water. If I broke my stare for even a second I lost track of where what it was.

"You must go inside," Mary said. "It can only hear you when you're in the water with it."

"It will kill me! It will devour me and have its supper! I'm no fool! Are you sacrificing me to this creature?"

"This is your choice," she said.

My instinct told me I couldn't go in the water. The thing filled nearly the entire lake. I pictured walking into the water and it covering me, smothering me, dragging me underwater with it—bringing my limp body toward its beak-shaped mouth. That had to be its plan.

"It has no mouth," Mary said.

"I don't want to be in this world if Jesse can't be here with me," I said. My mind seemed to flip in on itself. "If this thing took him then I guess I'll have no choice."

What happened next was a blur. As I put one foot in the Wabash Lake, the dark thing in the water moved back. When I'd swum in the lake with Jesse and Mary, the bed was dark. We'd been stepping on this thing the whole time and we hadn't even known it. Damn. Maybe Mary was right. I still was not sure how she came to be or how any of it was happening to me, but I knew, somehow, deep within, that I needed to have faith.

In no time I was up to my waist. The water was warm, which it hadn't been the other day. The air was warm, as well. The thing still moved away from me as I stepped inside. I turned one last time and my eyes met Mary's. She smiled and blinked once. I nodded and lowered myself inside the water. What followed happened faster than the details may lead you to believe.

Once I turned around, I saw nothing but darkness. The thing was going for the kill. It was smothering me. I was soon going to die.

Only I didn't. Instead, I took a few steps forward and saw that I was on a ledge. An endless cavern dropped down into the earth as far as I could see, ending in what looked like a bottomless black hole. The thing had covered the hole. I lowered myself into a sitting position so that I wouldn't step over the ledge and drop down. There was a tidal pull I could sense coming from the tunnel and I didn't want to be pulled down inside.

I felt something watching me and looked up. The thing was above me and I met its stare. Two flat grey eyes, each as big as my head, scanned me. Mary was right: I saw no mouth, although I did see two slits just under its eyes. Its movements were graceful and slow. Around its edges, I saw dark nubs like fingertips rolling across its rim—they looked to me a lot like they might be playing piano.

I gasped and swam. I looked up and found I was much deeper than I'd thought. When I first stepped inside the lake, it felt as though I were only a few feet under. Somehow, I'd sunk the length of several men.

I thought of Jesse sick and in bed and I didn't want to die. *He's going to need me. He needs to get better. He shouldn't be suffering like this. Take me, if that's what it takes. Take me in his place.*

The thing's eyes met mine.

It was just us swimming in here and having a good time. We didn't want any of this. We didn't need any of this. We didn't want to bother you none. Please. Let him be. You can have me if you need something. He'll miss me but he still has the world in front of him. He can do things I'll never be able to do. He can make things better. I can't. I'm just taking up space here now. I'll tell you what? I'll trade you, big guy, and maybe you can hear me the same way she can hear me. So just take me and throw me down that big hole you got there or whatever you need to do, but just let little Jesse free.

My mind raced with memories of my son. I remembered our room in New York where he was born, Mary's parents standing around, our friends. I remembered his first few nights as clear and as real as new. I felt his little fingers curling around my thumb. I heard his baby cries blending into his laughs. The smell of his hair so vivid I swear he was right there with me.

I saw him on the train jumping on the seats to get a better view as we rode from New York and across the plains. I heard his voice asking me if we were going to be okay. "We're always going to be together, right Poppa?" he asked.

"Of course," I told him. "Of course. Ain't nothing going to get in the way of that."

But it had.

Pictures of him racing across the field chasing some creature or another filled my head. It seemed I saw something just like that every day of my life in Diamond Creek as I passed him and went to work for Doctor Norton in the vineyards. Oh, to just have one more day! To have endless days!

I looked upward at the thing floating above me. It lowered itself onto me and as soon as our skin touched, I felt fire and pain worse than anything I can ever tell. My head filled with colors, exploding as if the heavens were on fire. I couldn't help but wiggle and try to break free. No matter. I was stuck in its grasp and nothing I could do would fix that.

When I woke, I was on the shore and I was alone. I sat up and got my bearings. I was soaked through. All my limbs were there. Everything worked. Nothing was out of place. I had a headache from all hell and I was sore, but that came as no surprise.

Mary was gone.

I stood and poured out my canteen. Then I went to the edge of the lake. The bed was dark. The water rippled, but the river bottom did not move. I searched for its eyes and could find none, them being on its underside.

Kneeling down, I filled my canteen with water from the lake. I stared at the dark bottom, and when I pulled the canteen from the water, I saw the slightest twitch.

Then I turned and took the first steps back home. Beneath the fading night, the stars shimmered against the deep blue sky.

Far below in the valley I heard the railroad workers singing again.

May we walk this Eternal Valley
May we walk this land in peace
May we find the Place We're looking for
May this Eternal Valley ever be

I pictured Jesse and knew soon I'd raise my canteen to his lips, and knew its lake water would cure him, and soon thereafter I'd hear his laughs and watch him run, and knew one day soon all I'd seen would just be a curious story I'd tell.

Taylor Grant

BLOOD

March 10

Yes, it's really me. I've missed you terribly. Please make sure and destroy this letter after you've read it. Your mom would lose her mind if she found out I had hidden this in your room.

I know it's been tough for you since your mom and I got divorced. The worst part of this whole situation is that you were caught in the middle. But I didn't choose this—your mom did. I still can't believe she got a restraining order against me—that was unnecessary and downright cruel.

No matter what happens from this point forward, I want you to always remember that you're the greatest thing that ever happened to me. Period. And some day, when you become a parent yourself—I hope—you'll understand first hand, just how deeply the love runs between a parent and a child. I wish that for you.

I snuck this letter into your room because some things happened while you were sleeping. It will undoubtedly disturb you when you hear about them. I want to make sure you understand what those things mean.

You were too young to understand before now. And even now, some of what I'm about to tell you will be difficult to process. But I've always talked to you like an adult and you've always been mature beyond your years.

More importantly, what I have to say can't wait any longer. Not after what happened tonight.

We've never discussed my childhood, and I know you've been frustrated by that. But there was a good reason. A lot of bad things happened in my youth that your mom and I knew you weren't ready to hear about. And to be honest, your mom doesn't even know the half of it.

But you will be able to handle the truth. I know you. Your mother hasn't beaten that open-mindedness out of you yet—though I know she's tried. I suppose you're too much like me that way.

You know that my parents were killed right in front of me at a crosswalk. Run over by an 86-year-old man who should never have been allowed to drive. But that's pretty much all I shared. I don't think I mentioned that I was 11 years old at the time (it's hard for me to believe you are two years older than that now).

As you can imagine, I was devastated—I loved both my parents very much. My mom—Meredith—ran her own home business selling women's cosmetics. She was a classic workaholic and we didn't get to spend a lot of time together. However, my dad—Max—loved to spend every moment he could with me.

Dad was a big geek before being a geek was cool. His had a boundless passion for science fiction, horror and comic books. And some of my favorite memories are of hanging out with him at the comic book store or going to a Sunday matinee movie. There was nothing better in the whole world than sitting next to him with a bucket of greasy popcorn and watching a good ol' creature feature.

Dad was the science teacher at my school. He was a humble man; loving and generous in spirit. He was everyone's favorite teacher because it was obvious he cared about every kid who passed through his class. In fact, sometimes I was a bit jealous of how close he was with his students.

And yet I knew he loved me most, because unlike many men of his generation, dad was never afraid to express his feelings.

If not for his early influence, I never would have been exposed to the wonder of comic books and become a writer myself. I know how much you enjoy reading the comics I've created—well, you can thank my dad for that. He inspired my love of storytelling.

Don't get me wrong, I loved my mom—but there was a bond between me and my dad that that is very similar to the one between you and me.

After dad and mom died, I thought about killing myself. I wanted to be with them in heaven. When things were at their worst, I'd hear dad's soothing voice in my head. He would tell me not to do it, and that the afterlife wasn't something I should rush into.

Dad visited me in my dreams all the time, reminding me how much he loved me. He told me he would always watch out for me, and protect me—just like he did when he was alive.

I believed him. And those visits kept me going during the worst of my childhood.

Unfortunately, there was no one on either my mother's or father's side who could (or wanted to) care for me. So I ended up in the foster care system, which basically it means I stayed with temporary families. They get paid by the state to take care of underage kids who don't have anyone else.

Some people take in foster kids in the hope that they might adopt them someday. Those are the best kind of foster parents. Others do it for the money or reasons so despicable I refuse to talk about them.

My first foster parents—Joel and Lucy Carmichael—were the bad kind. Things were simple with Joel. He asked you to do something and you did it. Otherwise you got a punch in the stomach or a slap across the face. There was no negotiating. He was not a good man, but at least he ignored me most of the time. That is, unless he wanted his feet rubbed (disgusting!) or a chore done.

The kindest thing I can say about Joel is that he didn't actively torment me.

His wife Lucy Carmichael, on the other hand, was four hundred pounds of pure evil, an amorphous mountain of flesh—with no beginning or end. Granted, I was only eleven years old and most adults seemed like giants to me, but Lucy made most grown men look small by comparison.

Whenever our family went out it was like an endurance test of public humiliation. The cruelty of strangers is something I never got used to. Lucy didn't react to mean-spirited comments from others, though. It was as if the layers of blubber had formed a protective shield against insults. Or as I once imagined, her rage was absorbed into her folds of fat, stockpiled for later use on me and the other foster kids.

There were three children in the Carmichael family, Molly, Jamin, and myself. Molly was fourteen years old and quite hardened for such a young age. But she had lived under the cruel dictatorship of Lucy Carmichael for several years, so it was understandable. Jamin was a four-year-old African American boy, and a sensitive, damaged soul—afraid of his own shadow. Molly and I did our best to protect him from Lucy's abuse, but we could only do so much.

Unlike most kids, who couldn't wait to get out of school, I dreaded leaving, because it meant I had to return home to the beast's lair. "The Beast" is what Molly, Jamin and I called Lucy behind her back.

Making matters worse, the Beast rarely left the house unless she had to, which meant we kids rarely left the house either. The Beast had two reasons, and two reasons only, for having us there. And they had nothing to do with being loving or supportive to foster kids. She simply wanted slave labor and the extra money the state provided. She needed it to support her enormous eating habit, which fell somewhere between grotesque and astonishing.

Even as big as she was, I could scarcely believe how much the woman ate in a single day—like a human garbage disposal that grinded, churned, and eliminated a never ending supply of processed consumables.

Everything the Beast ate was prepackaged, of course, because she couldn't be bothered to take the time to cook anything—for herself, her husband, or us. Cooking might take time away from eating, or her favorite pastime: watching trashy TV.

The Beast never missed a soap opera.

Molly, Jamin and I lived on a completely different diet than the

Carmichaels—the only criteria being how cheaply they could feed us. That usually meant generic cereal or a Top Ramen knock off that tasted like shredded styrofoam soaked in salt water.

If we were lucky, the Beast would give each of us a single Oreo cookie. There was always a bag of them sitting on a fold-out tray permanently stationed next to the living-room couch.

Two things you could always count on at the Carmichael house: back-breaking work, and new and innovative ways for the Beast to torment us.

On the weekends and after school, Molly, Jamin and I mostly did housework. We kept their two-story house immaculate. We vacuumed, washed all of the clothes and bedding, ironed, and cleaned every room until it was spotless. We did this every day without fail—even if we were sick (which was often, due to our terrible diet). There was no slacking in the Carmichael house—at least, not by the foster kids.

But all of that was a piece of cake compared to when we had to clean the Beast herself. She was too large to reach most areas—including the unmentionables—so it was up to the "scrub team" as she called us to clean her as she stood naked in the bathtub like some monstrous golem formed from fat rather than clay. That was an hour-long horror show of which I will gladly spare you the details.

Joel worked as a security guard with odd hours—so he was rarely around. And while he wasn't as fat as the Beast, he was no slouch in the eating-like-a-pig department either. The man could barely tie his own shoes laces due to his gargantuan belly. We thought it was hysterical to imagine him trying to chase down a bad guy. We tried to find the humor in everything—it was the only thing that kept us sane. Whenever I could make Molly and Jamin laugh, it was a good day.

If the near starvation, endless work, and lack of love wasn't bad enough, there was the physical abuse we faced on a daily basis. The Beast had a terrible temper and would fly into an uncontrollable rage at the drop of a hat. It was always uncalled for, of course, and I suspect a result of her self-loathing. She had little to no self-control in all aspects of her life—including beating us.

The Beast once said that harsh discipline was her way of educating us. We all knew it was horseshit—she simply used us for venting her endless reservoir of anger. But God forbid any of us ever expressed our own emotions. On those rare occasions that we dared, we always walked away with a fat lip, black eye, or welts on our backs.

We tried complaining to several caseworkers who visited us, but most of those people were already overloaded with cases or quit soon after. I think I we had five different ones in two years. There were never any investigations.

So, on one particularly awful day, I decided to do something about it.

It was a Saturday afternoon, on a blistering hot summer day. We were cleaning the house, as usual, when Jamin accidentally spilled some bleach on the carpeting in the bathroom. It left a large white spot that we couldn't fix or hide (God knows we tried).

When the Beast discovered the ruined carpet, she forced Jamin to hold his hands in a bowl of bleach for so long that his skin blistered and bled. The poor little thing had permanent tissue damage after that.

When I saw Jamin's terrible wounds, I nearly lost my mind. I stormed into the living room where the Beast sat on the couch watching TV and eating a giant bowl of macaroni and cheese. I started yelling and throwing things at her— anything I could get my hands on, including a thick cookbook that hit her on one of her chins and left a bright red mark. I called her every name I knew at the time. It all came pouring out of me, as if I were vomiting words.

I suppose child psychologists would say I was "acting out". That is, acting out what was inside of me, which was two years' worth of pain, hostility and aggression.

None of my outrage helped Jamin, though. All I got for my troubles was the worst beating to date, my left arm broken in two places and a badly split lip. This, of course, was explained away to the doctor as a bad fall in the playground.

On the drive there, the Beast turned to me at a stoplight. She stared at me for an uncomfortably long time, and her deadened eyes reflected her dark thoughts. Finally, she said, "If you tell the doctor what happened, I will slit your scrawny little throat—and no one will ever find the body."

I never spoke of what she'd done... until now.

That night, dad visited me in my dreams again. But this time it was different. *He* was different. The warm smile that usually greeted me was now an enraged grimace. He had transformed from a guardian angel to an avenging one.

The dream was so vivid that I remember it to this day. My dad's presence was as real as if he were standing in the room with me. I realize this is hard to believe, but trust me when I say that there are emotional bonds between people so strong they can transcend death.

As in life, dad said he would always watch over and protect me—no matter what. All I had to do was call out his name and no one would ever cause me harm.

When you're in a dream, everything seems reasonable, relatively speaking. Isn't that the purpose of dreams and fantasies? It's the one place where our minds can enjoy wish fulfillment without consequences, even if that involves enacting revenge on our enemies.

At that moment, I knew how I wanted the Beast to pay. My dad merely nodded at me in understanding.

Soon after my dad vanished from my troubled dreams, Molly, Jamin and I were awakened to horrifying screams. There was a terrible *crash* from somewhere in the house that shook the walls.

Molly gathered me and Jamin and we hid in our bedroom closet. I remember seeing the whites of their eyes, shining with fear. But I wasn't scared. Somehow...some way, I knew dad had returned to protect me.

We heard the deafening sound of gunfire—most likely from the big Smith & Wesson Joel kept in a drawer near his bed. We immediately flattened onto the floor.

Jamin began to sob as Molly did her best to comfort him. There were more terrified shouts—from both Joel and the Beast, *thuds* against the walls, glass shattering, and then all went quiet.

None of us dared move.

We remained hidden in the darkness for what seemed like the longest hour of our lives. The neighbors must have heard the war going inside our house and called the police. Several cops broke down the front door, searched all of the rooms, and eventually found us huddling in the dark.

They escorted us out of the house covered in blankets. We were told to keep our eyes closed on our way out. But of course, I didn't. Though I had a limited view, I could see that the carpet was soaked in what looked like a lake of blood.

And then I saw the Beast for the very last time, on the floor and nearly hidden behind the large living-room couch. Or rather I spotted her hand; it was pale and blood-spattered, and as big as a pie plate.

It wasn't attached to her body.

Over the following weeks, there were a million questions asked, a battery of psychological tests, unhelpful counseling from overworked social workers, and whispers of a maniac killer when no one thought I could hear. Eventually, Molly, Jamin and I were split up and sent to separate foster homes.

I never heard from either of them again.

To this day, the murder of Joel and Lucy Carmichael remains unsolved.

Now, only you and I know the truth.

I have more to tell you, though. So play close attention.

My next foster home placement was with Jennifer and Roman Henderson; they were decent, hardworking folks in their mid-fifties. Jennifer managed a pet store and Roman was the co-owner of an auto shop that specialized in exotic cars. I believe that initially, they had good intentions as foster parents. And though things turned out badly, they were never truly to blame.

The problem was a monster named Frederick—their biological son.

Frederick was a psychopath. You've probably heard that term used in movies and such. It's a serious personality disorder. Psychopaths don't feel love, guilt, remorse, or have the ability to empathize with their fellow man.

In other words, they tend to be assholes. And at thirteen years old, Frederick was already the biggest asshole you'd never want to meet.

One of the most insidious things about psychopaths is that the really smart ones can hide behind a mask of normalcy. They often have the ability to act as if they care about others, or use charm to manipulate others to their own ends. And believe me, if they gave out Academy

Awards for psychopathy, Frederick would have had a whole trophy case full of Oscars.

Frederick managed to dupe almost everyone into thinking he was a normal boy with a high IQ. At the very worst, he was considered a bit eccentric. In fact, the only people who ever saw Frederick's true nature were the unfortunate souls that crossed him. And even that was rare because Frederick usually got his revenge without the victim knowing that he had targeted them.

Like I said, he was smart.

I didn't understand this at the time, but I have since realized that the reason Jennifer and Roman opened their home to me is because they were looking for an emotional connection they couldn't get with their son. And having another child wasn't an option, since Jennifer was fifty-five at the time.

When I think about how wonderful my relationship is with you, I can see how hard it must have been for the Hendersons to have such a cold-hearted boy. I believe they hoped (consciously or unconsciously) that a foster child would help fill that void. And the truth is, I was just as anxious for an emotional connection.

Things went as well as could be expected for the first six months to a year. Having my own room was a godsend as there had been zero privacy at the Carmichaels' house. Frederick was initially courteous and polite; he even made a big show of telling everyone I was his new little brother and that he was going to take good care of me. I almost cried when he'd said it, because I so desperately wanted to believe it.

I think that was the hardest part of all. For a long time I didn't want to believe that Frederick was evil. He had a way of making everyone feel special. It was his way of luring people into a false sense of security, so he could take advantage of their good nature.

For example, he had all of the teachers at school wrapped around his little finger. He had learned at an early age that flattery would get him everywhere. And he played to their egos like a seasoned pro.

But there was one teacher—Mr. Milligan—who was on to him. Milligan was the history teacher, highly intelligent, and a veteran of the public school system for over twenty years. He'd seen and heard it all, and he didn't buy into Frederick's bullshit.

That was his first big mistake.

Frederick was the smartest kid I've ever known. Smarter than some of the teachers, I expect. But he hated schoolwork. He felt it was beneath him as he always aced his tests, undoubtedly due to his damned near photographic memory. He was able to cajole, deceive and talk his way out of homework constantly.

Mr. Milligan, however, was an old school teacher, and for him I think it was the principle of the thing. When he assigned homework he expected it to be done. It didn't matter to him that Frederick was good at taking tests.

This infuriated Frederick. I know because he talked about it incessantly, as if Milligan were his arch-nemesis, hell-bent on destroying him by simply asking him to do the same thing everyone else had to do.

One day I left one of my books under my desk in history class. When I went back for it, I found Frederick in the room pointing his finger at Mr. Milligan, who was sitting on the edge of his desk, red-faced and sweating. When they saw me, they both froze and didn't say a word.

I hurriedly collected my book and raced out of the room.

On the bus ride home, I asked Frederick about it. At first he didn't want to tell me what had happened—but quickly conceded. He had an enormous ego; it was impossible for him to keep such a grand victory to himself.

Grinning like a shark, he said, "I told Milligan he better stop trying to touch my private parts, or I was going to report him to the administration."

I stared at him—stunned. "Did he?"

He patted me on my shoulder as if I were a naive child. "Of course not. But now that old fucker won't bother me again. Not unless he wants his career to end in disgrace."

And he was right. From that day forward, Frederick didn't turn in a single homework assignment—yet he always got straight As. I was simultaneously disgusted and envious.

Over the next year, I watched as Frederick lied, cheated and stole from other students, teachers, and his own parents. And even though

I caught him stealing from me several times, I never told on him. As the foster kid I did everything possible to avoid any kind of drama. I lived in fear of decreasing my chances for adoption. My tactic worked, because over time I was the only person Frederick confided in.

I learned that he had two passions: candy and chemistry. And this was what he spent all of his stolen money on. That first summer I watched in awe as he created all kinds of cool and interesting chemical reactions with various household items.

There were some dilapidated homes about two miles from where we lived in an abandoned development project—and Frederick had chosen the most remote one as his personal science lab. It was a simple one-story three bedroom place—but for a kid, it was like having an entire castle for your clubhouse.

Frederick liked to show off with chemical magic tricks, like turning water into fake wine, creating invisible ink, and even fire breathing. But that was just kid stuff that he allowed me to see. What I later discovered was that his real interest in science lay in developing poisons to use on animals and people he didn't like (which was pretty much everyone).

He tried to keep his poison experiments a secret from me, but I pieced together what he was doing over time. He created his own concoctions using commonly found chemicals like ethylene glycol from anti-freeze. His most prized possession was a vintage kid's chemistry set from the Fifties—before manufacturers were forced to make them less dangerous. It contained harmful chemicals such as cyanide and a concentrated iodine solution.

I noticed that sometimes Jennifer and Roman would get sick not long after they scolded Frederick, which was a rare occurrence in our house. Both were heavy coffee drinkers, and one morning after Jennifer yelled at Frederick for not cleaning his dishes, I saw him pour a tiny packet of powder into her cup when he thought no one was looking.

A short time later, she suffered vomiting, diarrhea, and terrible stomach pain. This happened to both she and Roman multiple times. At the time, they dismissed them as digestion issues or food poisoning, as they never would have suspected their son.

The poisonings happened at school regularly. Frederick didn't know I was on to him, but I watched him closely in the lunchroom and while we ate snacks at recess. He had become masterful at sprinkling his mixtures onto other student's food without getting caught.

Inevitably, his victims became sick soon after—often sprinting for the bathroom to keep from shitting their pants. Frederick always wore a satisfied grin when this happened.

You're probably wondering why I didn't tell on him. Well, I wanted to—more than anything. But I was scared of so many things back then. I was afraid that no one would believe me, or that if he found out I might be poisoned myself. But mostly I was afraid of being sent away.

Besides—it wasn't like he'd actually killed anyone.

I did consider telling Jennifer and Roman many times, but I knew they were in denial about having been poisoned, if they suspected anything in the first place. I mean, no one would want to believe their own flesh and blood could be capable of such a thing. After all, what would that say about them?

Maybe you've heard the old saying: "Don't shoot the messenger", which means don't get mad at the person who delivers the bad news. Well, I was convinced that if I told Frederick's parents what I knew about their son, they would hate me.

They ended up hating me anyway.

That first Christmas the Hendersons bought me a bike. It's hard to express how grateful I was at the time, and how much I adored that cherry red BMX Diamondback. Suddenly I had the freedom to go wherever I wanted and I explored everywhere on that bike.

It was one such Saturday afternoon when I had driven down to the comic book shop to pick up the latest issue of *Captain America*. I also bought a copy of the horror magazine *Fangoria* for Frederick because the only movies he'd sit down to watch were the scary kind.

I remember thinking he was probably up to his usual tricks at the clubhouse, since that was where he spent nearly every weekend. So I was excited to ride up there and give him his gift. It was about midday when I got there, but I didn't see his bike anywhere. After calling out several times, I decided to go inside.

I knew he would be furious if he found out I'd been snooping around without him, but my curiosity was just too great. Inside the abandoned home, there were piles of candy wrappers everywhere (Frederick bought a lot of black licorice because he knew I hated it and wouldn't ask him for any), a few bottles of household chemicals, a poorly hidden stack of porno mags he'd stolen from his dad, and a couple of tattered beach chairs in the living room that we'd rescued from someone's garbage.

The living room and kitchen was where we always hung out, and Frederick's house rule was that the other rooms—jokingly referred to as the west wing—were off limits. That was fine with me, because honestly, the place gave me the creeps.

As I looked around, the wind whipped against the exterior, whistling through the cracks and causing the ivy growing through a break in the wall to sway and grasp, as if it were reaching for me. If it hadn't been a bright sunny day, I might have left right then. The clubhouse wasn't the kind of place you wanted to be at night. There were three bedrooms and a bathroom. There was nothing of note in the bathroom except what looked like a few drops of dried blood in the sink—though I couldn't be sure. The first two bedrooms were empty except for a few spider webs, but the master bedroom at the end of the hall had an assortment of long forgotten items left behind, probably since before I was born.

There was a half-empty, dried out paint can, a dirt-encrusted paint roller, a handful of crusted old batteries, and two big pieces of black tarp covered with what looked like decades of dust.

To this day, I'll never know what caused me to check under that tarp—just a feeling I guess. But when I pulled it away, I noticed the outline of a trap door built into the floor. Did Frederick know about it? And if he did, had he tried to hide it with the tarps?

I heaved at the rusted metal ring on the trapdoor and it swung open with a loud creak. My heart threatened to pound its way out of my chest as I stared into the dark void below. A terrible stench wafted up, causing me to dry retch.

As my eyes adjusted to the blackness below, I noticed a small red lantern on the second step of the stairs leading down. What caught my eye was that it looked relatively new. I reached down and lifted the lantern by its thin metal handle, inspecting it.

When I turned the dial it came to life and the sudden glare hurt my eyes. I was stunned that the batteries still worked.

I knew it must belong to Frederick.

Gathering every scrap of courage I could muster, I stepped down into the waiting darkness. As light played along the walls and revealed the basement's secrets, my breath caught in my throat.

It was worse than I could have imagined.

The walls were decorated with a nightmarish collection of animal's dissected bodies, limbs, heads, and the shriveled remains of internal organs. Though some were impossible to identify, I was able to pick out the limbs and heads of countless lizards, mice, a couple of raccoons, and several garden snakes.

I could only hope that the poor creatures had been poisoned and killed *before* their dismemberment.

As I continued to explore the macabre exhibition, I spotted twenty to thirty glass specimen jars lined up on the floor filled with a menagerie of the dead. Inside floated whole bodies of puppies, kittens, baby opossums, squirrels and skunks. Anguished faces seemed to scream from inside the liquid that preserved their suspended forms. Their fur was matted and their eyes wide, as if the mercy of a quick death had been denied them.

As I stared at the assortment of glass tombs, I was filled with disgust and outrage. It was maddening to think that so many innocent creatures had been killed for no other reason than to satisfy the whims of a twisted boy.

I didn't know it at the time, but what I was witnessing were classic signs of a future serial killer.

I swung the lantern to my left and moved toward the center of the basement. There was a plastic fold-out picnic table that had been permanently discolored by untold amounts of bodily fluids. God only knew how many dissections and other unknown experimentations had been carried out here.

But the worst of it was what looked up at me from the center of the table—the heads of eight recently decapitated tabby kittens—perfectly lined up together, all staring at me with deadened eyes.

Nausea overcame me and I threw up everything I'd had for lunch. I panicked, because I knew Frederick would see and smell what I'd thrown up. He'd know someone had invaded his killing room.

I searched the room for rags to try and clean it up, but all thoughts of that disappeared when I heard a creak from the stairs behind me.

I spun around and the light of the lantern caught the murderous look of Frederick, just a few feet away. He was crouched on the bottom step of the stairs, holding a vicious-looking knife.

"So what do you think?" he said, and the grin on his face chilled me to the bone.

He began moving toward me. "I've learned how to preserve bodies really well, don't you think?"

I had been backing away unconsciously, and jumped when I collided with the wall behind me.

I was trapped. There was no way out without a fight.

"I've never tried to preserve a person before," he said, sizing me up. "But if I chopped you up into small pieces, well…who knows?"

I didn't hear anything he said after that. I was lost in my own frantic thoughts, wondering how in the world I could survive this encounter, and realizing that I probably wouldn't.

I thought of my dad then, and his promise to watch over and protect me—and a terrified voice in my mind called out to him for help.

I had no frame of reference for what happened next, and I didn't understand what I'd seen until much later. It all happened in a matter of seconds.

There was a glint of steel as Frederick raised the knife for the killing blow. Behind him, the shadows formed into a dark wraith, vaguely shaped like a man. It swallowed my would-be killer within its swirling mass and I heard his muffled screams.

Then came the grotesque sounds of bones snapping, flesh ripping, and a human body folded inside out. If it had continued longer I would have screamed myself. But the grisly scene ended moments later, and all that was left of Frederick was a dismembered pile of refuse—not unlike the perverse trophies that adorned the walls.

As my eyes adjusted to the darkness, I could see hands that looked like living smoke reaching for me. I winced at their cold touch. Suddenly I could hear my dad's soothing voice in my mind, and the fear that gripped me soon eased to a familiar comfort.

Then the wraith was gone.

What happened over the ensuing months was a complicated legal mess that would take me another hundred pages or so to explain. But I did contact the police and told them most of what I knew about Frederick Henderson. I simplified the story and didn't mention the part about him trying to kill me. I told them I'd only discovered the hidden basement that day while looking for him—and that part was true.

Not surprisingly, I was removed from foster care with the Hendersons soon after. It was obvious they couldn't look at me without being reminded of that tragic day...or what their son truly was.

The one piece of good news was that the police cleared me of any blame for what happened to Frederick. Hell, the medical examiner couldn't even explain how his body had been turned inside out. And I was also absolved of the animal killings, since they determined that most of them were from years past—long before I lived in the area.

I had also buried the recent kills in the woods far from there.

The next few years were a revolving door of foster families. Unfortunately, the older you get, the lower your chances of getting adopted. Everyone wants the young kids. So I bounced around like a pinball for several years. Some families were decent but short-lived, others were terribly lonely, and a few were outright abusive.

I could have called out to my father during those times of abuse. But I thought it would be better to simply run away. I'd seen enough death to last me a lifetime. In fact, escaping from foster homes was like a bad running joke for my caseworkers—and I became quite good at living on the street for weeks at a time.

When I turned sixteen I got a fake ID and joined the Navy, which (mostly) kept me out of trouble for the next four years.

The rest of it you pretty much know. The military helped pay for college, and that's where I met your mom. The rest, as they say, is history.

As for my dad, he was always there for me in one form or another. He continued to appear in my dreams, and sometimes in the most unexpected places.

Soon after you were born, I woke in the middle of the night and found my dad standing next to your crib. You were giggling at him. He looked exactly as I remembered; lean, handsome, and with a thick shock of black hair.

He turned to me and offered a knowing look, and something passed between us. I knew at that moment that you and I would have a connection that was the same as me and my father.

That was the last time I saw him.

Earlier I wrote that there are emotional bonds between some people that are so strong that they transcend death—and that's the point of telling you all of this.

We are blood. Now and forever.

Now I'm afraid comes the hardest part of what I have to tell you.

Your mother divorced me so she could be with your new stepdad (I refuse to use his name), but she also made sure that my rights were taken away. Custody decisions are usually biased in favor of mothers—especially when there are accusations of abuse.

But we both know the truth; your mother is the one who has abused you. I suppose that's the tragic irony of all of this. In my attempts to protect you from your mother, she figured out a way to use the system against me.

And once I lost you, I lost myself.

Your mother never told you the truth about what happened to me, because she knew you would blame her.

She didn't tell you I took my own life six months ago.

I won't go into the gruesome details here. There is no reason to dwell on that. I can't undo what I've done, no matter how much I regret that decision. All I can do now is deal with the cards I've been dealt.

What matters most is that you know I will always love you, and that I will never leave you again. Ever. You will see me in your dreams. I will be there when you call for me.

And this brings me to tonight and the last, perhaps most important reason I am writing you this letter. I hear your thoughts. And I feel your pain. We are connected this way.

I know that three bullies have tormented you in school for some time: Peter Kopp, the gang leader, Jerry Falanga, the pig-faced punk, and J.R. Cutler, that whiny red-haired boy. These demons have made your life a living hell these past few months. And for that, I am truly sorry.

I know you have relived their bullying in your dreams because you have called out to me many times. Do you remember what you wished for?

Well, I visited those boys while you slept tonight. And I promise you that Jerry, Peter and J.R. will never torment you again. In fact, they will never torment *anyone* again.

You will learn about this soon—and when the news breaks there will be many ugly rumors and none of them will be true.

Only you and I know the truth.

If anyone ever tries to harm you, just call out my name.

This brings me to my final request as I leave you to think about the many things I've told you. I know you have mixed feelings about your mother and her abuse, and strong feelings about the man she chose over me. And I understand your anger at her for keeping me from you.

The question is: what do you want to do about it?

Goodbye for now. I'll see you in your dreams.

I love you with all my heart,

Dad

William F. Nolan
AMONG THE TIGERS

"Goddammit, Jimbo, our guys need to get into the air!" Ted Jarvis declared, as a shell sliced the sky above their small dugout. Cold bit into them. "When is this lousy weather gonna break?"

Jimmy Tucker shrugged, pulling his coat tighter around him. "Don't ask me. God doesn't tell me stuff like that."

Jarvis spat into the banked snow. "I don't believe in God, I believe in dead Krauts."

He was a tall heavy-set man with prematurely gray hair. His beard and mustache were frosted with ice.

Jimmy Tucker was lean and clean shaven. He was eighteen and looked twenty-five. War had aged him. He shivered, clapping his gloved hands together. "This damn cold is killing me!"

"The cold won't kill ya," grinned Jarvis. "A tank shell will do the job."

"Thanks for your optimism." Jimmy shifted his cramped position in the dugout, adjusting the weight of his rifle. "Can't see shit in this fog. Where's our regiment?"

"Up ahead somewhere," replied Jarvis. "No way to find 'em now. We're better off staying put. Wait for reinforcements."

"And what if they don't come? We got no food left, a half-canteen of water, and damn little ammo. We're fucked!"

"Shut up and listen." Jarvis tilted his head toward a creaking, grinding sound in the near distance. It grew steadily louder.

Jimmy looked worried. "Tanks !"

"Yeah," nodded Jarvis. His voice was bitter.

"Tanks."

Jimmy squinted, trying to make out moving forms through the massed trees. Fog, damp and opaque, hugged the ground.

"Sounds like Panzers."

"Yeah," muttered Jarvis. "Clearing the way for the big boys. Those King Tigers weigh like hell. They need room to move."

Jimmy drew in a frosted breath. "Will they spot us?"

"Not in this soup. Just keep your head down."

"If they do spot us we're dead meat." Jimmy gripped his rifle. "I saw a Tiger take out a Sherman like it was a cracker box. Krauts got the best damn tanks in the war. Their armor is—"

"Shut yer yap!" growled Jarvis. "I gotta think about where to go."

The grinding clatter of the tanks increased. Closer. Much closer.

"Go? You said we should stay put."

Jarvis scowled. "So I changed my friggin' mind. Fog' s thinning. We can't depend on them not spotting us. Gotta move. Find the main road." He gripped his rifle. "Stay low and follow me."

Jarvis slung his weapon over his left shoulder and, in a half-crouch, began weaving through the snow-draped trees, away from the rumbling tanks.

Jimmy Tucker was right behind him.

Twilight in the Ardennes. Chilled rain was falling in bitter sheets, a shower of cold needles stabbing the ground. Having failed to locate the main road, they spotted a shell-battered two story house a few hundred feet ahead. A large section of one wall had been blown away, and the windows were boarded.

"I'm freezing my butt off," Jimmy groaned. He was breathing hard. "I'm beat . . . can't keep going. Gotta stop."

"Okay, Jimbo, we'll see if anybody's still alive in the house, " said Jarvis. He climbed the slanting wood porch. "Maybe we'll find some chow in there."

Jimmy nodded weakly. "At least we'll be out of this frigging rain."

Jarvis pounded a gloved fist against the door. It was opened by a young girl with a knitted shawl draped over her shoulders. In her mid-twenties, slim-bodied and attractive. Her eyes were dark with the stress of war.

"Howdy, ma'am." Jimmy tried to smile, but his lips were numb. "We're American, and we need —"

She broke into rapid French.

"She's speaking frog," declared Jarvis. "Can't understand a damn word she's saying."

"Oh, but I also speak your language! I took English in your United States." She waved them in. "But please to enter. There is food and warmth for you."

They stepped inside, stamping icy snow from their boots. Crude repairs had been made to a section of fallen roof. A fat iron stove near the far wall sent out shimmering waves of heat.

"We surely do appreciate your hospitality," said Jimmy, pulling off his helmet to reveal a crew cut.

"Yeah. Damn good to feel warm again," said Jarvis, stripping his gloves and rubbing his hands at the stove.

"I'm Alayna," said the girl. "It is a pretty name . . . from my mother. She, too, was named Alayna."

"Ted Jarvis—and he's Jimmy Tucker. We're trying to find our regiment. Got separated when we were pinned down in the woods."

"You live here alone?" asked Jimmy.

"No," she said. "I live with my Aunt Grace. She made me attend school in your New York. After graduation I came back here, to Belgium, to be with my parents."

"Where are they now?" Jimmy asked.

She lowered her head with sorrow shadowing her eyes. Her voice was very soft. "They are dead. The Germans killed them."

"Yeah," nodded Jarvis, "the Krauts are good at killing. How is it that you and your aunt survived?"

"One of your Sherman tanks drove the Germans away," she said, "but I'm sure they'll be back."

"Then why stay?" Jarvis wanted to know.

"Auntie is too weak to travel. She is in bed upstairs. It is hard for her to walk. I have to stay here—to care for her. But you must be so hungry . . ."

"We surely are," declared Jimmy. "Last of our rations gave out two days ago."

Alayna headed for the kitchen. "I'll fix some hot food for you. It won't be fancy. The Germans took nearly everything. All I have is stale bread and canned beans."

"That'll be fine," Jarvis assured her.

As they ate, Alayna asked about the war. "I thought you Americans were winning."

"We are," said Jarvis. "We've been advancing farther each day but the Krauts are still putting up a helluva defense. They fight like frigging tigers!"

"I don't understand war," the girl admitted. "All the blood and senseless killing. I don't understand."

"Ask Hitler," said Jimmy. His tone was bitter. "He started this one."

Alayna shook her head. "What do the Germans want?"

"Power and land mainly," said Jarvis. "Right now they want to capture Antwerp."

"The port?"

Jarvis nodded. "That's why Hitler launched this big kick-ass offensive. If they are able to take Antwerp they'll cut off four of our crack divisions . . . trapped between Kraut troops and the sea."

The girl was shocked. "Can they do that?"

"Maybe, but probably not. Talked to a guy I know at Field HQ and he heard that the Krauts are low on fuel and ammo. Their tanks are running out of gas. "

Jimmy nodded. "Once the weather breaks our flyboys will be out again bombing their butts."

"That is good to hear," Alayna declared, fire in her eyes. "They are brutes and savages."

The heavy sound of booted feet on the porch.

"Krauts!" yelled Jimmy, grabbing his rifle. Jarvis pushed Alayna to the floor amid a crackle of small-arms fire.

"Spotted our prints in the snow," declared Jarvis.

Alayna's aunt appeared at the upper landing, looking stunned. The girl jumped to her feet and ran toward the stairs.

Jimmy shouted, "No, Alayna! You'll be—"

A grenade exploded against the front door, blowing it wide. Two grim-faced German troopers pushed their way inside, firing as they advanced. The girl and her aunt were both hit, falling backward, blood bubbling from noses and throats.

"No! Oh God, no!" sobbed Jimmy.

Jarvis fired back at the Germans, killing them instantly.

Silence.

Smoke and silence.

Jimmy was holding the dead girl in his arms, her blood staining his uniform. "Those bastards! Those lousy Kraut bastards!"

Jarvis slumped into a chair, putting his rifle aside. "We got lucky. Only two of 'em."

Jimmy glared at him, gesturing with a bloody hand. "You call this lucky?"

"It's war, kid. People die in war."

A deep grinding rumble from the trees.

Jarvis stood up, peering through the shattered doorway. "Tiger! Edge of the clearing. Time to haul ass."

He pushed jimmy through the doorway as the Tiger's main gun opened up. Two heavy shells tore into the air, demolishing the house.

Jimmy Tucker did not look back as they escaped into the dark woods.

A dim sunup. Once again the fog had closed in, sharply reducing visibility. The rain had stopped, but the icy cold continued to knife through their clothing.

"We are totally lost," groaned Tucker. "Where in hell's the main road? This crap is so thick I can't even see the trees!"

"Yeah," nodded Jarvis, defeat in his tone. "If the Krauts don't nail us this weather will."

"I can help you," said a male voice very close to them. The speaker's English was precise, in accented French. "I can help you," he repeated.

A gaunt figure emerged from the blanketing fog as Jarvis swung toward him, bringing up his rifle.

"No need for a weapon," the gaunt Frenchman told them. "We are comrades. I only wish to serve you."

Jarvis kept his rifle trained on the dim figure. "Where'd you get those duds? I never seen a Frenchie dressed like you."

"It's a uniform from the first big one," said Jimmy. "I seen pictures in books. Even the helmet. World War One."

Jarvis glared at him. "How come he's out here alone in the middle of nowhere dressed like it's Halloween?" To the Frenchman: "You must be freezing your ass."

"Not at all. I feel neither heat nor cold."

"Damn weird," muttered Jarvis.

Jimmy was concerned. "Maybe he's lost, like us."

"No, no, my friend." The Frenchman's voice had a hollow quality; the fog seemed to swallow his words. "I am bound to this spot where I fell, attempting to aid a wounded comrade. Thus, with my task unfinished, I must forever roam these woods. It is God's will, and His will is not to be questioned."

"He talks crazy," Jarvis said. "Like some goddam preacher."

"Maybe he's delusional," muttered Jimmy softly. "War can do bad stuff to people."

"I can aid you in finding the way back to your regiment," said the dark figure.

Jarvis raised an eyebrow. "How'd the frig you know about us looking for them?"

"I know, "said the man. "I simply know these things. Now . . . may I help you?"

"Hell yes!" Jarvis was deeply sarcastic. "I suppose you can tell us exactly how to reach the main road?"

"Go forward for less than a mile and you will find a rough path through the trees," the gaunt man told them. "Watch carefully, for it is easy to miss. Follow this path and, in due course, it will take you to the main road. Your regiment is there, awaiting future orders."

And as suddenly as he had appeared, the gaunt Frenchman was gone, melting back into the shrouding fog.

Jimmy Tucker shook his head. "He was kind of wavery, like you could see right through him."

Jarvis spat into the snow. "Like he was a ghost, huh?"

"There was another battle here in the Ardennes, French verses Krauts, back in 1914," said Tucker. "Maybe he was in it."

"I don't friggin' believe in ghosts," said Jarvis. "The guy was a nutcase, plain and simple."

Jimmy shifted his rifle to ease its weight. "Let's go ahead, try to find the path."

Jarvis stared at him. "And you actually think there is one? Get real, Jimbo."

"Let's try," said Jimmy Tucker. "What have we got to lose?"

"Yeah," said Jarvis. He ran a hand over his bearded chin. "Whatta we got to lose?"

The path was there.

They found the regiment.

And never talked about ghosts again.

Peter Atkins

ALL OUR HEARTS
ARE GHOSTS

Los Angeles, 1934

First time Henry Burgess saw Addison Steele, the guy was getting himself shot.

Henry, first day on the job and excited to be sent from the production office on Melrose out to the Placerita Canyon studio ranch, parked his Austin Roadster—tiny amongst the big Plymouths and Fleetwoods favored by the cast and crew—and made his way across to where everybody was working hard on bringing *Outlaws of Calico Creek* to life.

People and equipment were gathered in front of one of the ranch's standing sets: a segment of a Main Street from the days of the old west; a general store, a corral, and a one-storey chapel. Henry walked toward them, glancing beyond the fragment of a town to where the canyon stretched plain and clear between its low hills and offered a view in the far distance of the Sierra Nevada, still snow-topped in late April.

"Quiet on set!" a voice yelled, and Henry froze in place like everyone else not actively involved in the shot. From a few yards behind the director's chair he watched as, up on the chapel roof and on the shout of *action*, an older man—lean, wiry, wearing a black coat and black hat—jerked his hand to his chest and staggered like he'd just taken a bullet between the ribs. Henry turned to see who'd shot him and felt like a rube when he saw that the actor playing the good guy, knowing he was out of frame, was simply standing and watching like everybody else.

The older man's body went limp and he fell from the roof, playing dead all the way down until hitting the bunched mattresses piled below the camera line.

At a nod from the director, an assistant yelled, "Cut! Moving on," and Henry waited for applause from the crew for the stunt but none came; they were all already busy shifting the camera and the other equipment across to where the next set-up was to be.

Henry moved after them in the direction of a scrub-covered hill with a narrow cave mouth at its base, waving the batch of revised script pages at the assistant director to get his attention.

The AD hung back to let Henry catch up. "Who are you?" he said, glancing at the pages but not taking them—Henry wondering if he was used to dodging process servers or something—and turned to wave the camera crew on.

"Henry Burgess," Henry said. "From the production office. New revisions." He fluttered the pages again. "From the writers."

"Oh, yeah," the AD said, and then turned again to shout across to the crew. "Grant! Get the damn horse inside!"

Outside the cave mouth, a wrangler, presumably Grant—a big guy in his early thirties, ruddy-faced, with scowl-lines permanently etched in his brow—was standing tugging at the reins of a roan horse which was refusing to be led into the narrow darkness of the cave.

Even Henry—no farm-boy, Boston born and bred, and fresh out of Princeton—could see that the horse was afraid. Could see too that Grant wasn't helping; taking a tighter grip on the reins, jerking them, trying to get the horse's head down as if he could simply drag its thousand pounds inside.

"God damn it," Grant shouted. "Get in there!" He reached out his other hand and swished a tight leather riding crop hard against the roan's flank. The horse reared and he cut at it again.

"While there's still daylight, Grant!" the AD shouted.

Henry saw the older man, the stunt guy who had made the fall from the chapel roof, walk out from among the crew to stand in front of the horse. "Mind if I try?" he said to Grant, holding his hand out for the crop.

Grant gave it to him, and the man held it low and loose at his side, Henry wondering if he was letting the horse see it was no longer any immediate threat. "Let go the reins," the man said to Grant, though his eyes stayed on the horse.

"Don't be crazy, Addison," Grant said.

"Let go the reins," the man, Addison, repeated, with only a shade more emphasis.

As Grant dropped the reins, the horse shivered and flexed as if ready to buck again. Grant stepped back sharply but Addison moved closer to the roan and breathed out through his nose into its flaring nostrils, murmuring softly and reaching a confident hand to stroke the animal's brow. A few seconds later, he'd walked the calmed horse into the cave and come back out to rejoin Grant.

The wrangler nodded a slightly resentful acknowledgement. "Shoot," he said. "You didn't even need the crop." He held out his hand for its return.

"Sure I did," said Addison, and slashed it across the younger man's face—once, twice, left, right—before dropping it to the ground. "But I'm all done with it now."

Henry was as silent and still as everyone else as Grant stepped forward, the welts already forming on each of his cheeks. Addison stood perfectly still, letting the man come ahead if he was going to.

But he wasn't going to, Henry found himself realizing, and wondered why—the wrangler had fifty pounds on Addison and was half his age. The director stood up from his chair and shouted, "Save it for wrap, both of you. We've got work to do."

"I'll let it go, old man," Grant said to Addison. "You're lucky we're on a tight schedule."

"Right," said Addison. "That's why." He turned to look at the director, gave him a wink, and walked away, Henry turning his head to watch him go until the AD's voice brought him back to business.

"Pages?" the guy said, with a show of impatience, like he hadn't been just as fascinated as Henry. Henry placed the revisions in his outstretched hand and asked if he could stay to watch a couple more shots.

"Don't you have phones to answer back at the office?" the AD said, and Henry wished he had a riding crop.

Second time Henry saw him, he was getting quietly and elegantly drunk.

The residential hotel on the eastern reaches of Wilshire was hardly the Waldorf Astoria but Henry liked it enough. He'd been there four days now, the cute redhead in the production office having found it for him after he'd spent a few minutes whining to her about how the apartment he'd been promised—hell, put down a deposit on—had fallen through. She'd said that several members of the company were rooming there. "Including you?" he'd asked—you know, taking a shot—but she'd wiggled her engagement ring at him with a seasoned efficiency and he'd retired gracefully.

The hotel's bar looked like it had never heard of the Volstead act nor its repeal, like it had been quietly open for business all through prohibition, though Henry assumed that that couldn't actually be true. He hadn't given it his custom yet but on this fourth night decided to treat himself to a beer. He'd got his first week's wages earlier that morning and had had a long day.

Addison Steele was standing there, in the same black outfit he'd worn on set, one booted foot on the bar's brass rail. There was a shot glass full of whiskey in front of him, and two empty beside it.

"I'd like to pay for that, if you'd let me," Henry said, walking up to stand beside the older man and gesturing at his glass.

Addison gave him a look. "Man's a fool to refuse a free drink," he said. "But a bigger one if he doesn't ask the reason."

"I liked the way you looked out for that horse," Henry said, and saw a slow recognition come into Addison's eyes.

"Right," he said. "You were over to the Canyon Monday last."

"Henry Burgess," Henry said, putting out his hand. "From the production office."

"Henry," Addison said, after he'd shaken his hand. Not addressing Henry, simply weighing the word in his mouth and finding it not entirely to his taste. "Anybody ever call you Hank?"

Henry told him that no, nobody ever had, and Addison nodded like that was perfectly understandable. "I'd like to call you Hank," he said. "Unless you have any objection to that?"

"No," Henry said, amused, kind of pleased, but keeping it to himself. "None that I can think of."

"Well, alright," Addison said, and raised the shot glass in Henry's direction before throwing the whiskey down in one and flicking an upraised finger at the bartender to bring him another.

"My friend Hank will be paying for that one," Addison said to the bartender, "but I don't want him held accountable for the several more with which I intend to chase it."

The bartender nodded, and Henry waited till he'd walked away. "Talking about names . . ." he said, letting it hang.

"Yeah?"

"Addison Steele?"

"What about it?"

"It's a stage name, right?"

"A *stage* name?" Addison said, like the very idea of such a thing was bizarre. "No, Hank. It's not a stage name. I've worn it close to forty years now."

"So you weren't born with it?" *Born* with it? Henry being polite. If the guy'd worn it for forty years, he'd have been at least twenty-five when he first tried it on.

Addison cocked his head. "Full of questions, aren't you, Hank?" he said.

"I don't mean any offense."

"None taken, son." Addison took a sip of his next shot, staring at the mirror behind the bar. Staring *through* it, Henry thought, to somewhere very far away in time. He'd just about given up on getting an answer when Addison turned back to him.

"The name was given to me by a friend," he said. "At a time when I had sufficient reason to let go of the one my people had christened me with."

"Oh," Henry said, wondering what *that* story was but not ready to ask. "Reason I asked is, because it's a … well, it's not a *pun*, exactly … a play on words, I guess." Desperately avoiding the word joke. "A literary *jeu d'esprit*." Jesus Christ.

"A *jeu d'esprit*, huh?" Addison said, a little glint in his eye. Amused by the words but pronouncing them perfectly.

"It's the names of two eighteenth century writers. Addison and Steele. Editors of *The Tatler*. And *The Spectator*."

"Is that right?"

"It is."

"Huh," Addison said, and was silent for a moment, looking through Henry like he'd looked through the mirror. "Well, the friend in question was an educated lady," he finally said. "And her sense of humor always favored the sly."

"It's a good name," Henry said. "Must read well on the posters."

Addison smiled, kind of. "I don't get my name on movie posters, son. I'm just another bad guy in black. Someone for the hero to pick off. I get shot for a goddam living, Hank. Been doing it a long time. Been shot by Bill Hart and Bronco Anderson, been doing it since before the movies learned to talk."

Henry was eager to ask him about his life before Hollywood started paying him to die, because he could smell real western history on the man, but Addison—perhaps mindful of his manners, perhaps for reasons of his own—turned the conversation to Henry's own story and just how a kid with a degree from a fancy school back east could think it a good idea to come out and work as a glorified errand boy for the hacks at a B-movie factory, a move which Addison, although politely indirect about it, plainly considered to be a symptom of a sadly undiagnosed mental illness.

They continued to talk, and Addison continued to drink—the impressiveness of his intake matched only by the impressiveness of how little it seemed to affect him—and Henry thought he'd heard the last of the man's secret history until they were almost done for the night.

"Know what she said to me once?" Addison suddenly said, out of nowhere, out of a conversation about gunfights and wasted bullets—*you do it right, it only takes one*, he'd thrilled Henry by saying—and the other ways in which the movies got it wrong.

"Your friend, you mean? The educated lady?"

Addison nodded, and Henry asked him what it was she'd said.

"She said, 'All our hearts are ghosts'."

Way he said it, it sounded like a quote from something, Henry thought. Thought too that it sounded like the saddest thing in the world, but he was, after all, a little drunk himself. "What does it mean?" he said.

Addison paused before replying, covering it by throwing down his last shot. "Damned if I know, Hank," he said, slamming his emptied glass down onto the bar like an unseen director had told him it was a good way to end the scene.

Henry was damned if he knew either, but he watched Addison stare again into the bar's mirror after he said it and figured it for the first lie his new friend had told him.

Third time he saw him, he drove him upstate to kill the richest man in Houghton County.

Henry'd been taking sandwich orders in the office when he was urgently re-assigned. It was the last day of the *Outlaws of Calico Creek* shoot and Addison Steele had ruined everybody's morning by not showing up for work at the ranch location. Henry was told to drive back to their hotel and get him out to Placerita as fast as he could.

There was no answer to Henry's repeated knocking on Addison's door but a bellman eventually unlocked it for him, a phone call from an enraged studio executive having overcome any scruples the hotel management felt about letting anyone short of a cop into the room.

The room wasn't empty, but clearly deserted. The belongings were few, but were all tied in neat and ready-to-be-disposed-of bundles in a way that suggested Addison had no intention of ever returning for them.

On a circular occasional table, two items had been bound together with a thin red ribbon and were standing beside a newspaper clipping and the envelope in which it had been mailed. The envelope bore the previous day's postmark and the clipping itself was from a Lake Tahoe daily and was an obituary notice for a woman, a Mrs. Lester Cutter, who had died in Northern California's Houghton County the previous week at the age of sixty-three. Survived by her husband, it said, the founder of Cutter township and three times its Mayor.

Untying the bundle beside the clipping, Henry looked at the two things that Addison had thought worthy of a red ribbon rather than the twine with which he'd bound everything else he'd left behind. The first was an old photograph—so old that it was not on paper but on tin, its silvered image seeming so fragile that Henry feared his fingers could wipe it clean—and was a formally posed portrait of a beautiful young woman. Hardly more than a girl when the picture was made, Henry saw but knew—if only from the fierce and eager intelligence glowing from her dark eyes—that he was looking at an educated lady.

The other item was a book—published, Henry saw from the title page, back in 1894 and by an author with the unlikely name of Lafcadio Hearn. It was called *Shadows in Running Water; tales and verse from the Japanese*, and there was an inscription on its fly-page in a beautifully neat copperplate. *To my dear friend Addison Steele*, it read, *who knew me well when both our hearts were alive. In affectionate remembrance, Marianne Cutter (nee Ryan).*

A worn leather bookmark protruded from the text-block and, at a gentle touch from Henry's hand, the book fell naturally open there, as if the bookmarked page had been looked at many times over the years. There were four three-line verses on the page and the last line of the third *haiku*, underlined long ago in pencil, read; *all our hearts are ghosts.*

"Let me spare you the suspense, Hank," Addison said, when Henry's roadster pulled up at the bench outside the Pasadena train station. "You are not going to succeed in your mission."

"You're not going to come back?"

"The prospect seems unlikely."

"I gathered that when I saw your room. Even though you left everything behind."

"Not everything," Addison said, and Henry knew at once what he meant, though Addison's coat was roomy enough to conceal whatever he might have been wearing at his waist.

"At least let me give you a ride," Henry said. "Train to Tahoe stops every damn half hour. And you'll still be twenty miles from Cutter when you get off."

Addison looked almost impressed. "Well, Hank," he said. "You've been busy with your research. And quick, too. You know, once you've got this picture business crap out your system, you should head up to San Francisco; I believe Pinkerton's still hiring."

Henry didn't say anything, just leant across to spring the passenger door. Addison didn't say anything either, just got in, and Henry let him stay silent for almost the first hour of the long drive, before opening with what he figured was his best way in.

"The book and the picture," he said. "Everything else, sure. But I don't get leaving them behind."

"I didn't want them buried with me," Addison said, and let that sink in for a minute. Then, in a gentler voice, "Besides, I figured it'd be you that found them."

Henry felt a rush of sentiment, but didn't surrender to it. "They're in the trunk," he said.

"Well, you look after them then."

"I'm hoping I won't need to," Henry said. "I don't know how this story's going to end."

"Oh, you know how it's going to end, Hank," Addison said.

"I do?"

Addison looked at him like he was stupid. "I thought you liked those western pictures," he said.

"Sure, but—"

"Then you know they all end the same way. Two guys pull down on each other and one of them dies."

"*One* of them dies," Henry said.

"That's something else the movies get wrong," Addison said. "Real life, both those idiots usually wound up dead. Unless one of them got real fucking lucky."

Henry waited another half-mile or so before saying, "Okay, enough about the ending. I want to know the beginning."

Addison looked out to the side of the road for a moment or two, to where the Southern California topography was slowly giving way to the harsher and less forgiving look of the north, and then back to Henry.

"Price of the ride?"

"Price of the ride."

So Henry heard a story from the tail-end of the boomtown days, from when tiny communities would grow a hundredfold in three years when the gold was leaping out of the hills and dwindle back to nothing in two when the seams were exhausted. But truth was this particular story could have happened almost anywhere because it was a story about people, about a young girl and her dreams and the young hothead who loved her for them and how she was lost to him and became another man's wife.

"Rich guy from the big city?" Henry said, thinking he knew how this part went. "Turned her head with fancy jewelry and fine manners?"

"Big city? Fine manners?" Addison said and Henry, ashamed, heard the older man struggle to keep the contempt out of his voice. "Jesus Christ, Hank, maybe you *are* dumb enough to be in the goddam movie business. I believe he may have been born back east, yes, but Lester Cutter had killed three men before he was twenty-one. And enjoyed it. Poor as dirt, mean as they come, and fast enough to back it up."

"So why did she—"

"She didn't," Addison said, and his voice got very flat and very cold and he told it quickly lest the scars of the ancient wounds start bleeding anew. "He raped her. Got her pregnant. And I'd've killed him the day I found out if her people hadn't forced a wedding the previous night."

"My God, Addison," Henry said, not knowing what else to say.

"God wasn't paying much attention," Addison said. "I've found that to be the case more often than not."

Henry gave him a moment. "And the child?" he finally asked.

"Lost almost at full term, along with the chance of others," Addison said. "But I was long gone by then. It was my last promise to her, that I'd pay no visit to her husband while she was still alive."

"And now, what, you're just going to *kill* him? Just find him and kill him?"

"We've been over this, Hank. I'm not going to *bushwhack* the guy. I'm doing her memory the courtesy of facing him down properly."

"You're going to knock on his damn door or something?"

"No need," Addison said. "He knows I'm coming."

"He *knows*? That's ridiculous. How does he *know*? Some old gun-fighter instinct?"

Addison just looked at him, letting him start to believe that that was in fact exactly right, before giving a little snort of amusement. "The modern world has its conveniences," he said. "I called him up on the telephone. Made a date."

"Christ almighty. And he *agreed*?"

"Of course he did, Hank," Addison said. "Lester always appreciated the opportunity to kill someone. And it don't matter how much money he's made, how sleek he's got. Guys don't change. Not guys like me and him."

Henry had nothing to say, just shook his head and stared out at the road ahead. Who the hell *were* these people, he thought. He knew the wild ones were still out there, of course. Papers were full of them. Pretty Boy Floyd, Baby Face Nelson. Dillinger. And it was they, Henry thought, with a stab of something lost, who were the true heirs to the men of the old west, not the shiny-suited heroes of the silver screen with their guitars and good manners. Those movie cowboys were just pretty lies made for boys like Henry. He had a wild animal in his car, he realized. A wild animal, no matter its charm and elegance. He really didn't have much to say for the rest of the drive.

They could as well have been back on the *Outlaws of Calico Creek* set, Henry thought. They were more than a mile from the modern township with its stoplights and paved streets and Woolworths and,

yes, movie theater. This was the slowly decaying old town, long abandoned, a ruined thing left to rot out of sight of all those people with
their eyes on the glittering American future and no mind for its past.
Chroniclers of his country's recent history had already coined a phrase
for places like this, Henry knew; *Ghost towns*, they called them. And,
standing here, he knew that they'd named them well.

There was nothing ghostly about Lester Cutter, though. He was
fully alive. Unlike Addison, he'd grown fatter with the years and the
fedora hat he wore, unlike Addison's Stetson, paid no homage to the
days of their youth. But his eyes were feral and excited and Henry was
instinctively afraid of him on sight.

"This is Hank Burgess," Addison said, before Cutter could ask. "He's
got no dog in this fight and I trust you'll respect that. He's just here to
take me home. You know, one way or another."

Cutter's half nod was unpleasantly amused. "Appreciate your thought-
fulness, Addison," he said. "I'd hate to have to call out the fire station
boys to clean up my mess."

Henry wondered if there'd be some kind of formal countdown, some
kind of etiquette and stated rules of engagement, but they both slipped
into it like old boxers back in the ring, old gladiators back in the arena,
pausing instinctively about fifteen feet from each other on the dry ne-
glected dirt that used to be a Main Street. There was no right or wrong
left in their scenario, Henry realized. No good or evil, no black hats or
white hats, nothing but mutual appetite and excitement. They both
waited a second or two, their atavistic clocks perfectly synchronized.
Savoring it, Henry realized. Jesus Christ. *Savoring* it.

And then—without a word, without a gesture—it happened.

Cutter was fast, just as fast as Addison had said, fast on the draw
and fast to fire, and his eye was as good as if the years between had
never happened. Three bullets had slammed into his opponent before
Addison's Colt had even cleared the holster. All in the chest. At least
one in the heart.

Henry's own heart lurched in despair as if he, not Addison, had been
the target. No, not despair. A terrible sadness, perhaps, but not despair.
Because Henry knew something that Cutter didn't; Addison Steele got
shot for a goddam living.

Addison didn't fall, didn't falter, taking Cutter's bullets like they were no more real than the many he'd mimed taking in the movies. His gun was in his hand, his arm was up and straight, and his aim was cold and true.

The man in the black suit may have already been dead, already been as much of a ghost as the town he'd come back to, but this ghost had its finger on the trigger of its Colt and enough will—or its memory—to squeeze it.

You do it right, it only takes one, he'd said to Henry. And, one last time, Addison Steele did it right.

The entrance wound was nothing, Henry saw, through eyes already wet with tears—a small, elegantly centered hole in Cutter's forehead—but the exit tore half the fucker's skull off and Henry watched Addison's old enemy hit the dirt before he did. Whether Addison's eyes saw it or not, though, was something Henry was never able to say.

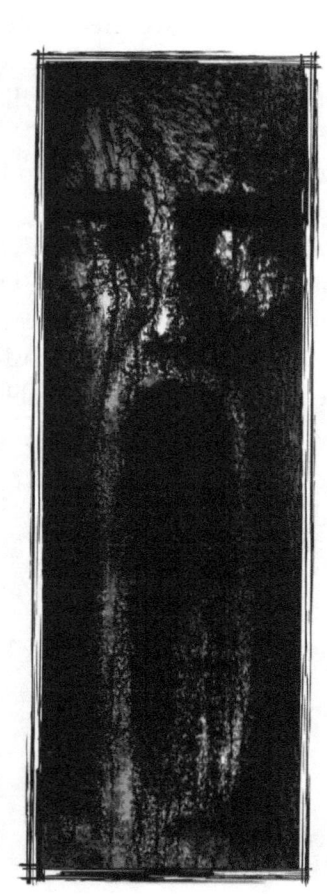

Michael D. Nye

THE ITCH

Marvin Tupps had an itch. Not the kind of itch you scratch with your fingers, earning the satisfying feeling that comes as your nails scrape along the skin. This was a different kind of itch altogether, an itch that spoke to the darkest corner of his being. This was an itch . . . to kill someone. The thing was, Marvin didn't have a particular someone in mind. He wasn't angry at anyone. No one had done him a wrong that would elicit such an act of retribution. But there it was—whispering to him—an itch that could only be scratched in one way.

The itch to kill had awoken one gray morning while Marvin was shaving. As he peered at his reflection in the mirror—the reflection of a thin (he liked to think "slender"), thirty-six year old with small brown eyes, a hawk-like nose above thin lips, and an almost non-existent chin—and positioned the razor to attack the last remaining bit of shaving cream and stubble, he caught a glimpse of sudden hunger and excitement in his eyes. Marvin could only stare, the razor poised an inch from his chin, as the idea of killing someone flowed through him. After a moment the itch faded and Marvin dismissed what he had seen in those eyes—his eyes?—as a trick of the slightly distorted light thrown off by the cheap glass of the mirror. He took one last downward swipe with the razor, and wiped his face with a rough, threadbare towel.

Now, three weeks later, Marvin was sitting in the one chair he owned—overstuffed and smelling of ancient cat urine—dressed only in boxer shorts. Scarfing down a bowl of canned chili he'd heated in his microwave, Marvin stared at the small television set that shared the top of the dresser with his keys, wallet and spare change. He wasn't watching the show; the sound was turned down too low to follow. Instead he was thinking about the same thing he had been thinking about since that first incident in front of the mirror.

The itch had progressively gotten stronger. At first it had been only a slight buzzing inside his head that would creep up on him in the late hours of the night, alone in his tiny studio apartment. A stray tendril here and there, worming its way through his brain. Now, however, the buzzing felt like a swarm of damn bugs was crawling around under his skin. And he somehow knew, was certain, in fact, that the only way to get rid of the itch was . . . to hunt.

Marvin stopped eating. The chili tasted like sawdust in his mouth. *Why do I keep thinking about killing someone? Yeah, there are some real creeps out there, but still . . . you don't just go out and kill them. That's . . . crazy.* Marvin put aside the half-eaten bowl of chili and stretched out on top of his bed. He closed his eyes, but knew that sleep wouldn't come easy. Every night when he would try to doze off, the idea would take hold again and itch at his brain; *What about the people out there who are really bad? The molesters who keep getting out of prison and molesting again. Or gangbangers who terrorize their neighborhoods and sell drugs to kids. And then there are the murderers.*

Maybe it would be okay to kill those people.

Maybe those people deserved to be killed.

The bugs had become increasingly more active. Marvin knew he had to do something, find some way of calming the almost constant buzz of . . . bug-energy. *Yeah, that's what it is: bug-energy.* Marvin got up and quickly dressed in the jeans, T-shirt and jacket he had earlier dropped on the floor next to the bed. He grabbed his keys, but as he reached for his wallet, decided that it would be better not to take it. His neighborhood, an older section of Los Angeles next to a half-empty industrial park, wasn't the kind of place you'd want to walk around in at 1 a.m. carrying a wallet, despite the meager amount of money his own contained.

Marvin stepped out of his old, brick apartment building. He breathed in the cool night air, and felt the bug-energy awaken to the possibilities. Marvin kept to the shadows as he made his way past his building and down the street. *Not much going on tonight,* he thought as he made his way to where there were several large old warehouses. On one a banner proclaimed, "Coming soon—the best in artist lofts!" The banner looked ragged and the building unused. A couple of blocks further down the street, Marvin saw a woman's head bobbing up and down in the front seat of a parked car, the driver leaning his head back, eyes closed. A few minutes later, on the next block, he watched a couple of small drug deals taking place.

After two hours of wandering around, Marvin realized he wasn't going to do anything. *What was I thinking I was gonna do?* he muttered to himself as he turned to head back home. His late night reconnaissance seemed to take the edge off the itch, however, and once home he was finally able to fall into a fitful sleep.

Over the next few days Marvin went to his job as a janitor at an inner city high school, a short bus ride from his apartment, and wasn't bothered by any thoughts of killing anyone, other than maybe whoever had thrown up in the library. He had to try to clean each book by hand, finally salvaging only a copy of the collective works of Robert Louis Stevenson.

—

The next Saturday night the itch hit him hard. As Marvin stood in his apartment looking out a grimy window, his fingertips etching streaks on the glass, he knew there would be all kinds of low-life activities going on a weekend night. The itch was tugging at him, drawing him out into the dark. It played at the edges of his mind, whispering, coaxing, teasing. And the bugs under his skin seemed to have multiplied. Marvin knew he had to go out again. Should he take a weapon? *What do I have?* The answer was—nothing. *I don't even own a hammer or a knife, other than the one butter knife I use to . . . well, spread butter.* He wasn't exactly prepared to start going on a killing streak, especially against murderers and rapists who, he figured, were probably armed to the teeth.

Marvin was in the shadows again, creeping along the street about two blocks from his apartment. Since he was unarmed, this was going to be just another look-see, a way to quiet the itch for a while. The bug-energy was excited about being out and about, however. The prey was out there, and the bug-energy wanted Marvin to find it. He had just turned the corner at Third Street when he saw something that made him stop and press deeper into the shadows. About a block from where he stood, a heavy-set, middle-aged woman was struggling with a young man. The man was dressed in jeans and a black T-shirt, and Marvin could make out tattoos all up and down his arms, though he couldn't see what they were. He had to look twice to realize that the young man had a grip on the woman's purse and was pulling on it, the straps stretched out taut like a tightrope, her hands grasping to hold on.

The purse snatcher gave one last hard yank and the purse was free. He turned and ran—in Marvin's direction! All kinds of thoughts raced through his mind; *Am I gonna do something? I'm no fighter. Maybe there's something . . .* Marvin frantically looked around for anything he could use as a weapon and saw an empty wine bottle near his feet. He grabbed it and ducked back around the corner. His whole body was vibrating like a tuning fork tapping on a piano wire. He could hear the purse snatcher's pounding footsteps getting closer.

Then suddenly the young man turned the corner and was in front of him. As if controlled by a puppeteer, Marvin's arm snapped up and swung the bottle as hard as it could at the purse snatcher's head. The sound of a "thunk" and the bottle shattered. The young man's head jerked back, his knees buckled, and he sank to the sidewalk. Marvin's heart was racing so hard he thought for a moment he might pass out.

Marvin was looking down at the young man's inert figure, the purse still clutched in his hand, when he heard cautious footsteps drawing near. The owner of the purse tentatively stuck her head around the corner. She looked at Marvin, then her eyes widened as they traveled down to the guy on the ground. By the way she stepped back it was obvious she was afraid to get near her assailant, so Marvin reached down and yanked the purse from his grip. He held it out to her and, like a nervous animal approaching to eat out of his hand, she reached out and took the bag. Marvin thought she would immediately turn away and leave, but she stood there looking down at her assailant.

"Is he . . . dead?" She whispered as if afraid her words might bring him back to life. Marvin could see that the guy was breathing despite a rather nasty gash on his forehead.

"No, just unconscious."

Still looking down she murmured, as if to herself, "You should have killed the bastard." Then she looked up at Marvin and stared him in the eye. "Thank you," she said and, clutching her purse to her chest, she turned and hurried off.

Marvin was still trying to process what he had done, when the guy groaned. As bad as it was that he had tried to rob the woman, Marvin didn't see him as a candidate for execution. Sensing the guy would soon be coming around, Marvin turned back toward his apartment building and hurried off.

His legs felt like rubber as Marvin climbed the stairs to the second floor of his building. Once inside his apartment, he let out a breath that felt as though he had been holding it for hours. He went to wipe his face and noticed a drop of blood oozing from his index finger. It came from a small cut, and as Marvin brought his hand up to his face to get a better look, he noticed the faint odor of wine. He embraced these new sensations like a badge of honor, then stumbled to his bed and flopped down. When the adrenaline rush had subsided, he felt the itch wash away and he drifted off to a deep sleep.

When Marvin woke, he had the vaguest memory of a dream where something glittered through a curtain. As he lay there and let the image refocus, he saw a silvery object emerge through the curtain. No, not emerge. Cut. Slash. A long, sharp, brutal knife ripping through the curtain. Then it stopped and he saw the hand that held the knife. And it had a small cut on it with a drop of blood. His hand.

Marvin lay there and thought about the knife. *It was really badass.* And the more he thought about that knife, the more he wanted it. *Why a knife—shouldn't I get a gun?* But when Marvin pictured the knife, the itch sent an excited pulse of bug-energy through him—more than when he thought about a gun. Maybe because with a knife he would have to get up close to his prey. Maybe because of the noise a gun would make. Or maybe just the practical consideration that a knife didn't require a background check. And Marvin sure as hell didn't want to wander around his neighborhood looking for someone to sell him an illegal gun.

The next day at work Marvin kept picturing the knife from his dream. Every time he did, his fingers would curl into a grip, as if they were already holding the knife. Yeah, he wanted that knife. That badass knife. Marvin thought about where he might get one. *There's a gun shop near here, so after I get off work, I'll head over there and see if they have knives—my knife.*

And the bug-energy sent a ripple under his skin.

●

A bell dinged as Marvin opened the door and went inside the gun shop. It was small in size but the shelves were stocked with traps, hunting jackets, fishing poles, and dozens of other accessories of the hunt. He looked around, unsure of what to do.

"Help ya, buddy?"

Marvin looked to his right. Behind a counter filled with hand guns stood a large man—a mountain man—tall and heavy-set, with a long, bushy gray beard. Not the kind of guy you see too often in L.A.

Marvin was nervous, definitely a fish out of water, but he managed to croak out, "Knife." The large man's eyes got hard and his right hand moved under the counter.

"You got one, or you want one?"

Marvin got a hold of himself and said, "I'm looking for one."

The large man chuckled and withdrew his hand from under the counter. "Well, you came to the right place." He nodded toward the rear of the store. "In the back, over to the left."

Marvin walked past racks of what looked like military-type rifles hanging on the walls behind counters full of handguns to the back of the store. He could see them as he got closer—a long glass case full of beautiful knives. There were small ones and large ones and everything in between. Marvin stood in front of the case and stared, hypnotized by the array spread out before him. His eyes traveled past the small ones; he needed something that would satisfy the itch. He was aware of movement and looked up to see that the large man had slipped behind the knife counter.

"What do you want to use it for?" The large man asked.

"I . . . um" Marvin stammered.

"You want to carve, skin, throw, or . . .?"

Marvin shook his head. "No. I . . . I want it for self-defense." That felt closest to the truth, but the large man stared at Marvin as if he had said the wrong thing.

"You want something for self-defense, you should be looking at the guns."

"No, it's gotta be a knife." It came out stronger than Marvin intended and the large man gave him another quizzical stare.

"Okay, let's see . . ." The large man slid open the rear of the case and Marvin watched intently as the man's hand passed slowly over the rows of knives. As his hand came to a beauty of a knife—not the biggest, but a real nice size—Marvin felt a buzz. Yes! That was the one! He nodded and the large man smiled and pulled the knife out, laying it on the counter top.

"That's a Tex Creek XL. It's got a 1095 Carbon steel blade with a Micarta handle and thumb ridge. She's a real beauty. You could carve all day with it, and it'd still be sharp enough to gut something at night."

The large man saw a light in Marvin's eyes and chuckled. "Go ahead, try it on for size."

Marvin reached out and picked it up. As his fingers closed around the handle, a tingle raced up his arm and the bug-energy hummed. The knife was heavy, but the right kind of heavy—solid and deadly.

"Step back and see how it feels." The large man said. Marvin backed up a step and moved his arm around, up and down, then a few circle movements. The large man stood there patiently, waiting. Marvin made some stabbing motions, in and out. He was sure they looked awkward.

"That's okay for your basic thrust and stab, but try holding it the other way," the large man instructed. Marvin switched positions and held the knife like he was stabbing down at somebody.

"Now, lower your arm and move it side to side while turning your wrist."

It took a couple of tries, but Marvin finally got what he was talking about.

"That way, if you miss going in one direction, you're ready to quickly slash in the other direction."

Marvin could see what he was saying. It all depended on how you wanted to stab. He'd have to practice a little, but this knife was the one.

"I'll take it."

The large man nodded his approval. "I'll even throw in a leather sheath and honing stone at no charge."

He opened a drawer under the case and brought out a plain dark brown leather sheath and a small gray rectangular stone. He slid the knife into the sheath and Marvin followed him back to the cash register. The large man placed the knife, sheath and stone in a bag. "That'll be one sixty-four, eighty-five."

Marvin's mind reeled as the price fully registered and he started stuttering, "A hundred . . . and . . ."

The large man smiled, then leaned in, all business. "I got other knives," he said. "Cheaper ones. But you get what you pay for. And if you're in a situation where your life depends on your blade, you don't want something cheap that might break off at the tang, ya know what I mean?"

Marvin didn't. He had no idea what the large man had been talking about ever since he had started describing the knife. Marvin swallowed and thought about the price. *Okay, how much do I have on my debit card? Maybe three hundred. Forget having chili for dinner the rest of this week. With my rent and shit, I'll be lucky to be able to afford Ramen.*

But he knew the bug-energy wanted it. And he also knew he'd get no peace from the itch if he went with something cheaper.

Despite feeling financially gutted as he left the store, Marvin also felt a growing sense of power. Not only did he have the knife, he had a purpose. He couldn't remember the last time he'd felt like he had a goal, something he knew was right.

Marvin spent the rest of the week after work, practicing. Stabbing, slashing, moving around, the knife becoming a part of him, an extension of his arm. By the end of the week, he felt more confident. Not an expert . . . but ready.

He could hardly sleep Thursday night, waiting for the weekend. By Friday night Marvin was nervous, excited, scared, and . . . ready to hunt. He left the apartment around 11 p.m. and, keeping close to the buildings, made his way up the street. Marvin's senses were attuned to all the sights, sounds, and smells. There was laughter to his left. And somewhere up ahead he heard the sound of glass breaking. The squeal of tires pierced the darkness from the next block over. The knife was in its sheath, attached to Marvin's belt, in the small of his back. He remembered some guy in a movie kept it there, and it felt like the right place for it to be.

Marvin prowled the streets past the warehouses and decrepit apartment buildings for a couple of hours and, except for small groups of people raising a little hell, there wasn't much happening. Around 1:30 in the morning he started feeling weary. He had been at work at 8 a.m. and wasn't used to all this walking. It was discouraging that since hitting the streets, he hadn't seen anything worse than a couple of kids breaking a car window and stealing whatever they could find of value inside.

Marvin was about to call it a night and head home, when he heard a muffled scream coming from a nearby alley. He cautiously approached the mouth of the alley and looked around the corner. Near the dead end he saw a man with a mop of frizzy hair holding a woman up against a wall, his beefy left hand was around her neck; in his right hand he held a knife. His face was almost touching hers as he spit out, "I said shut up! You and me's gonna have some fun." The woman was blonde, in her twenties, slender, and nicely dressed in a business suit. *She sure doesn't look like she lives around here*, Marvin thought. More likely she was someone who worked in a nearby office. Maybe went out with the girls after work on a Friday night for a few drinks.

Marvin stepped all the way into the alley, but the man was focused on the woman and didn't notice. Marvin's right leg was shaking so hard he thought it just might give out and send him crumbling to the ground. Marvin cleared his throat and spoke; the words coming out like a high-pitched squeak.

"Leave her alone."

Keeping the woman pinned, the man turned his head in Marvin's direction.

"This ain't none of your concern, asshole."

Marvin worked up some saliva and swallowed to clear his dry throat. "I'm making it my concern." He was so scared, he almost forgot about the knife. He reached back to his waist, grabbed the handle and yanked. His sweat-drenched hand slid off the handle, leaving him holding nothing but air.

Meanwhile, the man had started toward him, dragging the woman with his left arm. Marvin wiped his hand on his pant leg and reached back for the knife again. Grabbing the handle tightly, he yanked up and out it came. When he was about ten feet from Marvin, the man growled, "I'm gonna cut you, then I'm gonna have some fun with this little lady, after that . . ." The man stopped when he saw the knife. His eyes went wide and then, seeing the knife shaking in Marvin's hand, he chuckled and said, "Hey now, that's a nice knife you got there, buddy. How about we trade?"

After looking at all the knives in the gun shop, Marvin could tell that the man's knife was cheap. He bet it didn't cost more than ten or twenty bucks, tops. As the man drew nearer, Marvin noticed that he held the knife out in front of him, holding it the wrong way. Distracted, the man must have loosened his grip on the woman, because suddenly she twisted and was free. She screamed and took off running. As the man turned toward her in a futile attempt to grab her again, Marvin made his move.

Just like he'd been practicing, he swung the knife as hard as he could at the man. He wasn't aiming at any particular part of the man's body—he just wanted to make contact. And he did. He felt the impact, as if he'd hit a sack of flour. Then the knife was free again. However, Marvin was still moving, spinning away fast enough to cause him to trip over his own feet. Down he went—sprawled out on his back like an overturned turtle. He heard the man curse, and looked up. The man was standing there, looking down at his left hand which he held pressed to the side of his waist. It took Marvin a minute to realize that the flow of red seeping out from under the man's hand was blood.

As Marvin lay frozen on the concrete, the man's eyes, glazed and unfocused, shifted from his wound to Marvin. The man shook his head as if flinging away cobwebs and focused his eyes, squinting down at Marvin. A guttural sound like that of a wounded animal escaped from the man's lips and, with his right hand still holding the shoddy knife, he came screaming toward Marvin. Some instinct made him roll to the side and the man's knife hit the ground instead of Marvin. It splintered into two pieces and Marvin actually flashed on what the guy in the gun shop had said: ". . . if you're in a situation where your life depends on your blade, you don't want something cheap that might break off at the tang."

Marvin scrambled to his feet as the man dropped to his knees, a hand on the ground to balance himself. Marvin could have left him there; the wounded man was no longer a threat to the woman, who had disappeared, or to Marvin. Maybe the man would bleed out and die; maybe he wouldn't. But then the itch whispered and the bug-energy flowed through Marvin's body. This was the moment Marvin had been waiting for, the moment when he could scratch, the moment when he would begin a new journey.

It was time.

Marvin ran up behind the man and plunged his knife into the back of the man's neck, just above the shoulder. The man jerked up straight and Marvin thought he was going to get back up, but a moment later he dropped face first to the ground. Marvin stood there, knife in hand, and stared down at the body. He watched in fascination as an expanding pool of blood seeped from the man's neck. Slowly, as if emerging from a dream, Marvin became aware of sounds: a dog barking, a shout, and the distant sound of a siren. Had the woman called the police? Whether they were on the way or not, it was time to get the hell out of there. He turned to leave, but the itch wasn't done with him. As if being guided, Marvin reached down and put his hand in the man's back right pocket. When he pulled his hand out, he was holding the man's wallet. Before he realized what he was doing, he had stuffed the wallet in his jacket pocket. Now it was time to go.

Marvin looked around. There was not a soul in sight, but he crossed to another street, then turned and made his way back home, figuring if anybody saw him leave they'd point the police in the wrong direction. That's about as far as he could think at the moment. Pretty much everything else was a blur until he found himself standing in his room. He didn't even remember climbing the stairs to his floor.

Marvin walked into the bathroom as if moving through a vat of molasses. Flicking on the light, he looked in the mirror . . . and was shocked at what he saw. *How did I make it home? Did anybody see me?* Marvin was a mess. Besides looking disheveled, his shirt and jacket had a spray of blood along the front. Even though he could picture the knife going in, he hadn't been aware of getting blood on himself. He would have to take precautions the next time. If there was a next time. He'd have to think about that, but first . . .

As he attempted to wash himself off, Marvin saw that he was doing more smearing than cleaning, so he turned on the shower and, removing his shoes, stepped into the small cubicle with the rest of his clothes on. He was no sooner standing under the spray of warm water than a pink waterfall ran down his body and formed a pool at his feet that slowly twisted then disappeared down the drain. After a few minutes, he turned off the water and stood there dripping. *This isn't gonna work,* he thought. His shirt and jacket were still imbedded with dark pink stains. He was going to have to buy something that would be easier to clean; he couldn't afford to keep throwing away clothes.

Marvin peeled off his sopping wet jacket, T-shirt and jeans, and began stuffing them into a garbage bag. As he bundled his jacket into a ball, he felt something in the pocket. The wallet. He had forgotten about it. He opened it and saw a license, soggy bits of paper, and an unexpected bonus—forty dollars! He'd have to get rid of the wallet tomorrow. Jumping back in the shower, he scrubbed his entire body vigorously, then stepped out and dried himself off. He suddenly realized how tired he was and staggered over to the bed. He sprawled out on top of the thin blanket and closed his eyes.

That's when the images burst into his brain like fireworks. He relived every moment of the kill as if watching a movie in slow motion. His heartbeat rose to a crescendo, hammering against the wall of his chest. Then Marvin was floating through a warm sea of release, and felt that a great weight had lifted from his body. When the images subsided, he had an overwhelming revelation: the itch was gone, and only peace remained.

Marvin woke the next morning from a deep sleep. He stretched his arms and legs, then became aware of a sore spot on his thigh. He looked down and noticed a ragged circle of bluish-yellow discoloration. *What the . . .?* And then, in a rush, he remembered. Everything. It wasn't a dream. He had done it! A wave of energy enveloped his mind and body. He sprang from his bed, ravenous. Although he usually only had coffee and a donut for breakfast, today Marvin needed fuel. And then it struck him—he had an extra forty dollars!

Marvin got dressed and, on the way to a coffee shop over on the next block, he buried the garbage bag of bloody clothes under a layer of trash in a dumpster. At the small mom-and-pop coffee shop he treated himself to three eggs, extra bacon, hash browns and toast, all washed down with orange juice and coffee. After he had sated his newfound appetite, he stepped into the restroom and, stuffing the still damp forty dollars into his pocket, he washed his prints from the wallet. On the way back to his apartment he pulled out a paper towel he had taken from the restroom and, using it to hold the wallet, slipped it into a gutter opening.

Man, he was feeling great! Instead of bothering him, the bug-energy now flowed smoothly through Marvin's whole body and mind, giving him a rush of pure clarity. And best of all—no itch. Turning this new clarity to his next move, Marvin stopped into a Goodwill store and found a black nylon jacket. Something he could get blood on and it would easily wash off. *Does that mean I'm gonna do this again?* Marvin wondered as he left the store. Well, he wasn't going to ponder that question right now; he felt too damn good to worry about the future, a future he wasn't sure he'd have any control over anyway.

When he got home, Marvin kicked back and turned on his crappy little TV. No cable, just a pair of bent rabbit ears, but it got the local news. And there it was! An unidentified body had been found with several stab wounds. No word about a woman being attacked. The police, having found some meth on the guy, and no wallet, were looking at it as a drug-related robbery gone bad.

Marvin continued to follow the news on the killing, but after two days, when there wasn't much in the way of new developments, the media dropped any mention of it. The cops had finally come up with a name for the guy, but Marvin only half listened and had forgotten it by the time he turned off the TV. *Doesn't take a rocket scientist to know the cops are just gonna stick that murder in the open files along with all the other low-life killings,* Marvin thought as he grinned to himself.

Over the next couple of weeks, Marvin sailed through his crappy job, riding the bug-energy high. However, by the middle of the third week he could feel the itch crawling out from the deep crevasses in his brain and whispering that it was that time again. Time to hunt. The energy had begun to ebb and he had started getting a little edgy. He caught himself starting to shuffle, the spring in his step gone. That night he took the knife from under the mattress and slid it from its sheath. As he touched the cold hard steel, his fingertips buzzed and tiny electrical impulses danced up his arm. *Yeah, it's time,* Marvin thought, licking his dry lips.

Marvin had hopped a bus to a different part of town. Old single family homes with brown-grass yards were tucked around unmaintained four-story brick apartment buildings. This was where there were gangs. He had checked the bus schedule; the last one back to his part of town left in two hours. He hoped that would be enough time to find what he was looking for. When Marvin got off the bus, he pressed himself into the doorway of a closed shop, deep in shadow, and waited. A few cars cruised up and down the block, radios blasting. A small group of kids went by on the other side of the street, laughing and punching each other on the shoulder. He watched and waited. Every now and then he would reach back and allow his fingers to caress the handle of the knife.

After an hour of quietly standing in the doorway, Marvin began to reconsider his plan. Should he grab the next bus and find another section of town to prowl? His limbs were getting stiff, but he didn't want to be a target for a drive-by or a stop-and-rob by walking around. So he closed his eyes, took a few deep breaths, and tried to relax. That was when he heard them. A quick look up the street revealed two men—gangbangers— in their early-twenties, wearing the bright colors of their gang affiliation, jostling each other, and walking toward Marvin on his side of the street.

"You messed that dude up bad, homes."

"I hear that. Old man shouldn't have been walking on our turf."

Two of them. *Can I do this; can I take on two at once?* Every frantic beat of his heart sent electric impulses radiating through his body, and the itch said, *Yeah. Yeah, you can do this.* Marvin wanted to take another quick peek, but he could tell they were close. A few more steps and then they were in front of him. As they cleared the doorway, the one farthest away was looking in his direction and saw Marvin.

"What the fu . . .?"

Marvin stepped out of the doorway and jammed the knife deep into the side of the closest one's chest. As he went down, the knife slide out followed by a spray of blood. Marvin quickly swung the knife back in the other direction, knowing that the element of surprise was dissipating fast. The second banger lunged at him before he could complete the arc of the swing. He collided with Marvin and they both went down. The banger's body landed on Marvin and knocked the breath out of him. His hands found Marvin's neck. He was faster and stronger than Marvin had anticipated.

As they lay on the sidewalk, the banger's body pinning Marvin, the banger started to squeeze—his thumbs jammed into Marvin's throat, pressing hard. Fireworks exploded behind his eyes and he felt darkness closing in. But he still held the knife! He brought it up and down on the banger's back, but couldn't get the angle right to puncture through the banger's jacket and do any damage. The banger must have felt what Marvin was trying to do because he took one of his hands off Marvin's neck and swung his arm around trying to bat the knife away. The banger spat out, "You wanna stab me too? Is that what you wanna do? Ain't gonna happen, 'cause you're one dead mother!"

This was it, one last chance. Marvin brought the knife in toward his chest and, with the last of his strength, plunged it upward. It skimmed the banger's throat, cutting a shallow line, then plunged into the soft underside of his jaw and entered his mouth. The banger released his grip on Marvin's neck and grabbed at the knife, but quickly let go as the blade sliced into his fingers. That's all Marvin needed and, with a last burst of desperate energy, he slammed the knife up through the banger's mouth and into his brain. His eyes went wide and he stared at Marvin for what seemed like an eternity, then collapsed back down onto him. Marvin was lying there trying to catch his breath, turning his head in order not to inhale the spray of blood pulsing from the banger's mouth.

It took some effort, but Marvin shoved the banger's body off himself and staggered to his feet. He was covered in blood, so taking the bus back home was out of the question. The street was quiet, and a couple of blocks away he found a house with a garden hose at the entrance to the driveway. Marvin rinsed the nylon jacket and his hands and face the best he could, then walked the six miles back to his apartment. At that hour of night there were few people out, and when he did see a car or someone walking, he slipped into the shadows. It took almost two hours, but he finally made it home.

Looking in the mirror, Marvin still saw a serious amount of blood, but the new jacket cleaned up fine. He then hit the shower for a long, hot rinse off.

After the shower, Marvin paced the room. He was cranked up.

Exhausted, but wired. As much of a thrill as the double kill had been, he realized if he was going to survive, he needed to have a better plan. He'd think about that later. Right now he just wanted to bask in the glow.

Now that Marvin realized the itch was not going to subside—that in fact it was coming at a more or less regular rate of every couple of weeks—he knew that he'd have to work out a better plan than just cruising around waiting to get into a fight he might not win. The first part of the plan was to go out and look around when the itch hadn't taken over, when he was more or less in his regular state of mind.

That's how Marvin found himself checking out a nearby neighborhood on a Wednesday night. After a couple of hours of aimlessly walking around, he thought about having a drink. Marvin wasn't much of a drinker, but he spotted a neighborhood bar up the block. As he started toward it, a strong wave of bug-energy hit him. He stopped and looked over at the front entrance. It was one of those cheesy little dive bars found in many blue-collar neighborhoods: a neon tiki-style sign out front and dirty white plaster surrounding a dark wooden doorway. Every now and then someone hurriedly entered or staggered out—some weaving their way home on foot, others heading for a small parking lot next door and pouring themselves into a car. And that's when the solution came to him. *Yeah, that'd work. And it would be easy.* Another little buzz confirmed the idea.

It had been almost three months since Marvin had put his plan into action. It was so simple—drunks. He started going to other towns a short bus ride from where he lived. He figured the world wouldn't miss a few low-life drunks, and even better, they were an easy target. Best of all, the itch didn't seem to care who he killed. At first he waited and went after the ones who were so drunk they could hardly walk and who were getting into a car to drive home. Marvin figured that they might kill somebody, so it would be okay to kill them first. But then there were times when he couldn't wait for one who was getting ready to drive, and . . . well, the itch had to be scratched. Most were so drunk they didn't realize what was happening until his knife plunged into their neck. And it hadn't taken long to realize that grabbing them from behind, then reaching around with the knife kept most of the blood spray from getting on him.

Marvin's life now revolved around his twice-monthly kills. He thought of it as his fix. It stopped the itch and gave him a nice bug-energy high for a couple of weeks. The high made him walk with confidence. Even the kids at his school seemed to give him more respect. Of course, the drunks rarely had any money to speak of after drinking it all up, so he had deviated from his plan one night when he saw a well-dressed older man take out a bundle from an ATM.

The media started calling him "The Drink and Die Killer," which Marvin thought was kind of catchy. Most people didn't seem to be that upset with his killings—especially not after the news broke that a drunk driver had run over a group of kids in a school crosswalk. Another news story said that some people on the internet were rooting for him not to get caught. He liked the idea of having a fan club. *Maybe sometime I'll use the computer at the library and find out what they're saying.*

Marvin found himself looking forward to his nights out. More and more he felt at home on the street and enjoyed the power of being judge, jury, and executioner. On this night Marvin took a bus over to a town about an hour from his place. He was having to go farther away because the last time he was checking out a local watering hole he saw a police car cruising around. He figured that it was a good thing they didn't have enough cops to watch all the bars. He just had to break up any patterns and he'd be okay.

Marvin found himself in an industrial part of his chosen town—the kind of area that mostly shuts down after 6 p.m. Every business Marvin could see was closed except for the little neighborhood bar he was watching. Finally, around midnight, he spotted a good candidate. The man came out of the bar stumbling a bit. A skinny guy around fifty, dressed in jeans, flannel shirt, and work boots. Marvin followed him as he made his way to wherever he was going. Marvin caught up to him as he was about to pass an alley between two closed warehouses. He pushed the skinny guy into the alley and dragged him to the end. The guy was trying to make sense of the attack and mumbling, "Whaddaya doing? I ain't got no money."

That's too bad, Marvin thought. *I can always use the extra few bucks I pick up from time to time.* Like most of the drunks Marvin targeted, he reeked of booze and a lack of hygiene. The skinny guy struggled briefly under Marvin's assault, rearing up just as he stabbed him. Marvin's knife stuck in his chest as the skinny man fell forward, hitting the ground and driving the knife farther into his torso. Marvin was slightly bent over with his hands on his knees, catching his breath, and looking down at the skinny man. He began to feel the bug-energy high—that good feeling starting to flood his body.

He was reaching down to retrieve his knife when he heard a soft scraping sound. Forgetting the knife for a moment, Marvin straightened up and turned around. And saw him. He was standing in the shadow of a dumpster about ten feet from Marvin. There was no doubt in his mind that the man had seen him. What should he do now? Had he come to the point where he could kill an innocent bystander? The itch whispered that it would be self-defense; the man was a witness. His life or Marvin's. He squinted at the man in the dim light that filtered into the alley from a street lamp. The man was a good deal larger than Marvin. He looked to be over six feet tall and must have weighed well over two hundred pounds. He wore a long dark coat and a watchman's cap, so it was hard for Marvin to make out the man's features. But Marvin understood one thing—there was no way he'd be able to take him unless he got his knife back.

Marvin's mind raced through his options. In order to retrieve his knife, he would need to roll the skinny man over. And if he tried to do that—tried to grab the knife—would this guy run away and start yelling for the police, or pounce on him before he got the knife out? As Marvin stared at the guy, it dawned on him that the man wasn't reacting the way one would expect. He had now stepped out of the shadows and was standing in plain sight. Calm. He moved closer, looking from Marvin to the still body of the skinny man, showing no fear, just a kind of . . . curiosity. Marvin finally spoke, trying to use the bug-energy to sound strong and confident.

"What do you want?"

"I've been following you," the man said in a deep, husky voice.

Marvin felt queasy. "You've been following me?"

The man stepped closer. "Yes, for a few weeks."

Marvin recognized something in the man's eyes and didn't want to ask, but he couldn't stop himself. His throat was dry and constricted, but he managed to form a single word.

"Why?"

As the man reached into his coat pocket, the hint of a smile crossed his lips. "I have an itch," he said.

John Everson

DRIVING HER HOME

I was drunk the first time I picked her up. It would never have happened otherwise. I don't pick up hitchhikers. I've seen the movies. They never end well.

But I'd been sitting at Teehan's Tavern in Tinley Park for one pint too many, and on the way home I decided to avoid cutting through the quiet, old part of town and instead took the long way home. It was after midnight, so I drove down the always-busy Harlem Avenue—I didn't need the local cops spotting and pulling me over on the local roads when I was the only car on the road. I didn't *think* I was going to weave ... but better to blend in with a bunch of traffic. Once I reached 143rd Street though, I had to make a right and head down that lonely road through the forest preserve to reach the Midlothian Turnpike. It wasn't a long road, but it definitely was dark.

I saw her standing on the side of the road right after I turned the corner and the landscape changed from streetlights to dark, shadowed stands of trees. She had long chestnut hair, twined in a braided pony tail, and wore a tie-dyed, cropped t-shirt and Daisy Duke frayed denim shorts; an odd outfit for the end of September. Especially since it was a chilly night. When she put her thumb out, I didn't think twice. She had to be freezing.

I pulled over.

"Thanks, man," she said, when she slipped into the passenger seat. "I'm almost home, but I appreciate the lift."

"What are you doing out here this late?" I asked. "It's not safe to be walking alone at this hour."

I saw her shrug out of the corner of my eye. "There was a thing down at Donnie's," she said. "We played some tunes, danced a bit . . . but now it's time, ya know?"

"Well, I'd just be careful about walking a dark road at night," I said. "You never know who you might meet."

"Like you?" she said, and laughed. I wasn't sure if I should be offended.

"Life is for taking chances, and meeting new people," she said. "Otherwise you might as well sleep in a grave."

"Well, they always say, 'I'll sleep when I'm dead,'" I said.

"You don't seem dead to me," she said.

"Nope," I said. "And I'm not sleepin'."

Just then, WLUP-FM segued from Boston's "Don't Look Back" to CCR's "Susie Q."

"Oh, I love this one, do you?" she asked, leaning forward to bob her head.

"Sure," I said. "Hey, what's your name, by the way? I'm John."

"Marigold," she said. "But you can call me Mari."

"Glad to meet you, Mari," I said. "See—I took a chance and I'm meeting new people."

"Right on," she said. "But now you have to say goodbye."

"What do you mean?" I said.

"My house is just over there," she said, pointing to a place in the forest that looked as dark as the rest of the forested roadway.

I started to pull over, but didn't completely slow the car on the shoulder. "Where?" I asked.

"This is good," she said.

"There's nothing here!" I said, but hit the brakes. Outside the passenger's side window, the forest looked dark and foreboding.

"Sure there is," she said. "My house is just through the trees. If you look hard, you can see the light through there." She pointed just past the bridge we'd just passed over. "See the porchlight?"

I craned my head, and damned if she wasn't right. There was a faint light beaming back there in the trees, past the small pond that the road ran over.

"Thanks for the lift," she said.

She leaned across the seat and planted a soft kiss right on my lips. The scent of lavender teased my nose. My eyes widened in surprise, and she grinned.

"Live a little," she said. And then in a heartbeat, she slipped out of my car. I saw her begin walking down the gravel embankment, but then a pair of headlights came up in my rear view mirror. I raised my hand to shield my eyes from the glare, and when the car passed, and I looked down the path towards the trees and the overgrown pond... she was already gone.

I wiped a finger gently across my lips and took a deep breath before pulling back out onto the road.

I woke up the next morning with a headache and a strong memory of being kissed by a stranger on the side of the road next to the forest preserve.

"You didn't . . . really?" I asked myself, while brushing my beer-fuzzed teeth.

A tousle of bed-head hair nodded yes.

"Stupid," I said, and spit.

I drove down Midlothian Turnpike to 143rd Street on the way to work, just because. I'd been that way a million times, but I'd never seen a house tucked back in the forest. And I didn't that morning either. I'd have to stop and walk into the woods if I was going to.

Days passed and somehow the weekend came around again. The first weekend in October, which was a difficult time for me. You could say the beginning of October was the anniversary of the end of my life. And so to celebrate, I played one too many games of KISS pinball in the corner by myself at Teehan's . . . and probably had one too many Revolution IPAs in the process before finally driving home at 1:30 in the morning. Consequently, I took the long way again.

When I turned down the dark road leading through the forest preserve, it was like entering another world. The lights of the busy four-lane road disappeared and suddenly I was snaking between the dense stand of trees on a road that shimmered with a layer of early morning frost. I felt as if I'd turned into another world.

And just as I marveled at the beauty of the silent landscape, I saw her again. She was slumped over, sitting on the side of the road. Her feet were bare, and her hands gripped her calves as she hung her head between her knees.

I don't know what made me pull over. I don't buy Girl Scout cookies and I'm not the guy that gives money to panhandlers. And I have to admit, I'm not the guy who pulls over when someone has a flat tire. I keep to myself whenever I can and I try not to get involved in other people's problems. But a piece of me recognized her, as soon as I saw the figure on the side of the road. A minute later, I was kneeling beside her.

"Are you okay?" I asked. "Can I help?"

"Hey there," she answered, looking up from her knees. There was a tear on her cheek. "I remember you," she whispered. "The man who is afraid to live."

"I'm not afraid to live," I said. "What are you talking about?"

The side of her mouth turned up. Her eyes sparkled. Maybe it was just the tears, but her face seemed to flash with sudden humor. "Last time I saw you, I told you to live a little, remember? But here you're driving down the same old road."

"Yeah, and a good thing for you, too," I said. "What happened?"

She shrugged. "My old man's a bastard, that's all."

"Wanna talk about it?" I asked. My breath rose up in a cloud before my eyes.

"Not much to say," she said. I realized again that she was barefoot and in a thin yellow tanktop, when it was something like 30 degrees out.

"Do you want to warm up in my car, at least?"

Her shoulders shrugged. "Sure, I guess."

I held out my hand and she took it. Her fingers were thin, and soft. Gentle. Her nails were short, and unpolished. She leaned hard on me as she got up. I realized she was limping.

"What happened to your leg," I asked, once we were in the car.

"Jackson pushed me down the stairs," she said. "Didn't like it that I was out late last night. I didn't like it that he thinks he owns me."

"Doesn't sound good," I said.

"He's jealous," she said. "He thinks he is the only one I can love."

"Are you in love with him?" I asked.

"Of course, or I wouldn't be living with him. But Jackson needs to accept that he is not the only one. I love a lot of people. Life is too short to only be with one."

"Well, if you're seeing other people, maybe you should consider moving out, if he is going to hurt you," I suggested.

She shook her head. "My baby Caitlin needs a father," she said. "And he's sweet, when he's not angry."

"That's difficult," I said. I thought of the last bitter nights of my marriage, and my daughter who I almost never saw now, and all of the reasons I spent a lot of time these days at Teehan's. "If your baby grows up seeing you getting hurt, that's not good, though."

She nodded. "That is then, this is now. Hopefully Jackson will grow up before my baby. If not...we will see."

"Want me to drive you home?"

She nodded, and I pulled out onto the empty road. I remembered I had dropped her off near the bridge rails last time. You actually wouldn't know the road there ran over a bridge if not for those rails, it was so small. It just extended the road over a drainage creek near the pond.

A moment later we were there, and I pulled the car over and killed the lights.

"Do you want me to walk you home?" I asked.

She smiled. "I'd like that."

I got out and walked around to open the door for her. She smiled and accepted my hand as she got out of the car, and then led me down the shoulder of the road to a gravel path that wound through the brush and into the trees. The forest was dark, but the sky was clear, and I could see our way through the leaves by starlight. The moon's glow reflected off the pond that the path wound around. When I saw the clearing in the trees a little way ahead, Mari stopped me.

"Wait," she said.

We stopped. She slipped her arms around my neck. I responded, hugging her close.

"You're sweet," she whispered. "Thank you for being here for me now."

I didn't know what to say. I rubbed my hand on her back and she lifted her lips to kiss me. Her touch was soft and gentle. Electric. My lips tingled as she pressed against them, and when her tongue slipped easily inside my teeth, and wrestled my own playfully, I couldn't help but surrender. My hands roved down her back, and cupped the denim curves of her ass, pulling her tight to my hips.

Her answer was to break the kiss so that she could shrug the tank top over her head. She wasn't wearing a bra. Her chest was pale and her breasts slight but full with the milk she was making for her baby. Her nipples stood pink and erect in the cold.

"No," I said. "You'll freeze out here."

She laughed. "It's always warm in the heart," she said. And then she unzipped and pushed off my coat, and pulled the t-shirt over my head. "Hold your heart to mine and you'll see," she said.

My back was cold but she was right. As we hugged, there in the middle of the night, in the middle of a frigid forest, I felt her breasts crush against the hair of my chest and I felt as warm as I'd been in the car. Warmer, really... because my blood was pumping faster. The caress of her fingers through my hair was like magic. Every touch brought back memories of those times when I'd been happy with my wife, the only woman I'd ever really loved before or since. I barely noticed when Mari reached down to undo my belt buckle. I was lost in the feeling of her, and the intoxicating scent of lavender that filled my nose when she kissed me.

We lay down on top of our clothes on a bed of crunching oak leaves. Our lips and hands explored each other slowly at first, and then with increasing fervor. Every time she touched me I shivered with both heat and cold. She was like a live wire, jolting me with sensations I'd nearly forgotten in the past two years since my divorce. I suckled her chest and was surprised and a bit turned on when I tasted the rich water of her milk. And then she rolled on top of me, and with her hands on my chest, drew her thighs up to the place where we could truly join together. With my hands on her hips, I moved her slowly at first, easing our bodies together. And then I felt the slip and the pressure and the velvet wet heat of her, and we were truly one. She sealed us, yin-and-yang with a kiss, and together we moved, breathing together, rocking together, loving together.

When she reached her crest, our lips broke apart and she called out to the stars, "oh yes, at last, yes!"

My own moment followed and it felt as if my very life was draining from me in a wave that left me both full of sensation yet completely, blissfully empty. I was floating in a place between the frozen earth and the distant stars, joined to this beautiful creature with her pale features and long hair and soft hands that knew just how to touch... at last, she rolled in the crook of my arm and smiled.

"That was just what I needed tonight," she said. "Thanks for sharing your love with me."

"No," I said in a whisper. "Thank you for reminding me . . . how it can be."

She touched my lips with the tip of a finger. "It can always be that," she said. "But you need to *let* it be. Let it be. You have to live. Smell the flowers. Touch the sky."

She ran a finger down the chain around my neck.

"What is this?" she asked.

I lifted it and felt my face flush. "A memory," I said.

She lifted the locket that hung over my heart and with a fingernail popped it open.

"Who is she?" she asked, staring at the tiny picture of my ex-wife.

"Linda," I said. "The woman I used to love."

She nodded. "But no more?"

"I still love her. She left me."

Mari pulled on the chain until I could feel it pinch the back of my neck. "So," she said. "This is the chain that holds you down. Your anchor."

"I guess," I agreed.

"The past is past," she said, and lifted the necklace from around my head. "Let it be buried."

Something in my heart shifted at those words, and I knew she was right. As long as I wore that chain, I would never be able to move on. I would always be that lonely guy at the back of Teehan's. I tapped the back of the locket and Linda's face fell out, and slipped between the brown leaves.

"Here," I said. "Maybe you can put Caitlin's picture in it."

"Yes," she smiled. "That would be nice."

I slipped it over her hair, and the empty locket settled between her breasts.

She pushed herself away from me then. "I need to go," she said. "Caitlin will be hungry, and Jackson will be angry." She fished her panties from the leaves and pulled them on. When she tugged her jeans out from under me, I suddenly felt the cold all at once. The real world returned and I hurried to follow Mari's example. The goosebumps spread across my entire body like an ice wave.

I walked her towards the clearing, but then she put a hand on my chest. "I better walk the last part alone," she said. "But thank you."

I watched as she moved across the frosted grass towards a small two-story house tucked at the edge of the opposite tree line. There was a wooden porch in the front, but the windows were dark. I couldn't see much more than the glimmer of the moon on the windows, and the pitch of the roof as it met the sky. She opened the door and disappeared inside.

When I woke the next day, I was worried about a lot of things. I worried about my mental state . . . No matter how much I'd had to drink, how had I ended up doing it —unprotected—in the leaves of the forest preserve with a stranger . . . when there was frost on the ground? I studied myself naked in the bathroom, wondering if in my drunken idiocy, I'd contracted something from this weird, bohemian girl. At the same time, I also worried that I'd never again feel as amazing as I had in the short time I'd lain with her. Mostly though, I worried about her. Jealousy and free love and babies didn't mix well. Just read the newspaper on any given day. What had she walked into last night when she'd gone through that door?

As I forced myself through my morning routine, my head hurt, but my heart hurt worse. This was the anniversary weekend of my divorce. October 3rd. I'd never forget that date. The day my life ended. I guess Mari had been right the first time we met . . . I had been existing for the past couple years, but I hadn't been alive. The first time in ages that I'd felt anything but sadness in that cavity beneath my ribs was last night —well, actually this morning—at about 1:30 a.m. And that was with a girl who was cheating on her boyfriend. Nice.

I got through the day, with a million conflicting thoughts running through my head. That night, I was back at Teehan's, holed up in the corner once more with a beer in my hand and a lump in my throat. I saw the couples around the bar laughing and enjoying the night. Swaying to the old school classic rock on the jukebox. I saw the singles hitting on each other, cheerful desperation lubricated by shots of Jäger. A group of three guys threw darts nearby with a cute blonde; you could see them vying for her attention. They appeared to be friends, but all in competition. Who would she decide to go home with tonight? Typical barfloor soap opera.

It was too pathetic. And in the end, they were all going to get hurt. It just wasn't worth it.

But just as I thought that, I saw a flash of Mari's face, the memory of her intensity, as she straddled me last night. Those giving eyes and long sexy hair trailing across my cheek. It had been like she was looking into my soul. Like she had been giving everything that she was to me.

Wasn't a moment like that worth the pain and disappointment that usually grew up around it?

Maybe. Maybe not.

I slugged another pint back and sunk back into my own private pity party. Mari had given me a taste, but I wasn't likely to find it again.

I packed it in at last call. It was past 2:30 a.m. and the pint glass in front of me had been emptied too many times since 9 p.m. I'd met nobody, and talked to no one but the bartender. Though I *had* gotten my name into the Top 10 list on pinball. Small victory. At least until they reset the machine.

As I turned the corner on 143rd Street, part of me hoped that I would see Mari tonight. I knew it was the hope of a fool. It was super late; she'd be in bed, or if she *was* up, she'd be in a rocking chair nursing her infant. Hopefully she'd patched things up with her boyfriend. She didn't need me to muddy those waters.

Still, as I neared the bridge by the small pond, I took my foot off the gas, and stared into the dark of the forest that cloaked her house. It was warmer tonight, but the sky was thick with clouds; a misty rain had been falling for hours.

I was almost over the bridge when I saw a glimpse of pale legs moving fast against the dark prism of the forest. I veered the car onto the shoulder, stopped and got out. My forehead was instantly damp with mist.

"Mari?" I called.

The figure in the woods stopped. I hurried down the path I'd walked less than 24 hours before, and finally caught up to where she was standing at the edge of the clearing, a bundle wrapped in a blanket in the crook of her arm. "Mari, are you okay?" I called.

She shook her head. Negative.

I hurried forward and she held out her hand. "Don't," she warned. "He's crazy tonight. He doesn't think Caitlin is even his. I don't know what he's going to do. I've never seen him like this."

"Don't go back, then," I said. "Come home with me. Let him cool down. You and Caitlin will be safe with me for the night."

"Are you sure?" she said. I could hear the relief in her voice.

She was quiet in the car, and I didn't want to press her. The baby in her arms held her attention, and I focused on the road. There was no way I should be driving, let alone driving a baby. I focused on the dotted white lines on the asphalt, the speed limit signs, and my own speedometer. The rain clouded the sky and my headlights seemed to gouge tunnels through it as we sped along, the only car on the road. We were moving in a bubble through the night. Just us three. I felt a surge of protectiveness at that. Another feeling I remembered from long ago.

"You have to think of your baby," I said quietly. "You can't let this keep happening."

"I won't let him hurt Caitlin," she said.

"What if you can't stop him?" I asked.

"He's not like that," she said. "You don't know him."

I pulled into the garage at last and killed the engine.

"We're home," I said. "You can sleep in my bed with the baby. I'll sleep on the couch. In the morning, we can talk and figure out what you should do."

Mari shook her head sadly. "I know what I need to do. But what about you?"

"What about me," I asked.

"You're still not living," she said. "I knew it the moment I saw you."

I shrugged. "I lost the woman I loved. She didn't want to be with me anymore."

She fingered the chain I had put around her neck, and then lifted it from beneath her shirt to show me the locket. My locket. Now empty.

"There is more than one love," Mari said. "If you open your heart, you'll see what I mean." She smiled and shook her head. "I have the opposite problem; I love too much. Stop hiding from it and driving down the same dead end road."

She saw my reaction, and reached across to put her free hand on my cheek. "Do it for me," she said. "Let yourself love again. Live a little."

She leaned over and kissed me again, and my lips felt suddenly aglow with energy. My heart pumped faster, my mouth yearned to keep kissing her. But this wasn't the time. I had to get her and Caitlin safely to bed.

I got out of the car, and walked around to her side.

I opened the passenger door for her.

Only… she wasn't there.

Mari and her baby had vanished.

I looked around the garage and called her name. But there was no reply.

A chill ran up my spine and after looking again in the car, in the back seat, and around the garage, I finally gave up, and stumbled my way into the house.

And locked the door.

On Sunday morning, after a pot of black coffee and a healthy helping of self-doubt, I pulled on my jeans, and drove down to the bridge near Mari's house. I honestly wasn't sure what I was prepared to do if her boyfriend answered the door. But . . . I had to see her again. To prove . . . that she was real. Maybe I'd hallucinated the whole thing last night. But what about the night before? Was I really that far gone?

The gravel was wet and I nearly slipped walking down the embankment from the road. The path was interrupted by puddles, but I did my best to step around them. I saw the spot on the side where Mari and I had made love; I imagined the leaves were still matted down from us, not from the rain.

When I reached the clearing, I shook my head.

And blinked.

Could it really be the same clearing? I looked behind me and there was no place where the path diverged. Yes. This was where I had stood long after midnight the past two nights, first to say goodbye, and then to drive her home.

If that was the case, what I saw now could not be real.

But as I looked across the clearing again, what I saw was irrefutable.

There was no house across the way. There was only a chain link fence that scrub bush branches grew through and that trees from the other side hung over.

On this side of the fence, there was only grass.

And tombstones.

Some of the stones were toppled, and some spray-painted with graffiti. I knew suddenly exactly what this place was. And just as I realized it,

I saw a steel trashcan nearby with the name of the place stenciled on the side. I stood at the entrance to Bachelors Grove Cemetery. I'd heard about the place since I was in Boy Scouts. So many campfire stories had arisen from this hidden plot of land. I'd never been here before, never really known quite where it was. But I knew its long reputation as an abandoned cemetery, hidden somewhere inside Bachelors Grove Woods.

A haunted cemetery.

And here it was.

I'd been kissing a ghost.

I walked between the broken stones, reading the names and dates where I could. Some went back to the 1920s and 1930s. There were even a couple from the 1890s. But I knew unconsciously where to go. I'd probably noticed it from the moment I'd stepped into the clearing.

On top of one low grey stone, beneath the clouded Sunday sun, shone the glint of something silver. I bent to pick it up, and retrieved the chain I'd given Mari on Friday night.

Then I stared at the face of the stone. I knew what it would tell me, but I read the engraving anyway.

Marigold Plotnik
Born, April 23, 1950
Died, October 3, 1969

There was a smaller headstone next to hers, and my eyes welled when I read it.

Caitlin Plotnik
Born, January 18, 1969
Died, October 3, 1969

I heard her voice in the car last night. Quiet but sure. *"I know what I need to do,"* she'd said.

"What did you do, Mari," I whispered. "Why did you go home that night? What happened to you?"

I knelt by the stone, and tears slipped down my cheek. Not only could I not help her, she had been dead long before I was born. Another woman whose love I'd lost.

All of the things she'd said to me came rushing back. And I realized that maybe I hadn't lost her. Maybe I'd *called* her. How much of a chance was it that I saw her right at this moment in my life, the anniversary of my death . . . the anniversary of hers.

Maybe she had come back just for me. To give me a warning. A chance to give me a last chance.

"If you open your heart, you'll see what I mean," she had said. *"Stop hiding from it and driving down the same dead end road."*

I picked up the chain and put it around my neck. The empty pendant dangled next to my empty heart.

"Do it for me," she had said with her last kiss. *"Let yourself love again. Live a little."*

"Thank you, Mari," I whispered, and rubbed my fingers across the rough stone that marked her grave. "I won't forget you. Rest in peace."

"Life is for taking chances, and meeting new people . . . Otherwise you might as well sleep in a grave."

I took a deep breath, and left the cemetery.

I had a locket to fill again before I slept.

THE AUTHORS

Peter Atkins is the author of the novels *Morningstar, Big Thunder,* and *Moontown* and the screenplays *Hellraiser II, Hellraiser III, Hellraiser IV, and Wishmaster.* His short fiction has appeared in such anthologies as *The Museum of Horrors, Dark Delicacies II, Hellbound Hearts,* and *Ghosts,* and has been selected eight times for one or more of the various "Year's Best" anthologies. His most recent book, *Rumours of the Marvellous,* a collection of his short fiction, was a finalist for the British Fantasy Award. He is the co-founder with Glen Hirshberg of The Rolling Darkness Revue, an annual folly they commit at whatever theatre will let them. He blogs at *peteratkins.blogspot.com*

T. C. Bennett was born and raised in Los Angeles. His novella, *Phantom Carriage,* was first published in 2004 and republished in 2005. His short fiction has appeared in, *100 Doors To Madness* and in various other anthologies and magazines, such as *Dark Eclipse. Cemetery Riots* is his first foray into editing an anthology.

Hal Bodner is a Bram Stoker Award® nominated author who, while best known for his gay satire/comedies, often writes in the horror genre. The year it was published, his freshman vampire novel, *Bite Club,* made him one of the top-selling GLBT authors in the country. To this day, the royalties help keep him in the proverbial "cigarettes and nylons" —even though he quit smoking five years ago and never did drag. For several years, Hal wrote erotic paranormal romances, most notably *In Flesh And Stone*. His agent cringes when he refers to these books as "supernatural smut." He rarely writes erotica anymore, mostly because he has run out of interesting verbs to use when describing various intimate bodily functions. He is currently working on several thrillers which paint classic "noir" with a decidedly lavender glaze. Hal is legally married to a wonderful man, half his age, who never knew that Liza Minnelli was Judy Garland's daughter.

Tracy L. Carbone is a New England born writer who recently moved to Southern California where the sunshine is plentiful and her dogs can go outside without sweaters. Her horror and literary short stories have appeared in dozens of anthologies and magazines in the U.S. and Canada. To date, she has published five novels and a collection of her dark cautionary tales.

She is an active member of the Horror Writers Association, its Los Angeles chapter, and former Co-chair of the New England Horror Writers. She edited the New England Horror Writers' Bram Stoker Award® nominated anthology, *Epitaphs,* a creepy collection of horror stories and poems by the group's authors. She is excited to be back in the editing arena with *Cemetery Riots.*

She recently completed a new novel, *The Rainbox.* Please visit her at *www.tracylcarbone.com*

Karen Dent has worn the hat of actor, playwright, director, screenwriter, and filmmaker but since moving to Massachusetts, turned her creativity to writing fiction. Her short stories have sold in a variety of genres including horror, sci-fi/fantasy, mystery, YA, and middle-grade. The Sisters Dent have successfully collaborated on a number of projects, most recently, their short noir mystery, "The Death of Honeysuckle Rose" sold to Plaidswede's anthology, *Murder Ink.* Their one-Act play, *Young at Heart,* garnered the *Nebie Award* from The Firehouse

Center for the Arts, and their full-length romantic farce *Monkey Girl Blues* was picked to showcase in the New Works Festival also at the Firehouse. Karen is editing her first full-length novel, *A Case to KILL For*, a paranormal/noir, based on the same characters she created in "A Case To Die For" in *Damnation and Dames*. She is a member of New England Horror Writers (NEHW), Broad Universe, SAG, AFTRA, the Dramatist Guild, and Essex Writers and Artists Guild (EWAG). She graduated from The School of Visual Arts in NYC. *www.sistersdent. com*

Roxanne E. Dent has sold nine novels and dozens of short stories in a variety of genres including Paranormal Fantasy, Regencies, Mystery, Horror and YA. Her most recent short, "The Monster of Biscayne Bay," sold to the anthology, *Tales From the Lake*, Crystal Lake Publishing. In collaboration with her sister, Karen, "The Death of Honeysuckle Rose," a Noir Mystery sold to the anthology, *Murder Ink*, Plaidswede Publishing. They are currently writing another one with the same characters for Vol. II. Roxanne also collaborated with her sister on *Monkey Girl Blues*, and *Young at Heart*, plays put on at The Firehouse Theater in Newburyport. She has also written screenplays and directed her own three minute movie. Currently, she is completing a novel, *Beyond the Iberian Sea*, Book II of the *Janus Demon*, a paranormal fantasy, and putting finishing touches on *Miss Amalie Carter and the Dorian Generator*, a Steampunk novel.

She is a member of New England Horror Writers (NEHW), FWG, Broad Universe, and Essex Writers and Artists Guild (EWAG). *www. sistersdent.com*

James Dorr's *The Tears of Isis* was a 2014 Bram Stoker Award® nominee for Superior Achievement in a Fiction Collection. Released in May 2013 year by Perpetual Motion Machine Publishing, it joins his previous books *Strange Mistresses: Tales of Wonder and Romance: Tales of Mystery and Regret*, and his all-poetry *Vamps (A Retrospective)*, along with nearly 400 individual fiction and poetry appearances from *Alfred Hitchcock's Mystery Magazine* to *Yellow Bat Review*. As both a short story writer and poet, Dorr works largely in dark fantasy/horror with forays into science fiction and mystery.

An Active Member of HWA and SFWA, Dorr has been a technical writer, city editor on an area magazine, a full time non-fiction freelancer, a semi-professional Renaissance musician, and is currently keeper of a cat named Wednesday (for Wednesday Addams of the *Addams Family)* who's into mousing and plastic fake spiders. For more information he invites readers to visit his blog at *www.jamesdorrwriter. wordpress.com*, where Wednesday also has her own webpage under "Pages" in the right-hand column.

Dennis Etchison is a three-time winner of both the British Fantasy and World Fantasy Awards. His collections include *The Dark Country, Red Dreams, The Blood Kiss, The Death Artist, Talking in the Dark, Fine Cuts, Got To Kill Them All & Other Stories, A Little Black Book of Horror Tales and It Only Comes Out At Night & Other Stories.* He is also the author of the novels *Darkside, Shadowman, California Gothic, Double Edge, The Fog, Halloween II & III* and *Videodrome* , the editor of *Cutting Edge, Masters of Darkness I-III, MetaHorror, The Museum of Horrors* and (with Ramsey Campbell and Jack Dann) *Gathering the Bones.* Etchison has written extensively for film, television and radio, including 150+ scripts *for The Twilight Zone Radio Dramas.* He served as President of the HWA from 1992 to 1994. His e-books are available from Crossroad Press. His work is consistently meritorious.

John Everson is a staunch advocate for the culinary joys of the jalapeno and an unabashed fan of 1970s European horror cinema. He is also the Bram Stoker Award® winning author of *Covenant* and seven other novels, including the creature feature spiderfest *Violet Eyes,* the erotic horror Stoker Award finalist *NightWhere,* and his latest, the seductive backwoods tale of *The Family Tree.* Other novels include *Sacrifice, The Pumpkin Man, Siren* and The *13th.* Over the past 20 years, his short stories have appeared in more than 75 magazines and anthologies. His fourth fiction collection, *Sacrificing Virgins,* was released from Samhain Publishing at the end of 2015. For more information on his obsession with chili peppers, as well as his fiction, art and music, visit *www. johneverson.com.*

Ray Garton has been writing novels, novellas, short stories, and essays for more than 30 years. His work spans the genres of horror, crime, suspense, and even comedy. His titles *include Live Girls, Ravenous, The Loveliest Dead, Sex and Violence in Hollywood, Meds*, and many others. His short stories have appeared in magazines and anthologies, and have been collected in books like *Methods of Madness, Pieces of Hate, and Slivers of Bone.* He has been nominated for the Bram Stoker Award® and at the 2006 World Horror Convention he received the Grand Master of Horror Award. His novella *Vortex: A Moffett & Keoph Investigation* is now available as an ebook and in paperback. He lives in northern California with his wife, where he is currently at work on several projects, including a new novel titled *Monster Show.* Visit his website at *www.raygartononline.com.*

Taylor Grant is a two-time Bram Stoker Award® nominated author, Hollywood screenwriter and award-winning filmmaker. His work has been seen on network television, the big screen, the stage, the Web, as well as in comic books, newspapers, national magazines, books, and heard on the radio.

Several of Grant's screenplays have sold or been optioned by major Hollywood film studios such as Imagine Entertainment, Universal Studios, and Lions Gate Films. His fiction and non-fiction has appeared in multiple anthologies and magazines, including *Cemetery Dance Magazine,* as well as four Bram Stoker Award® nominated books. He edited and co-wrote the Bestselling horror comic book *Evil Jester Presents,* and his first collection *The Dark at the End of the Tunnel* received a Bram Stoker Award® nomination and was named "Best Story Collection" in the 2015 Solstice List, which recognizes excellence in horror literature.

Eric J. Guignard is a writer and editor of dark and speculative fiction, operating from the shadowy outskirts of Los Angeles. He's won the Bram Stoker Award®, been a finalist for the International Thriller Writers Award, and a multi-nominee of the Pushcart Prize. Outside the glamorous and jet-setting world of indie fiction, Eric's a technical writer and college professor, and he stumbles home each day to a wife, children, cats, and a terrarium filled with mischievous beetles. Visit Eric at: *www.ericjguignard.com*, his blog: *ericjguignard.blogspot.com,* or Twitter: *@ericjguignard.*

Jack Ketchum is the author of over twenty novels and novellas, six story collections, three books of nonfiction and a book of poems, *Notes From The Cathouse.* He's the five-time winner of the Bram Stoker Award®, the last for Lifetime Achievement. In 2011 he was elected Grand Master by the World Horror Convention.

Kelly Kurtzhals worked under the pseudonym Kelly Kursten when she was a standup comedian and TV writer, until the dark fingers of horror reached into her dreams and brought out her true identity. Now in the daylight breaks from her slavery to the dark muse, she works as an Emmy-nominated producer for E! News.

Richard Christian Matheson is an acclaimed bestselling author and screenwriter/executive producer for television and film. He has worked with Steven Spielberg, Stephen King, Dean Koontz, Roger Corman and many others. Matheson's critically-hailed fiction appears in his short story collections *Scars and Other Distinguishing Marks ,* #1 bestseller *Dystopia* and over 150 major anthologies, including many *Years' Best* volumes. He is the author of the suspense novel *Created By* and Hollywood novella *The Ritual of Illusion.* His work has been translated into ten languages. A professional drummer, he studied privately with Cream's Ginger Baker. He is president of *Matheson Entertainment.* Matheson's upcoming collection is *Zoopraxis.*

Kathryn E. McGee is a Los Angeles-based writer. She has an MFA in creative writing from UC Riverside Palm Desert, where she focused on horror and haunted house fiction. She is a member of the

Horror Writers Association and published a short story in the anthology, *Winter Horror Days* (Omnium Gatherum, 2015). In her work as an architectural historian, she writes building histories and consults on development projects involving historic properties.

Lisa Morton is a screenwriter, author of non-fiction books, award-winning prose writer, and Halloween expert whose work was described by the American Library Association's *Readers' Advisory Guide to Horror* as "consistently dark, unsettling, and frightening". Her most recent releases include *Ghosts: A Haunted History* and the short story collection *Cemetery Dance Select: Lisa Morton*. She currently serves as President of the Horror Writers Association, and can be found online at *www.lisamorton.com.*

William F. Nolan Over the past six decades, since he began writing professional fiction in 1954, William F. Nolan's short stories have been selected for more than 400 anthologies including many "Best of" volumes. He has 91 books to his credit and is justly celebrated as the author/creator of the science fiction classic, *Logan's Run* (major film, TV series, etc. available in various world-wide editions).

Honored by a host of awards, Nolan has been named a Grand Master, a Living Legend, a Lifetime Achievement Award Winner, and an Author Emeritus.

"Among the Tigers" is William Nolan's first war tale, set in Belgium during the Battle of the Bulge in WWII. We are proud to debut it here, as an example of a superior fiction from a writer who has never failed to deliver first rate entertainment.

Michael D. Nye is no stranger to horror and fantasy—as both an actor and writer/director. Michael wrote and directed the vampire feature film, *Night Tour* (in post-production), as well as the wrap-around segments for the horror anthology feature, *Grave Images*. As an actor, Michael has had many principal roles in films and television shows including: *Priest, Heroes, Torchwood, Westworld, Carnivale,* and *Eagleheart.* He's also played a zombie in several commercials. In addition to his work in film and television, his play, *The Big Farewell*, (a spoof on the noir detective genre) was produced on stage in Los Angeles. Michael has also written three books on acting, including *The Actor's Guide To Auditioning*. Please visit *www.facebook.com/night2tour* and on Twitter *@night2tour*

John Palisano's short fiction has appeared in many places. Check out: *Dark Discoveries, Horror Library, Darkness On The Edge, Lovecraft eZine, Phobophobia, Lovecraft eZine, Terror Tales, Harvest Hill, Halloween Spirits*, the Bram Stoker Award® nominated *Chiral Mad, Midnight Walk, Halloween Tales*, and many other publications. *Nerves* was his first novel. He is working hard on its sequel, as well as many other upcoming works.

His non-fiction has appeared in *Fangoria* and *Dark Discoveries*, where he's interviewed folks like Robert Englund, director Rob Hall, and Corey Taylor from Slipknot.

Currently, *Dust of the Dead*, his first book from Samhain Publishing, arrived in June 2015 with *Ghost Heart* on February 14, 2016, with *Night of 1,000 Beasts* to come in the very near future.

His work has been cited by the Bram Stoker Award® four times.

"Available Light" was nominated for the Bram Stoker Award® in 2013. "The Geminis" was nominated for the Bram Stoker Award® in 2014. "Splinterette" was nominated for the Bram Stoker Award® in 2015. "Happy Joe's Rest Stop" won the Bram Stoker Award® for best short fiction in 2016.

John's had a colorful history. He began writing at an early age, with his first publications in college fanzines and newspapers at Emerson in Boston. He's worked for over a decade in Hollywood for people like Ridley Scott and Marcus Nispel. He's recently been working as a ghost-screenwriter and has seen much success with over two dozen short story sales and his novel *Nerves* continues gaining critical and reader acclaim. There's more where that all came from. You can visit him at *www.johnpalisano.com* where you can learn about the artist and his upcoming projects.

Michael Sebastian is a fiction and comics writer, musician and film snob living in Los Angeles. He studied film at the University of Southern California and the Ways of the Force at Clarion West.

Chet Williamson has written in the field of horror, science fiction, and suspense since 1981. Among his many novels are *Second Chance, Hunters, Defenders of the Faith, Ash Wednesday, Reign*, and *Dreamthorp*. His most recent publications are *The Night Listener and Others* (a story collection from PS Publishing), *A Little Blue Book of Bibliomancy* (Borderlands Press), and *Psycho: Sanitarium*, an authorized sequel to Robert Bloch's classic *Psycho* (St. Martin's Press).

Over a hundred of his short stories have appeared in such magazines as *The New Yorker, Playboy, Esquire, The Magazine of Fantasy and Science Fiction*, and many other magazines and anthologies. He has won the International Horror Guild Award, and has been shortlisted twice for the World Fantasy Award, six times for the Horror Writers Association's Stoker Award®, and once for the Mystery Writers of America's Edgar Award. Nearly all of his works are available in ebook format at the Kindle and Nook Stores.

A stage and film actor (his most recent appearance is in Joe R. Lansdale's film, *Christmas With the Dead*), he has recorded over 40 unabridged audiobooks, both of his own work and that of many other writers, available at www.audible.com. Follow him on Twitter *@chetwill* or at *www.chetwilliamson.com*.

awolfromelysiumpress.com